Blood Runs Thicker

a&b

Blood Runs Thicker

A Medieval Mystery

SARAH HAWKSWOOD

Allison & Busby Limited
11 Wardour Mews
London W1F 8AN
allisonandbusby.com

First published in Great Britain by Allison & Busby in 2021.

A CIP catalogue record for this book is available from
the British Library.

First Edition

ISBN 978-0-7490-2715-5

Typeset in 11/16 pt Adobe Garamond Pro by
Allison & Busby Ltd.

The paper used for this Allison & Busby publication
has been produced from trees that have been legally sourced
from well-managed and credibly certified forests.

Printed and bound by
CPI Group (UK) Ltd, Croydon, CR0 4YY

For H. J. B.

Chapter One

Harvest time 1144

'Cease your whining, woman.' Osbern de Lench snarled at his wife, pushed her roughly from him and strode out into the sunshine, which was at such odds with his mood. It had been a bad morning and his temper had long since frayed. Nobody did what he told them; everyone failed him. He yelled for his horse, and berated the man who brought it in a hurry for not having it ready. The groom cringed, expecting a blow, which he promptly received. It was one of those days. The man knew that he would have been chastised just the same had he been walking the lord Osbern's horse up and down, since he would have been accused of daring to assume his lord would ride, even though he did so every day at the same hour before noon. He held the stirrup, studiously looking down at the dusty toe of the leather boot, which enabled him to step back smartly and avoid the half-hearted kick aimed at him. Osbern pulled his horse's head to the right, and cantered away with imprecations upon his lips and the dry earth rising in little clouds behind him.

'There are days, too many of 'em, when you would wish the lord Bishop of Worcester or the lord Sheriff held this manor themselves,' grumbled a tall man, wiping a scrap of sacking across his heated brow as he came round the corner of the barn. He nodded towards the receding horse and rider. 'What cause had he for ire today?'

'Who knows, other than our lady?' The groom shrugged.

The tall man glanced towards the hall and frowned.

'Get you out to the Great Field. Since I will still be here, I will attend to his horse upon his return. We need every man we can with sickle in hand if we are to get the harvest in before the weather changes, and Old Athelstan swears it will within two days.'

The groom was about to ask why Fulk the Steward had himself returned, but thought better of it. The steward might not strike him as the lord Osbern would, but he had a sharp tongue in his head if aggravated, and he already looked less than delighted. Perhaps it was simply an inauspicious day. The groom hoped Fulk would be wary of the lord's horse upon his return, lest it lash out. The old grey mare might have mellowed in temper a little with age, just as her coat had paled to the colour of snow, but horses might be as prone to ill-temper as men.

The steady rhythm of his horse's hooves calmed Osbern, as did the very routine nature of his ride. Every day, unless the weather was so foggy as to make it ridiculous, or so inclement as to make

8

it foolish, he rode up the hill that overlooked his manor and sat for a half hour, contented, surveying it. People could be difficult, and often were, but the land changed only by the seasons, and this was his land. 'Lord of the Hill' his villeins called him, always behind his back, but he knew of it and rather liked the appellation. It might be held of William de Beauchamp, the lord sheriff of the shire, who in turn held of the lord Bishop of Worcester, but Osbern's sire and grandsire had lived here, been buried here, and this was his. He knew each ridge and furrow, every tree, and had taught Baldwin, his heir, to value it as he did. At noon the sun was on his back and the hill's soft shadow cast upon the green-wooded slope to the fields below. His grandsire had cleared the very top when he first took seisin, thinking to create a motte and bailey to show how he was above the old ways and the old lord, the English Alfred. As the story had been handed down, however, he had got no further than felling the trees. His lady had so berated him for foolishness in wanting a breezy hilltop when he could keep a far better eye on his villagers down where the cluster of dwellings were focused about a little church and the stream, that he had changed his mind. Instead he had turned the Saxon hall into a barn, just to prove his Norman superiority, and built a grander hall. The barn still stood, and the new hall also, but the old church was nothing more than the footprint upon which Osbern had now overseen the erection of a new place of worship, adorned with fine carving from masons who had worked on far grander ecclesiastical buildings than a manor church. The building was roofed again, and within the week it would be fully decorated, the walls fresh and white, the arch above the chancel step chevroned in red and yellow ochre. It declared to all who entered that Osbern de Lench was a lord of means, and pious also. It would help his soul when the time came, just a little, he thought, for God alone knew how much there was for which to atone. He crossed himself and was thinking of the next world rather than this and was thus caught off balance when his horse jibbed and came up short as he was confronted.

'How come you are here?' he enquired, his brows drawn together. He was surprised, and a little annoyed, but not in any way frightened, which was not a bad state in which to die, all things considered.

The rider was in his middle twenties, well dressed, and with a serviceable sword at his side. He entered the village as though he owned it, and he might as well have, for this was Baldwin, son and heir to Osbern de Lench. He frowned at there being nobody coming out to take his horse, and then shook his head at his own stupidity. He had been thinking of other things, of the future, and completely forgotten that he had passed communities all bringing in their harvest as he had returned from his sire's manor in Warwickshire. There the harvest had been finished three days past, but it was a small manor, and the steward had been so panicked that the weather would break that he had begged Baldwin to let him commence the harvesting even before their neighbours. Baldwin liked the harvest time, seeing the culmination of the farming year, assessing the yield, the possible surplus to sell, even the act of cutting the grain stalks, which had such purpose. He had even been known to join in during his adolescence, just to show off his strong arms, though his back thereafter ached from the bending. He had not done more than survey the labours this season. He turned his horse about and headed towards the Great Field, a half-smile on his face.

The pale grey mare, almost white with age, trotted into the empty bailey and ambled towards the stables, where it halted before the shut door. The main gate was open to receive the cartloads of gathered sheaves to be threshed in the barn, which stood within a dozen yards of its grander replacement as the lord's dwelling, but the bailey was otherwise deserted. A woman, very heavily pregnant, emerged from one of the simple cotts with a midden pail. She glanced into the bailey at the sound of the horse stamping its hoof upon the compacted earth. She looked puzzled, and then waddled slowly into the enclosure. Her hand went to her mouth, for a horse to return riderless meant something bad. She dithered. With everyone bringing in the harvest there was no man to alert, and it did not occur to her to enter the hall and call for the lady. She had only ever entered it upon great feast days when the lord broached kegs of ale and had a hog roasted to celebrate the nativity or Easter. She tied the reins of the bridle to a ring driven into the wall, and set off with a slow gait, frowning in determination and concern, towards the fields. It was some time before men came running back, the harvest forgotten, following as fast as they could after a grim-faced Baldwin de Lench. They came to a halt, chests heaving, staring at the now-unsettled grey mare being calmed by the lord's heir, whose own mount stood abandoned in the bailey yard.

'Did he go up the hill?' cried Baldwin, and nobody needed to ask who 'he' was.

11

'Aye, messire Baldwin.' The groom came forward and took the horse, soothing it where the agitation of Baldwin de Lench had failed. 'He went up as usual.'

'And I saw him, just as always, up there.' A lad of about twelve pointed up the hill.

'So he must have fallen on his way back, and not long since.' Baldwin paused, and then yelled for the steward. 'Fulk, where in Jesu's name are you?'

A few moments later and the door into the hall opened. Fulk, who was not only tall but broad-shouldered, seemed to fill the doorway. He was wiping his hand across his mouth. In normal circumstances Baldwin would have made a guess that he had been imbibing his lord's wine illicitly, but these were not normal circumstances, so it was ignored. The hand dropped before the action was complete.

'Messire Baldwin.' He sounded surprised, and not overjoyed. Then he saw the horse. 'Sweet Lady Mary!'

'Take two men and fetch a hurdle. If the lord Osbern has fallen and not yet come home, swearing at his horse, he must be hurt and either on the Evesham road or the trackway up the hill. I will ride ahead, and you come on as fast as you can.'

Fulk nodded, tight-lipped, and jerked his head towards two strapping young men. As he strode towards an outbuilding a woman emerged from the hall. She looked wary, and if Fulk had not been best pleased to see Baldwin de Lench, her look was more of loathing.

'I thought I heard . . .' She stopped and stared at the horse, then crossed herself. 'A fall?'

'If he took a tumble then the horse did not come down, I

12

would swear oath to that, my lady,' piped up the groom, who had been feeling the grey's legs. 'Not a mark upon her, nor added dust upon the flanks or saddle.'

'Praise be for that,' came a mild voice. Father Matthias stepped forward. 'Best you wait within, my lady, and direct preparations of the lord's bed. Mother Winflaed, you will be needed.' He looked to an older woman, the village healer, who pursed her lips and went swiftly for her medicaments. 'We can pray also.'

The lady de Lench let herself be guided back into the cool dark of the hall.

'If salves are all he needs then prayers have indeed been answered,' muttered Baldwin, remounting his horse and heading for the gateway. 'Run, you bastards!' he cried over his shoulder at the two men now grappling a hurdle and wondering how best to carry it at speed. They looked to Fulk the Steward.

'He said run, so best we run, lads. Come on.'

The rescue party departed, and the villagers, caught between the desire to get back to the harvest and a feeling that they ought to remain, milled about rather aimlessly, talking in hushed tones.

Baldwin de Lench rode back into the village slowly, since his horse bore both himself and his father's body slung across its back. What use was a hurdle for a corpse? He was pale, and when he called out for the priest, his voice shook a little. For a moment he was angry beyond belief that everyone simply stared at him and stood stock-still. He swore. He wanted to dismount, but he was not actually sure that his knees would not buckle. He called again, even more hoarsely, and Father Matthias emerged from the

13

hall, without haste. He stared at the body, crossed himself, and was almost pushed aside by the lady de Lench.

'It cannot be true,' she cried, running in a flurry of skirts to the body of her husband. She lifted the cloak that covered it and took the head in her hands, gazing at the face as if she expected him to speak. 'Osbern. Osbern!' Her voice rose, she let go of the cloth and stepped back very suddenly, crossing herself, and began to weep. Baldwin looked down upon her bent head.

'Tears of grief, or of guilt, lady Mother?' he asked softly, but she raised her head as quickly as if he had shouted at her. He always gave her the title with sarcasm, for she was perhaps no more than five years his senior.

'What do you mean?' Her hands, which had been clasped tightly together before her mouth, went to her breast. 'What do you mean, Baldwin?'

'I mean he wed you for your looks and to give him more children, and all you bore him was that whelp you dote upon. What sort of a wife does that make you? And where is Hamo himself?'

'He is not here. He . . . he went out with his hawk this morning.'

'Did he, indeed?' Baldwin's lip curled, and his face regained some of its colour. 'And did he by chance go alone?' Her face gave him all the answer he needed. 'He did. How . . . interesting.'

'You cannot imagine he would harm his father, mes . . . my lord,' interjected Fulk the Steward, watching both of them.

'No, not with his own hand. Too weak and watery for that, my little brother Hamo, but his hand might have given silver to others, yes?' Baldwin dismounted now, taking his leg over

14

his horse's withers and jumping to the ground. His knees held firm. He drew back his cloak with what was almost a flourish, revealing Osbern de Lench bootless, swordless, and in only his undershirt and braies.

'He was robbed? So close to home?' The priest sounded amazed. 'He was but going up the hill as always.'

'Yes, "as always". Everyone here knows he does . . . did so. No stranger would. So perhaps it was a great mischance and lawless men set upon him, having by some strange coincidence turned off the Evesham road to go up the hill, but I doubt it, I doubt it very much.'

The lady de Lench, apparently speechless, cast the steward an imploring look, and he shook his head.

'But why? Why would any of Lench seek the death of the lord Osbern?' Fulk, frowning in perplexity, voiced the question. The nods from the other villagers were designed to associate themselves with that question, but many were dwelling upon incidents when their lord had been far from popular. The lord Osbern in his ire had been free with boot or hand, even the flat of his sword, and his tongue scathing, even if half his swearing was in Foreign and its niceties lost upon them. There were also memories among some of the women of the man, in his youthful years especially, when handing out violence was not all he did; sometimes he took. Old resentments rose, old fears too, for although Osbern de Lench could hurt nobody now, his heir was in the same mould; moody, intolerant and physical. Perhaps it was not so much 'why?' as 'why now?'. All the things that had caused mutterings and whispered oaths had gone on for ever, and there was nothing new or special. Besides, had not all been in the Great Field with the harvest? It could not be a villager, and of those who knew the lord Osbern's habit of riding each day at the same hour to survey his land, there only remained the stripling, the younger son.

Baldwin de Lench said nothing. He glowered at them, daring them to think other than as he thought. He could not himself think why his half-brother would see their father dead, since it would profit him nothing, but there must be some cause, hidden like a snake in the long grass, that he could discover.

'My lord,' Father Matthias's voice was soft, supplicating, 'would you have the lord Osbern laid now in his hall or in the church?'

'In the church.' It was the lady who spoke, and she sounded surprisingly determined. 'Its rebuilding meant so much to him, so very much. Take him there. I will come and do what is needed,' she shuddered, 'though it is a terrible thing to have to face.'

'God will give you strength in this hour, my lady,' assured the priest, 'as he does to us all.' He crossed himself yet again and, seeing that the lord Baldwin looked not so much grief-stricken as angry enough to commit murder himself, commenced an *Ave Maria*, which he hoped would give time for him to calm himself.

The villagers took up the familiar cadence, heads bowed, the lady de Lench began to weep again, and Baldwin muttered the prayer through gritted teeth. What Father Matthias dreaded was the swift return of Hamo de Lench from hawking. However godly a man, his added prayer was not heeded, for even as Fulk the Steward and the taller of the two hurdle bearers lifted the corpse from across Baldwin's horse there came hoofbeats, and a

16

dun pony was pulled up short in the bailey. The rider was small, still boy more than man, though he was beginning to broaden a little at the shoulder. His voice had broken but sounded as if he were as yet surprised at its depth, and there were odd notes to it. Hamo would have flung himself from his pony, had he not had his hawk upon his wrist. He was a solitary lad, who loved his hours with his bird of prey, and would as often go out alone as with a servant to carry it. As it was, he dismounted in an odd mix of scramble and care. He was frowning.

'What has happened? Mother, how comes my father is dead?' He looked to the lady de Lench, now wringing her hands again, but before she could give answer, his half-brother took two strides to him and hit him across the face. He staggered back, and the hawk flapped in alarm and to regain its balance.

'You know what happened. Sweet Jesu, there is even blood upon your sleeve. Did you actually watch? Did you get so close you could be sure he was dead?'

The youth blinked, and when he spoke his voice had risen an octave in fear.

'The . . . the blood must be from a pigeon that Superba took. I let her enjoy one and kept a brace for the pot. If I had seen our sire in danger I would have come to his aid. It is my duty.'

'Aid? What aid could you be?' spat Baldwin, derisively. 'You can barely wield a sword without whining that it makes your wrists ache. Would you spout Latin at an attacker, or plead with them to be gentle? You could use a dagger, though, if only you could bear the sight of wounds, or mayhap this shows you are not so blood-shy as you have pretended. Was the blow that killed him yours?'

'He could not do so. He loved his father, and his father loved him' The lady de Lench rose in defence of her son.

'Giving in to your pleadings for generosity and gifts was not love.' Baldwin leant forward, his eyes narrowing. 'You will not get away with it, stripling. You hear me?'

'My lord, think straight, I beg you.' Fulk the Steward, still holding the sagging body of Osbern de Lench by the shoulders, spoke up. 'There could be no cause for Young Messire to do such a thing. What gain would there be?'

'He speaks true. What gain is there to me in our father's death? None. It is you who gain.' Hamo pointed a wavering finger at his half-brother.

'I have been the heir of Osbern de Lench from the moment I was born. I have no more reason to wish his end today than yesterday or ten years past. I do have greater reason to grieve than all others, though we raised our voices at each other sometimes.'

'My lord, this death must be reported to the lord Sheriff, William de Beauchamp, and to the lord Bishop also. He will not permit thieves and cut-throats to go unpunished in the shire. He will find out the truth of all.' Father Matthias spread his hands, placatingly.

'I know who did it,' growled Baldwin, 'and if William de Beauchamp wants to take his corpse—'

'No!' cried the lady de Lench, stepping to stand in front of her son. 'It is because you hate him, hate me, nothing else. Hamo, get you to the church. Pray for your father's soul, and you, Baldwin, I defy you to drag any from their prayers and kill out of malice only. Shame upon you. Your sire lies cooling, barely an hour dead, and you are thinking only of yourself. Think of him. Let us all think of him. You ride to Worcester, Fulk, to the lord Bishop and lord Sheriff, and ensure the lord Sheriff or his deputy comes back here. We ought to set about a hue and cry, for at the least some sign may be found of which way the killers departed, and if strangers are seen from Evesham way, they can answer if they have seen anyone who looked lawless or not.'

'It is my manor, not yours, lady. I give the commands.' Baldwin clenched his fists.

'Then act the lord, not the jealous brother,' she flung at him. 'If I give commands it is because you have failed to do so.' Her bosom heaved, and her eyes, eyes that had spent years being downcast and submissive, outstared the new lord of Lench. It was he who coloured the most, and he who looked down. She felt guilty but elated, and it showed. When Baldwin raised his eyes again, he saw that look.

'When my father is buried, think where you will live, lady, for it will not be here, I swear it. Your dower is a miserable hole my sire never saw but once and pissed upon when he did. So I make you welcome of it and expect to see you crawling back to your own sire, and oh, how little he will want you. A nunnery might be best, then you can pray for my father and for your son's soul.'

'You cannot harm . . . Fulk, ride swiftly to Worcester.' Her brief confidence evaporated in an instant, and Fulk looked to Baldwin. After all, he was the lord, and his master now.

'Yes, go away and tell all. But if you are not swift there will be no need of sheriff or men. You can tell William de Beauchamp that, from me.'

'And what about the harvest, my lord?' An aged man, rather bent and lacking his front upper teeth, asked a pertinent question. Deaths or no deaths, the harvest was vital and the weather not likely to hold fair.

'We bring it in. That is what my father would have said, and I say it also. Leaving it so we starve next summer does neither his soul nor our bellies any good. Back to the Great Field, all of you, and no time for whisperings and gossiping.'

A few minutes later and Baldwin was alone at the oaken door of his manor house. He ran his hand through his hair and closed his eyes, just for a few moments.

Chapter Two

'I do not see it as sensible at all, my lord.'

Hugh Bradecote stood with folded arms and a look which could best be described as obdurate. His wife's cheeks reddened with anger and she was ready for an argument.

'I will not see you put yourself at risk, Christina.'

'What possible risk could there be in me going out to see how the harvest is advancing before it is all brought in?'

'You might have tripped over, and you did not tell anyone where you were going.'

'But it was to the North Field, not . . . York, and I am not incapable, just with child. Besides, almost the entire manor from swine boy to Father Achard is out in the fields, so I had nobody to tell except Nurse.' She huffed. 'Stop treating me as if I had no more wit than baby Gilbert.'

'Then act like the sensible woman you are and obey me.'

She looked mulish, and her bosom rose and fell rather distractingly.

'You play the tyrant.'

'No, I play the husband. It is a good role.' His calm voice infuriated her the more.

'And sometimes they are one and the same.'

He stepped close to her then, unfolding his arms so that he could hold her, though she stiffened and leant away from him.

'No tyrant. I just want you safe and . . .' He closed his eyes for a moment.

'Hugh, this is not about me, but about you. How can I make you understand there is nothing to fear? I keep telling you that what happened to Ela will not happen to me.'

'You cannot promise that.'

'No, I cannot promise, but I can tell you with certainty. This child will be blessed.' She relaxed a little and placed her hands upon his chest.

'It is not just the child, Christina. It is you. I could not bear to lose you. I have said it so often.' It was true. It still gave him nightmares, the thought of her suffering as Ela had suffered, dying as Ela had died.

'You will not lose me, my love.' Her voice softened, and she stroked his cheek. 'But do not turn me into a wasp-tongue wife with over-cosseting. I am enjoying being with child, with your child, as I have never done before, and now it has quickened . . . I feel as if I am doubly alive.'

'I am no tyrant,' he repeated, but it was more of a plea than an assertion.

'No. But you are an overcautious lord. I will be dutiful and obey,

22

but only in that I will not go outside the walls of the manor without telling you or Alcuin the Steward. I am happy. Be happy with me.' She gave an encouraging smile, and he bent to kiss her, even as he heard voices in the passage that crossed the end of the hall. They curtailed his kiss, and he turned as Serjeant Catchpoll appeared in the opening, looking disconcertingly cheerful, and followed a few paces to the rear by Walkelin, his serjeanting apprentice.

'Why is it that when you look like that, Catchpoll, I worry?' Bradecote's lips twitched.

'Like what, my lord?' The cheerful look became his death's head grin.

'Like that, you wily bastard. Have you come to drag me in to Worcester?'

'No, that I have not.'

'Then . . .'

'I have come to drag you off to Lench, where the lord Osbern de Lench has been found dead and the heir is keen to see his brother hang for it.'

'This fills you with joy, Catchpoll?'

'Well, I looks at it this way, my lord. The lord Sheriff has been in a temper for days over some squabble with his kindred and lashes out at all in range, which mostly means me, and the wife has been scolding me since the day before yesterday for breaking her best pot so . . .'

'So investigating a killing is as good as a treat for you?'

'Seems fair to say so.'

'And for me?'

'Well, we cannot all be happy, my lord.' Catchpoll sounded the voice of reason.

Christina laughed, and shook her head. It occurred to her that however much she loved having her lord at home, it would do him good to have something else to think about than her thickening figure for a week.

'You must go, my lord, and ensure that brother does not end brother without cause. You need have no fear,' she paused, for her true meaning was between herself and her lord, and then continued smoothly, 'for the harvest is all but in, and Alcuin will oversee the threshing. I shall do no more than admire the hard work and ensure there is ale for parched throats at the end of the day.'

'Are you . . . ?'

'Must I command you to your duty, my lord?' Her eyes held a twinkle.

'No, but . . .' He sighed and grinned, though a kernel of concern remained within him. 'Take yourself a beaker of beer, Catchpoll, and you also, Walkelin, and I will be ready by the time you have drained it. We can reach Lench before nightfall if we are not sluggards.'

'We are not, my lord, but I cannot say the same for my horse,' complained Walkelin.

'Well, you just kick him more, so as I do not have to kick you afterwards,' said Serjeant Catchpoll, still looking as though upon some treat.

Hugh Bradecote withdrew into the solar with his wife, who indicated that the nursemaid should leave the chamber with a waft of her hand. Bradecote took his son from her arms, and Gilbert Bradecote batted his sire's cheek with a pudgy hand. He laughed.

24

'Good,' declared Christina. 'I want you to depart without gloom. These things do not take months, but barely weeks, and if anyone is to be worried, it is me, for I shall do nothing but get rounder of belly, and you will likely attempt foolishly brave things.'

'I have too much care for my wife and son.'

'Did you have that when you launched yourself into the Severn when you cannot swim?'

'No.' He had the grace to blush. 'But there are no rivers near Lench, and I swear to you, love, that never again will I launch myself into deep water, even after a murderer.'

'Small comfort that is, but I shall take it, nevertheless.' She came close, stroked a hand down his cheek and offered her lips. At which point both discovered that kissing was remarkably difficult when one of the couple had an infant in their arms who resented not being the centre of parental interest. Giving up, Christina took the baby from him, smiled ruefully and complained about 'jealous men'. She watched in silence as Hugh packed a few things into a rolled blanket. He looked at her as he finished.

'I will take care.' It was his promise.

'Yes.'

'And you will take care also.'

'Yes, my lord. I will take care also. Now, be gone, so that you may return the sooner.'

'So, Catchpoll, what do we know, and why does one of Osbern de Lench's sons want to hang his brother? Other than brotherly dislike,' Bradecote asked, as he urged his big grey into a loping canter.

'It is a half-brother, my lord,' interjected Walkelin, before Serjeant Catchpoll could reply.

'Well, the less likelihood of love betwixt them but . . .' Bradecote still looked to Catchpoll.

'We got a tale that was as twisted as a maid's plait, and no, young Walkelin, that is not something to grin at. The steward of the manor came, on a horse sweated up and nigh on dropping, and him little better. He had gone first to the lord Bishop, as if that would be of use, and had been sent straight on to the lord Sheriff, and with some priest at the man's elbow, forever butting in to be helpful and thus muddying things further. All we know for sure is that the lord Osbern de Lench was alive this dawning and dead by a little after noon, his body found by his heir, Baldwin de Lench, after his horse came home riderless. The body was pretty nigh stripped. The lord Osbern was keen to ride to the top of the hill above his manor each noontide, so the son thinks whoever killed him, or had him killed, knew this. He also thinks it was his little brother, er, half-brother, though the steward cannot think why, and has threatened to hang him before we reach Lench unless we are swift. The lord Sheriff sent the steward back upon a fresh horse, not a very good one, mind you, and with a strict command that Baldwin do nothing until our arrival, on pain of the displeasure of the lord Sheriff of Worcestershire. The depth of this displeasure was . . . made very clear.'

'Then if Baldwin ignores the advice he is a fool beyond belief. Nevertheless, I think we do not make the journey at an easy pace, Catchpoll.'

'I feared you was going to say that,' sighed Walkelin, resigned to sore heels from kicking his reluctant mount.

'Well, I can at least entertain you upon the ride, for this is a family where they have killed each other before,' the serjeant declared.

'Go on.' Bradecote was not going to let his jaw drop like Walkelin's.

'It was when I was as Walkelin is now, my lord.'

'Still making mistakes and riding a beast that is barely a horse?' Bradecote's lips twitched.

'Perhaps a few less-than-sound decisions,' conceded Catchpoll, 'but the horse was better.'

'And I haven't made a mistake in . . . a long time, my lord. Not a big one.' Walkelin was not totally sure that the undersheriff was in jest.

'That depends on your idea of big, young Walkelin.' Serjeant Catchpoll was secretly very pleased with his protégé's progress but would not want him to know its extent. 'Now, back then, Lench was held by a man called William Herce, a widower who had married a very comely young woman. He was quite envied, right up until she did for him. He was a jealous husband, and rightly so, for she grew tired of her balding lord and turned for her pleasure to another man, though she never revealed who he was, indeed cried her innocence throughout. When the husband came too close to knowing the truth she poisoned him.'

'How was it proved her blame, and how was it known she had a lover?' Bradecote frowned. He could not but think of his Christina and her mistreatment by her first husband. A woman that abused might seek escape if not through taking her own life, then that of her abuser, whatever the risk to her immortal soul. 'I would have thought if she were the lady of the manor and he died, it would be accepted as an accident.'

'A man don't die blue-lipped, after thrashing about and screaming of many-headed beasts just because he ate too many herb dumplings, and at a meal he shared with his lady and sons. It was poison, right enough, and most like slipped in his wine. She tried to claim it was some mischief from the wise woman in the village who had been treating him for the scarlet toe, which gave him great pain.' Catchpoll saw the undersheriff's frown deepen. 'I heard off an apothecary that the Foreign is something like goot.' The frown eased, and Bradecote nodded in understanding. 'She used nightshade in the poultice for that, and that alone, she gave her oath. The wise woman was sworn for by all the village as one who had done nothing but good her whole life, aye, and had a softening of the heart for the man since she was but a young wench and he had more hair and a roving eye. There was no cause for it to be her, and just to take any doubt from it all, the wife had been asking about the poultice and what was in it.'

'Then that does give how, but not why, Catchpoll.' Bradecote was being as dogged as Walkelin.

'The lover was real, though he had neither face nor name to the end. She had taken to slipping away of a forenoon, if her lord slept late after much wine, and always came back in good spirits and smiling. The swine boy said as he had heard her in the woods, laughing and talking to a man, for he heard a man's voice and Foreign speech. He never saw, for he thought seeing might mean being seen and his life cut short by a lordly dagger, which was most likely true.'

'But that is not quite proof, surely?' Walkelin had been listening intently.

'Not of why, but since we had no doubt she did it, and none other had cause or way of doing it, it was good enough. The manor went to the elder son, Osbern, the man now dead. He must have been no older than sixteen, I reckon. The younger son, Roger, was given the manor that came from his mother at marriage, and somewhere not in the shire. Osbern was always "Osbern of Lench", not "Osbern Herce", presumably because he felt it was unlucky. Did not mean he avoided a sudden death though, after all.' Catchpoll gave a grim chuckle, as though he felt a man trying to avoid his *wyrd* was foolishness.

Despite the sheriff's men making best speed to Lench, it was early evening when the trio arrived in the village, and they slowed to a walk to follow a cart through the gateway into the bailey. A lad was leading the oxen, and a gathering of villagers followed it, the oldest and youngest to the rear. They all had stooped shoulders and lagging steps.

'The harvest waits for none,' murmured Catchpoll.

'True enough, and I wish I was at home for my own, but there.' Bradecote knew there was no point in worrying about it, for Alcuin the Steward was as trustworthy as they came, and his lady would, whatever he said, be taking an interest in how much progress was made each day. It was the better part done as he left. It struck him that this scene was so ordinary that it was hard to imagine they were about to seek the killer, or killers, of the manor's lord.

A man emerged from the hall, a man looking worried and

29

even more tired than the harvesters. He nodded at Catchpoll in recognition and made obeisance to Bradecote.

'My lord Undersheriff, I am glad you are here. The lord Baldwin is within and the lady de Lench.'

'And no hangings yet.' Bradecote did not make it a question, merely a seeking confirmation.

'No, my lord, not that it has been easy . . . Glad I am that you are here. Messire Hamo is in the priest's house, away from the eye of the lord Baldwin. Kenelm,' the steward jerked his head at one of the younger men, 'take the lord Undersheriff's horse and the others thereafter. I will take you in to the lord Baldwin, my lord.' He bowed again to Bradecote, and did as he said.

The hall was as all halls, rather dark and pleasantly cool after a warm ride. Upon the lord's seat at the end of it sat a man perhaps ten years younger than himself, judged Bradecote, and a man unused to the position. He gripped the oaken arms rather firmly, and half rose before thinking it better to assert his own authority by remaining seated. It did not bother Bradecote, though he heard Catchpoll's hissing intake of breath. Serjeant Catchpoll was very jealous of the importance of the office of undersheriff.

'I am Hugh Bradecote, the lord William de Beauchamp's undersheriff, with Catchpoll, the lord Sheriff's serjeant, and Walkelin, trusted man.' Bradecote thought it showed Walkelin was not just a horse-holder but would not mark him as someone the servants had to treat with caution and in whose presence hold their tongues. He felt, rather than saw or heard, Catchpoll's approbation.

'Baldwin de Lench, lord of Lench,' responded the seated man, and totally ignored the lady sat a little to the side of him.

She was fair, rather pale, and had a look that was half fearful and half proud. Not used to being lady of the manor either, thought Bradecote, assuming she was Baldwin's wife, for she looked younger than her years.

'I would have word with your hus . . .' Bradecote halted as her eyes widened in shocked surprise, and Baldwin de Lench interrupted.

'I am not wed. That is my sire's grieving widow.' His voice dripped with sarcasm.

'My apologies, lady, for the error. I would not distress you with hearing details you might otherwise prefer to remain unknown to you, so perhaps you would care to withdraw to your solar.'

'My solar, not hers,' muttered Baldwin.

'What details might upset me when I have washed the body, seen the wounds, my lord Bradecote?' Her voice was soft but did not waver.

Catchpoll sighed. He far preferred corpses untouched by respectful tending, for he could learn more from them, but it was a natural thing to have done.

'If you wish to remain, then—'

'I do not want her present.' Baldwin stood up. 'She will interrupt to keep telling you her son is nigh on a saint.'

'No saint, but not so great a sinner, and not one who would kill his sire,' she riposted.

'Then I will speak with you both, one after the other, and to your son, my lady, after that.' There was such animosity between the pair that Bradecote thought nothing would be achieved with them together. 'But first we must see the body of Osbern de Lench.'

'He lies before the altar, my lord,' said the widow.

'Thank you. We will not be long.'

'I shall come with you.' Baldwin looked suspicious.

'No. A corpse is treated with respect, but it is not fitting for kin to have to observe.' It had been a hot day, but Bradecote thought the stiffening after death must be setting in by now. 'We will not be long.' He nodded, as though dismissing them, and turned upon his heel. He had asserted authority, and only the low mutter from Baldwin showed that the new lord of Lench had realised too late that it had been imposed.

The church was silent except for the sound of a lone voice chanting in Latin, which faltered as they opened the door and stepped within. A priest with greying tonsure turned his face to them and gave a respectful nod, then finished the prayer and crossed himself before rising from his knees. He noted Bradecote's garb and demeanour.

'You have come from the lord Sheriff, my lord?'

'We have, Father, and we need to see the body, though we interrupt your prayers.' Bradecote spoke gently enough but would clearly not brook demur.

'God hears the silent prayer as much as the one that is voiced, and from any place. Would you have me leave you?'

'It is your church, Father.'

'It is God's church, my son, and in a way Osbern de Lench's, for he spent much to make it as you see, resplendent, honouring the Creator. The colours are barely dry upon the stone, but there, in comparison with the Glories of Heaven it is but a hogcote, and I pray that the soul of the lord Osbern might, in time, reach them.'

32

'What sort of man was he, Father? Do not answer to praise the dead but to be honest with us. It helps us, I promise.'

'Not an easy man,' the priest sighed, 'for he was afflicted with a temper and of recent years a leaning to the heart-sick. It was as if sometimes he hated his own person but took it out upon others. Love of self to excess is sinful, for it means ignoring others, but hating self can be as bad. The only thing that truly delighted him, always, was the land. He would go up to the top of the hill every day if he could see the manor below and the weather was not foul, and just look down on it and be eased. He always seemed less angry upon return.'

'His family pleased him though?' Catchpoll crossed himself before the altar and began to draw back the cloth that covered the body, giving silent thanks that the body had not been shrouded by the widow. He sounded almost casual, as if the answer would be just a pleasantry.

'Yes, but . . . like an ebb and flow of tide, not all the time. Of course the lord Baldwin is too alike to his sire for them to have been always in amity. There were ravings from both sides, much stamping and roaring, like stags before the rut, but they respected each other. The lady, she is the second wife, and I think it hard sometimes to fill that role if the first was loved. The lady who bore Baldwin and his sister died when he was but a boy of six or seven, and those who were here then will tell you the lord Osbern grieved mightily, but wed again three years later, taking a very young wife. I think he feared having only the one son to inherit, life being always out of our own hands. I came to the parish that year and christened the child she bore him, messire Hamo, but the travail was difficult and she was barren thereafter.'

'And this younger son was rejected?' Bradecote frowned, listening, but whilst watching the silent interrogation of the body by Serjeant Catchpoll, who would undoubtedly have spoken out loud to it had the priest not been hard by. Walkelin stood beside the body also, but might have been mistaken for a respectful mourner, his woollen cap gripped in his hands and his head bowed. 'It seems unlikely unless the boy showed some marked imperfection. If a man wanted another son and got one, would he not rejoice and dote upon him?'

'What might give you . . . ? Oh, the lord Baldwin accusing his brother . . . that is, I am sure, just their dislike and jealousy.'

'So you are saying Hamo was preferred, then?' Bradecote's frown became more pronounced. He looked away from the body and straight at the priest, knowing that he would hold the man's gaze. Catchpoll was now getting Walkelin to help him turn the body over. It was not dignified.

'No. But . . . it is hard to explain, my lord. The lord Osbern liked to command and be obeyed, yet despised those who submitted to him. The lady de Lench learnt the lesson, I fear painfully, early in the marriage, and the meeker she became the more he railed at the slightest failure. She would not stand up for herself, only her child, but she also taught the boy not to annoy his sire. Messire Hamo is a quiet lad, watchful, careful. He does not trust, I think, and you can see why. He is clever, for I taught him to read and even write a little, which is more than his sire or brother could ever do, and he learnt to get what he wanted by only ever asking when the moment was propitious. The lord Baldwin just asked when the idea hit him and was thus often rebuffed. So the lord Baldwin, who hates the lady who took his mother's place, not least because she is beautiful and young, also hates her son who seems to get what he wants and be favoured. This is so even though he knows his sire loved him for being his firstborn, and in his own mould and that of his mother. She was, they say, a raven-haired, headstrong woman. Rare fights they had, according to the woman who nursed the two babes, but always ended in another sort of passion, if you understand me.' The priest blushed. 'Perhaps that is why he picked the opposite second time – he could not bear someone so like unto her.' He paused. 'It is one thing I think a priest can never quite understand, the many tangled bonds of man and wife in the flesh and in the heart. I have found in my life the love that is compassion, not passion.'

The undersheriff said nothing. He felt he had enough tangled bonds in the family of the dead man without adding the influence of a long-dead wife, though the past so often bore down upon the present.

'My lord,' Catchpoll's tone meant that he did not need to say 'come and look'.

'Excuse me, Father.' Bradecote went to join his men and positioned himself between the corpse and the priest.

'Several knife wounds, my lord, but it was the one up under the ribs into the heart as did for him in moments.' Catchpoll spoke quietly.

On the cleaned and cold body the wounds looked rather unimportant, just a few places where the pale skin was split for the width of a knife blade, one low in the belly, one upper right and one a little wider just below the ribs and slightly to

35

the side on the left. There was something wrong about them as a group. The undersheriff opened his mouth to speak but Catchpoll jumped in first.

'No other marks upon the body, my lord.' Catchpoll's voice was devoid of any emotion. If this was all that the serjeant had gathered from the body, Bradecote felt he would sound far less unconcerned. There was more, but Catchpoll was not going to discuss it now.

'Thank you, Serjeant.' It was his turn to sound wooden. He turned to address the priest. 'We can leave you and the mortal remains of Osbern de Lench in peace, Father.'

'I could have told you as much as you have learnt, my lord. I was with the lady when she washed the body.' The priest sounded mildly peeved, as though a deceit had been wrought upon him and he could not work out what it was. 'There was much blood in the undershirt, and both dust and dirt all over him from where he must have been dragged to the ground by whoever set upon him, and the three wounds.'

Catchpoll coughed. As signals went it was hardly subtle, but the priest was thinking of his dead lord and not attending.

'The law needs to see, not just hear, reports,' said Bradecote, by way of reason and dismissal, and sounding as official as possible. 'Sometimes we notice things others miss.'

'Ah yes, I see.' This seemed to cheer the priest a little. It was just the way things were done. He understood ritual. 'God aid your discovery of the wicked.'

'Amen to that, Father.' Bradecote gave him a tight smile and walked out into the evening warmth. Catchpoll and Walkelin followed. The trio did not head straight back to the hall, but

36

walked to the stable and went within, where only the horses' ears twitched to listen to them.

'Well, Catchpoll, why were those wounds all wrong, and what else did you learn from the lord Osbern de Lench?'

'Not enough, but then it is rarely enough and more questions than answers, though it gives us a start, my lord. It gives us a start.' The serjeant pulled one of his ruminating faces. 'I sort of need to start at the end. The priest assumed the body was dusty because some lawless men dragged the lord Osbern from his horse and did for him on the ground. Nice idea if lawless men were ever there, but I doubt that, a lot. We will see well enough when we gets to see the place he died.' He paused for effect, but Bradecote only raised an eyebrow. Walkelin did not hold back.

'But there were three wounds. A planned killing you would think would have one clean one, but robbers are hasty.'

'There is something not right about the wounds though, Walkelin.' Bradecote frowned. 'Three different places and the knife held with the blade horizontal for all three. Random yet no haste.' He shook his head, and Catchpoll sighed.

'You have it that far but no further, my lord, eh? Those wounds alone show us there were no robbers. If a man is brought down, heavy and sudden, from a horse, you would think there would be some mark, a scuff of skin, just somewhere, though I grant that is not most important. What is important is those wounds. For a start, the two into the belly went in straight, stabbed down into his innards, blows to a man lying on his back. But the thrust that killed him was delivered upwards, not straight as if down into the chest of a man on the ground, Besides, most robbers would more likely slit a belly or throat, or

37

drive the knife straight down through the windpipe, from what I have seen of their ways.'

'So the wound that killed him was the first, and when he was mounted.' Bradecote frowned. 'The other two were after death and just for show. That was it. They made no sense because they were with intent but no passion, no anger. I had expected several close, repeated blows, slashes, battle wounds. He was not ambushed, and he let his killer in close, so he knew them. Were they on horseback too?'

'The wound was a little towards the side, and none of the horses in this stable other than yours, my lord, is a tall beast, nor was the lord Osbern a lanky-bodied man. I reckon as the knife was thrust in at about five and a half feet from the ground. Walkelin, get on that horse there, the grey.'

'You are more his height, Serjeant,' mumbled Walkelin.

'But I am stiffer of limb, so up with you.'

Walkelin did a little bounce to lean over the horse's withers and scrambled onto its back. It turned its head to stare at him but did nothing more than stamp a foot.

'There, my lord. There would be a saddle, true enough, but since Walkelin is taller than the dead man he accounts for a bit of that. Also if I pulls him a bit towards me like so,' he reached and grabbed Walkelin by the front of his cotte and pulled, 'the distance shortens a little. The knife entered about here,' he poked Walkelin hard enough with a finger for him to grumble, 'and even though striking upwards would have far less force from a man on the ground, what it went through was soft flesh into the heart, not breaking bones. Not saying it is more likely, but any man of reasonable height could do it.'

'So we still only have that he was killed by someone on a horse or on foot. Doesn't get us closer, Catchpoll.' Bradecote folded his arms as Walkelin slid from the grey.

'Yes, but we knows he wasn't killed by no robber, and it was someone he recognised, like you said. No stranger would get knife-close to his side, either way.'

'Which means we will find the killer, because they are still here.' Walkelin sounded delighted.

'And just how many men are still here? A village full.' Catchpoll grimaced.

'But it is harvest. Everyone would be in the fields, Serjeant, from men-at-arms to oldmothers.'

'Except our killer? Fair point, young Walkelin.'

'We are ahead of ourselves.' Bradecote was not going to leap ahead to a line of thought that might be too narrow. 'I agree with what you say. The killer was not unknown to Osbern de Lench. I go no further, yet. Let us hear from the son who found the body, and then we will also see where he was found. Come on.'

Chapter Three

Within the hall it was as though those present had been turned, like the wife of Lot, into pillars of salt, for they seemed not to have moved and the atmosphere suggested that nor had they spoken. Baldwin de Lench still looked uncomfortable in his father's place, and the widow was staring at her folded hands in her lap. Her face was impassive, but those hands were gripped tightly together. Bradecote was unsure whether she was angry, frightened, or both. The one thing she did not look was grief-stricken.

'So, you have seen my father's body. It is clear what happened. He was stabbed.' Baldwin looked tired and was even more tetchy.

'We have, but knowing that a man died by knife or arrow, sword or stone is but a very little step upon our path to who did the deed.' Bradecote was unruffled. 'I said I would speak with you after seeing the body, and I will, but if it was you who found him, I would have you speak as you lead us to the spot. We have an hour until full dark and can still learn much that is fresh. On foot would be best, unless it is far, which I doubt.' Catchpoll had already remarked that only a lord would bother to ride to the top of the little hill, since it could be no more than a few furlongs from the hall to the very top.

Catchpoll did not test this reckoning by paces as they set off out of Lench upon the Evesham road, which rose to the southward. He listened as intently as his fellows while Baldwin described how he had come from the Great Field, as soon as a woman had appeared from the village, gabbling that his father's horse had returned home alone.

'My thought was the obvious one, that his horse had stumbled or been frightened by a rising bird and jibbed, and my father had been caught unawares and fallen. He was not home even as we reached it, so he must have hurt a leg, twisted a knee, perhaps even broken a bone. I ordered Fulk the Steward to bring two men with a hurdle as fast as they could manage, and set off myself, upon my horse, to the spot.' He paused. 'I did not expect to find his corpse. We leave the road here and it is but the track to the hilltop, not one taken on the way from anywhere. No casual passer-by killed my father, my lord Bradecote.'

Bradecote noted the more polite appellation. He was glad the man was calmer.

'And you knew he would be here because he had told someone it was where he was heading?' The undersheriff already knew this was a habitual journey, but it was good when everyone said the same thing.

'It could be no other around the noon hour, and besides, a lad saw him up on the hill, almost silhouetted as he liked to be, with the sun on his back and his manor before him. He used to say the land was the one thing that would never change beyond the circle of the seasons, never betray you. "Lord of the Hill" the people here called him, and I shall be as him and do as he did.' Baldwin made it sound a vow. He halted. 'There, that is the place. He pointed to a patch of earth the same as any other but did not go closer. 'He was lying upon the ground, his eyes open, staring Heavenward, and he was dead. God have mercy upon his soul.' He crossed himself.

Catchpoll went forward first, his back bent, looking as though he sought some small precious item lost among the grass and dust. Then he called for Walkelin, with his young eyes, to follow his path. He knelt, grunting, and Bradecote was not sure if it was his usual complaint about his knees or acknowledging some detail that proved something to him. He let his men study the ground and spoke to Baldwin de Lench.

'You say whoever killed him knew him well enough to know his habit of coming up the hill, yet he was robbed of garb and . . . was there a dagger?' There was no reason the man would wear his sword, but he might have been a man who always had a dagger at his belt.

'Either the killer thought to disguise their deed as robbery, or was paid to kill and the dagger and clothing were an added gain. I regret its loss, for it was a good one.'

'Yet they did not steal his horse,' commented Walkelin,

rubbing his finger in a horseshoe imprint upon the ground. The weather had been dry, and the lord Osbern took the same path every day. He was not sure if it was new or days old.

'It must have been frightened and headed home to its stable before they could catch the reins.' Baldwin shrugged. 'If they were paid, then it was bad luck for them, but not worth chasing after it and being seen.'

'Where did you dismount, my lord?' enquired Catchpoll.

'Right by the body, but no doubt the hoof prints are mostly my father's mare's. Fulk and the two men arrived, out of breath and some time after me, of course. You may see where the hurdle was laid upon the ground to place the body upon it.' Baldwin de Lench seemed suddenly to have sloughed off the anger that filled him in the hall, and it was noticeable. Well, thought Bradecote, the very first shock was ebbing, there were others to take up the burden of discovering the killer, and he might just have reached the strange numb stage of grief, if grief was strong in him. Most likely it was that he was away from the lady and the young half-brother whom he must loathe. Here, in the warm onset of a late summer night, the mantle of lordship had truly fallen upon him, and those two did not exist. There was only the hooting of an owl and the final rustlings in a rookery as the birds settled to rest – sounds which went beyond the generations of men, their births and deaths.

'You say he was facing skywards, on his back. Was there anything about him, beyond the wounds, that you recall? Anything particular?' Bradecote saw Baldwin de Lench's frown, one more of irritation than perplexity.

43

'I did not think beyond his death. He was my father, and he died by a man's intent.'

'Must have been bad, my lord, with all that blood.' Walkelin did not look up, but shook his head, sadly. Catchpoll hid a smile. The lad really was learning the craft.

'Blood is blood, and I have seen it, but the undershirt was very wet with it, and I do not know about his leather tunic, for it was one open down the front, and besides, it is gone.'

'A good cloak for winter, a fine leather coat, such would I be glad to have if not too stained.' Walkelin knew his path and kept to it, but Catchpoll, on his hands and knees, raised one finger in covert warning. Go no further.

'Who is to say why they near stripped him?' Baldwin de Lench sounded annoyed now. Men-at-arms were to be spoken to, not there to offer views. 'Does he always bleat so much?' He looked at Bradecote.

'Not if he doesn't want a boot up his arse.' Bradecote kicked Walkelin, casually, though the blow was more a push to the buttock with the sole of his boot. Walkelin obligingly fell over, muttering. De Lench looked more approving. It was clearly the way he treated his inferiors if they displeased him. 'Mind you, the question is valid.'

'Robbery was just a way of covering up what happened, my lord Undersheriff. Mayhap they took more than what might be of use just to make it all the clearer. Had they but stolen his boots it would seem wrong.'

It was not an unreasonable suggestion, and Bradecote nodded, as if he agreed. 'It fits.'

'Of course it does. That miserable stick of a youth that I am assured is my half-brother by blood is crafty, not bold of hand. He would watch, yes, but prefer that to striking the blow.'

'Why do you say it was him?' Bradecote sounded interested, not sceptical. It encouraged the giving of information.

'Because he was not in the Great Field with the harvest, nor in the hall. He was out hawking, and alone. He came home after the body was brought in and was all agitation, but that was an act. He is sly, and he cares for nobody, not even his own mother much. I have seen him look at her, look as if she was some mystery he could not unravel. He watches always, speaks but little and is as poisonous as an adder. He killed my father, had him killed.' The man sounded sure.

'But why?' Serjeant Catchpoll did not fear a boot, not only being patently more senior than a man-at-arms who might get his arse kicked, but also being further away, and looked up. 'My lord, paying others to kill is not hot blood. It is a plan, with a reason. So why?' He sounded respectful, which Bradecote knew was not something he did by nature. This was as much an act as the kicking of Walkelin.

'I am not the lord Sheriff's man. It is your task to discover that. I am just saying it was him. I know it.'

The tetchiness, thought Bradecote, might actually be natural to the man.

'Seen enough, Serjeant?' He sounded commanding.

'Yes, my lord.'

'Then we return to the manor. The light is going anyway.'

The quartet walked back in silence. In the hall the candles had been lit, and Fulk the Steward was talking to a maidservant bearing the

45

clear remains of a meal. It reminded the sheriff's men that they had empty stomachs. There was no sign of the lady de Lench.

'Where is she?' growled the lord Baldwin.

'My lady was tired and had the headache, my lord. She begs your forgiveness, my lord Undersheriff, and has retired for the night.'

'The bitch! She just wanted to keep the lord's bed. Serve her right if I pull back the curtain and—'

'She is your mother, my lord.' Fulk sounded horrified.

'She did not bear me. There is no blood between us.' Baldwin sneered.

'Holy Church's words,' the steward chided.

'Do you obey all of Holy Church's words, Fulk?' The sneer lengthened.

Fulk blushed, and lowered his gaze.

'Well, I will not make her share my bed, but nor will I share my solar with her and sleep in the other bed. Not tonight. My hall is at your disposal, my lord Bradecote. We sleep here when we have eaten.'

Sleep did sound a good idea, and food even better. Bradecote doubted Catchpoll or Walkelin had taken more than the odd beaker of small beer and perhaps a crust since first light, and he had certainly not done so. He had no intention of waking the lady, but hearing about her son from her might give another view before they spoke with him. That would be for the morning.

'Steward, you will see that messire Hamo comes to you and does not leave your dwelling. We will speak with him on the morrow.' Bradecote thought he looked more able to restrain the youth than the mild priest.

'As you wish, my lord.'

'And Walkelin will be lodged with you also, lest your watch be less than needful.' That made for added security.

Walkelin was caught between relief that he would not have to share the same chamber as the lord Baldwin, who looked as if he might as easily kick other men's subordinates as his own, and regret at being out of any muttered exchange of views between Serjeant Catchpoll and the lord Bradecote.

'Shall I bring your roll, my lord?' Catchpoll was so unlike a servant that Bradecote could have laughed out loud.

'No, Serjeant, I want to see my horse is bedded well for myself.'

It was the excuse they wanted. Having Baldwin de Lench in the chamber with them would prevent mulling over anything learnt thus far.

'If we are going to spend much more time among the horse dung and hay munching, we might as well bed down here,' grumbled Catchpoll, when they entered the stable. 'Pox on the man for not taking to the bed he knew. It was good enough for him last night.'

'But last night it was his and now it merely belongs to him. Sweet Virgin, how he hates the lady his sire wed.' Bradecote shook his head.

'Hates now, my lord, but was it hate born of something else?' Walkelin, who had decided that his watch would commence after he had taken any private instructions from his superiors, looked thoughtful. Those superiors stared at him. This was deep thinking.

'Go on, young Walkelin. Your loins are the youngest.'

Catchpoll, realising what he was saying, grinned his death's head grin. 'Tell us the lust of youth.'

'Well,' the flame hair met the rising blush to the brow, 'a mere lad he was when his sire took a new wife, but when he left boyhood and became a man she was what, no more than twenty, beautiful and being used by his father in the same chamber. A curtain can hide sights, not sounds. An easy step it would be to hear, and dream, and if ever he overstepped the mark and she rejected him, or mocked his youth, well, love and hate, Serjeant, you have said, are close as lovers themselves. One became the other, and festered. If we had not been here tonight, would he have torn back the curtain from hate and sinned with her against her will? Who would stop him?'

Bradecote winced. It was not a nice thought, but likely enough.

'You know what,' remarked Catchpoll, looking at the still-blushing Walkelin, 'I have often moaned at you for thinking with your *beallucas* but I think they give you wisdom in this. Makes good sense, I agree.'

'But he cannot wed his father's wife, nor whore her, openly. Even if he loved her, not hated her, there is no reason to kill his sire.' Bradecote spoke as if to himself.

'And it was the other son who was absent. The lord Baldwin was in the field with the harvesters, my lord. He could not have done so.' Walkelin did not wish to dwell on carnal matters, at least not other men's. Dwelling on what he had been doing with Eluned, the kitchen maid, just after sunset last eve, that was worth dwelling on, but in private, and with a grin on his face.

'Yes. I ramble.' Bradecote scratched his nose. 'So, in the short time we have before the rumbling of my belly is louder than my voice, was there anything learnt from the place where Osbern de Lench died, and does it prove anything?'

'There was the hoof prints from two horses, my lord. One set heading up the hill and the other down.' Catchpoll was confident. Walkelin looked amazed. 'The one coming down must have been the dead man, returning from his gazing upon his lands, and the one going up met him.'

'But how do you know they was from today, Serjeant?' Walkelin stared at him.

'There was others, I grant, and the ground is quite hard, but there were signs that a horse coming down the hill stopped and stood square. Its toes dug in a little, and only the marks of a standing horse would be side by side. The traces of the horse heading up the hill were less certain, but there was fresh horse shit where it must have stood.'

'But were not the second set of marks those of Baldwin de Lench's horse when he came to find his father?' Bradecote frowned.

'Ah no, my lord. You see, I found the standing prints not where he said he stopped when he dismounted. There you could see the scuffs from the hurdle being dropped, and not footprints but disturbing of the ground, from feet, the dragging of the corpse, and no doubt the lord Baldwin kneeling by the body. Flower stems were broken off, and there was a trace of dark, dried blood. No doubt the body was rolled before it was stripped. The two horses I speak of met so the riders were close, knee to knee, you might say.'

49

'So the killer was mounted, my lord. They had a horse, which discounts most of Lench,' said Walkelin.

'Or had access to a horse for at least as long as it took to trot up the track and do the deed,' amended Catchpoll, looking about the stable. 'We have the lord Osbern's grey and the two horses of the sons, both of which were not here. The other horse is the one the lord Sheriff sent the steward back on, so the beast that came to Worcester was here.'

'But if you aren't used to riding a horse you fall off a lot. I know I did when I first had to ride,' said Walkelin.

'You still do.' Catchpoll grinned.

'But you were a town lad.' Bradecote remembered riding bareback as a boy even before he had a lordling's pony. 'On a manor most lads have been up on a horse's back, whether they risked a thrashing for it or not. They vie to bring in my horse from grazing, and would not lead it all the way. A few manors even have a horse for a cart, not the plough oxen. It may not be as likely but . . . and there is a groom who will be confident with the animals here. It is possible.'

'And we have been happy to think the killer is here, my lord, but lords know their neighbours and their neighbours know them,' declared Catchpoll, with a grimace. 'The Lord of the Hill name must have been known for miles about, and his habit. If the father was like the short-tempered bastard that is the son, as the priest said, we may have to cast our net wider.'

'I pray that is not so,' Bradecote groaned. 'Let us hope that our speech with the young Hamo in the morning makes all clear. The only trouble is, I think that Baldwin de Lench takes a path and cannot step from it. His very certainty makes me doubt he can be right, and if he is not, we are as in this stable, in the dark.'

'You listen well, young Walkelin, if the steward's wife is loose-tongued over the meal. We may learn more from others one step back from this family at each other's throats.'

'Er, he is wifeless, Serjeant. A serving wench told me.' Walkelin looked pleased to reveal something that the serjeant did not know, but a bit sheepish.

'Then you'll be eating with the servants, and even better. More tongues to wag. Just make sure yours doesn't . . .' The lecherous look on Catchpoll's face, even in the gloom, needed no more.

'Upon which we part.' Bradecote interrupted him. 'You have a mind like a—'

'—single man of twenty summers. Yes, my lord. It keeps me young.' Catchpoll grabbed his bed roll. 'Your belly is rumbling loud, my lord. We eats and sleeps, and God grant us wisdom on the morrow.'

'Amen.'

Chapter Four

Hugh Bradecote woke to the sound of Catchpoll coughing and hawking into the cold hearth and grumbling about his knees. The serjeant walked past him, a little stiffly, and headed out into the cool of early morning, if not to commune with nature then to answer its call. Bradecote stretched his long limbs, sniffed and sat up. Baldwin de Lench was lying on his stomach with his head pillowed on his arms, still oblivious to the world. At least the lady would have slept safely, thought the undersheriff, getting to his feet and rolling up his blanket. They had learnt nothing over the meal except that his cook made a good pottage with the added delight of a portion of spit roasted pigeon, not that a brace of pigeon went far between three. Catchpoll had not been offered any of it, for it was kept for the lord, the lady and the undersheriff, with none even for the lad whose hawk brought the birds to ground. The fact that the lordling had gone out hawking and returned with game did not mean much, since a good bird and good fortune might have brought down their dinner soon after he rode out.

Bradecote went outside and found Catchpoll shaking water from his face and hair, having thrust both in a bucket of water. He reminded Bradecote of a grizzled old hound.

'Better?' enquired Bradecote.

'Much.'

'De Lench still sleeps.'

'Good. Them as has real work is already about, so we should have time to speak with Walkelin and see if he learnt anything, nice and quiet like. Most everyone will be off to the field as soon as they may. There's streaks of red in the dawn and a smell in the air makes me think they have today, if lucky, to get in their harvest.' Catchpoll sounded less than hopeful.

'I wish them luck then, for theirs is mine also. We were well over halfway when I left, but I could not say for sure we would end today. Mind you, Alcuin, if he feared rain, would have all to work before the sun was full risen over the horizon.'

'But the steward here has more to worry him than the harvest. Ah, here is Walkelin.'

Walkelin, his red hair looking tousled and his eyes bleary, emerged from the steward's modest dwelling beyond the palisade without looking up, and relieved himself against a nearby tree as his superiors walked from the enclosure to join him. When he turned round, they were but a few paces from him, looking mildly amused.

'Greetings to you also, Walkelin,' murmured Bradecote.

53

'Having got that off your mind, did you learn anything from the servants or Hamo de Lench himself?'

'My lord,' Walkelin ignored what he had just been doing, 'I cannot say anything about whether he had his father killed, but he is an odd one and no mistake. And that is the view of everyone else, not just me.'

'So, tell us.' Bradecote led the trio away from the cluster of low cotts that made Lench and leant against the solid trunk of an ash tree, folding his arms before him.

'The lord's servants do not think their lot will be better under the lord Baldwin, because they say he is as like unto his father as one pea in a pod to another, with an added dash of his mother's temper thrown in. Moody was the father, and moody will be the son, and all had best watch out when he snarls. I asked, all innocent, if they would have preferred if the young lordling Hamo had the manor in his stead, and they laughed outright. Seems he has a mind that drifts, lives in a world all his own. He does not shout at them or act powerful, but never speaks to them unless he gives a command, and then assumes it will be done because servants . . . serve. He has never goosed a maid, takes no interest in the land and talks to his hawks rather than people.'

'He sounds simple, but the lord Baldwin was all for him being clever and crafty.' Catchpoll frowned.

'Well, it depends on how you mean both, Serjeant. He can read, and he can write also, even chooses to do it, little notes on vellum he keeps in a box that nobody must touch. Not that anyone would know what they meant. One woman said he made her flesh creep, because he was watching everyone all the time, the way a cat watches a mouse. Sort of interested, and yet as though they were different animals.' He dropped his voice. 'She thinks there were elves at his birthing.' Walkelin was not sure how seriously to take elves. His oldmother had told tales of them as if she had seen them herself, and they were not happy tales.

Bradecote looked sceptical. 'He was clever enough also to get what he wanted by choosing his time with his sire. He understood him well enough.'

'But, my lord, that would not be difficult, just from watching and learning. He would not need to understand him. The lord Baldwin, for example, must have understood his father, a man formed like himself, but blundered into requests like a boar in the forest. He understood but did not think.' Walkelin was not put off.

'And was this thinking lad awake when you returned to the steward's home?' Catchpoll thought direct knowledge better than talk of elves and weirdness.

'Yes, for a while. He said he did not like Fulk's dwelling because it smelt of chickens, and he would rather sleep in the church.'

'With his father's corpse laid before the altar?' Bradecote raised his eyebrows.

'Aye, my lord. No wonder you are surprised. So was Fulk. He said he could not sleep there with the body in the church. And then messire Hamo looked at him and said it was but a corpse and his father was on his path to God's Heaven. He made it sound as though he was walking to Evesham . . . just ordinary.' Walkelin shook his head. 'When Fulk told him it was your command that he remain, he folded his arms and told Fulk to take his chickens to the hall so you could put up with them. Then, when Fulk shooed them out, he lay down, turned over and went to sleep. Er, the chickens were taken to Fulk's neighbour.'

'We can be grateful for that.' Bradecote looked thoughtful. 'It will be interesting to hear the picture of her son that the lady gives us. You stay to guard the lordling, Walkelin.'

'As you wish, my lord.'

The lady de Lench was at that moment in heated argument with her husband's son, who had turned on her when she emerged from the solar and told her in no uncertain terms that she would not sleep another night in the lord's bed. Once his father was in the earth she would be gone, and he cared not whether she went to her own father or the guest hall in Evesham Abbey.

'But I do, and I say she stays.' Hugh Bradecote stood in the doorway, Serjeant Catchpoll behind him. 'Until this is ended and the killer of Osbern de Lench taken, she stays.'

'Through what need? She could not have killed him. Look at her.'

Bradecote looked. She still looked younger than her years, and there was a birdlike fragility to her. Without taking his eyes from her he spoke to Baldwin.

'Yet you say, as if it were fact, that your brother,' and he intentionally omitted the half-blood relationship, 'paid men to kill your sire but discount the lady? Why?'

'Me? Kill my lord?' The lady de Lench actually jumped at the suggestion. 'What good could come to me from his death? What he threatens,' she pointed at Baldwin, 'is no more than I have always known he would do. I lose all.'

Catchpoll was looking at the pointing finger, or rather her wrist now showing from the sleeve of her gown. There was bruising upon it, the sort of bruising that would come from a very hard grip.

'Where came you by the bruises, my lady?' The serjeant had seen women over the years whose husbands treated them roughly, when in drink or from plain ill-temper, though of course in this case it might be they came from Baldwin the son, not Osbern the husband. What had passed before the sheriff's men had arrived the day before was unknown, but unlikely to have been amicable, if Baldwin had been all too ready to hang the son of her body.

'Oh, I am not sure. I am one who bruises at the slightest thing, and oft times forget whence they sprang.' It was said airily.

It was the husband then, thought Catchpoll, but wondered if she protected the dead from fear of the living, or as something she could barter for Baldwin pressing the case less harshly against the young Hamo.

Bradecote's thought was that she was not a good liar, which might assist them in other things.

'What matter are her bruises when you are seeking my sire's killer?' Baldwin snarled. 'I have given you all you need so why do you not—?'

'You may leave the hall, and we will speak with the lady de Lench here or in her solar.' Bradecote spoke with authority and made it hers still, at least until the body was buried. He also did not much like Baldwin de Lench, so annoying him was a pleasure. It certainly worked. The new lord of Lench grew very red in the face, opened his mouth as if to defy him, then saw the amusement on Catchpoll's grizzled countenance. The man was clearly waiting for the entertainment. Well, he would not get it. Instead, Baldwin declared he would go to the Great Field and see how the harvesters progressed. If he was wanted then they must come to him there. It was the best he could do, and it was not much. He strode out, fuming.

'You may be more comfortable in your solar, lady,' said Bradecote, gently.

'Yes, I . . . I thank you, my lord.' She led the way into the solar and Bradecote followed, indicating that Catchpoll keep a little back by the open door between it and the hall. It felt less intimidating with the sheriff's men apart, yet he would be able to hear all that was said and speak also. She sat upon a seat, with a low back and arms which she gripped as if they gave her strength.

'I am not here to frighten you, my lady, but to find out truth.' Bradecote looked squarely at her. 'Your lord was killed by someone who knew his habits, and who had cause to wish him ill. It was someone he recognised.'

'It was not my son. Hamo would not kill his father.'

'I did not say that it was. But we have no idea of who liked or loathed the lord Osbern.' It gave her the chance to advance alternatives to it being her child.

'Osbern was not liked, my lord Bradecote, by anyone, when truth is spoken. He was a difficult man to like. He was respected, and by some he was feared, but he was not liked. Yet many people are not liked and still they are not cut down in

58

blood. He was pious, for all his anger. The new church you see is proof of his generosity to the Church, and he prayed, every night he prayed, silently, before he retired, sometimes with tears upon his cheeks. I never saw him humble before any man, but I would give him his due and say he was humble before God.'

'Was there any man whose dislike might have given rise to hate? One may spring from the other.' Bradecote was watching her face and realised that she was already struggling to keep the image and impression of the man who had been her husband until yesterday. He was becoming some dream, lost upon waking.

'Raoul Parler, who holds Flavel from William de Beauchamp, the lord Sheriff, has been in discord with him these three years over something that Osbern would never discuss, and Walter Pipard, who has the one half of Bishampton from Roger Pichard, long ago declared that he would not permit Osbern to set foot on his land upon pain of death. Mind you, those two are at odds themselves, neighbours but not neighbourly. There were bad words between Osbern and Corbin FitzPayne, over at Cookhill, but he is dead now, so . . .'

'Do you know the cause?' Bradecote felt a knot form in his stomach. He had not known Corbin FitzPayne, only of him, but it touched home, and Christina. He knew that Christina prayed for the soul of her late husband and had thought him a good man, but she had barely mentioned him since their marriage. Christina was a beautiful woman. Had Osbern de Lench given offence to her lord by word or deed concerning her?

'A silly thing. Osbern bought a horse from him, and a week later it took and died of a colic in its belly. Such things happen, but Osbern kept saying he had been cheated and sold a sick horse.' She shrugged. 'It could be so with him. Anger need not have roots of truth.'

Hugh Bradecote relaxed. Christina had said nothing when Osbern de Lench's death had been mentioned, but her heart was in the present and her dreams of the future, and the past she had consigned to the past. She may indeed never have known of the horse or its demise.

'I see what you mean about not liked, my lady.' Bradecote paused for a moment. 'How was he with his son, your son? Harsh? Cold?'

'No.' There was vehemence in her tone, too much.

That was a lie, or at least half a lie, thought Bradecote, and he sensed Catchpoll on the alert.

'My lady de Lench, your son Hamo was not here when your husband was killed, and none can vouch for where he was. The lord Baldwin seems very convinced it was, if not Hamo's hand, then Hamo's silver, that was responsible for the death.'

'That is just jealousy, hatred. Baldwin was the one Osbern shouted at the most. Always yelling at each other they were, and it was Baldwin that Osbern had sent to his manor at Tredington, over by Shipston. He said it was to see that the steward did not panic and cut the harvest far too early, but I know it was to let his blood cool. He was refusing to accept the match that my lord thought fitting for him.'

'But Baldwin was here, came from the harvest here, when the grey came home riderless.' The undersheriff was patient.

'I was nearly as surprised seeing him as I was the horse, my lord, for I had no warning he was returning.'

'He did not sleep here the night before?'

'Oh no. He was at Tredington, as I said, and had been for over a week.'

Catchpoll was thinking, going over exactly what he had been told, and his face screwed up in concentration.

'My lord, we was not told a lie over this, just nobody was asked. The lord Baldwin said he came from the harvesting, that is all.'

'Yes.' Bradecote did not want distracting from learning the relationship between Osbern and his younger son. He kept his eyes on the lady. 'If father and elder son scrapped like dogs, how was it between Hamo and his sire? Did they argue also?'

'Hamo does not argue with people. When he is angered it is frustration. He is a quiet boy, solitary. He has spoken of entering the church at Evesham, and I think it would suit him.'

'He is pious, like his father, lady?' enquired Catchpoll.

'He . . . he would like the order, the calm of each day following the same pattern, the absence of chatter and small things. He likes to know.'

'Know? Know what?'

'Everything.' It was her turn to frown, her smooth white brow furrowing. 'Our son . . . my son . . . is not interested in the flesh, or in friendships. Even from a babe his question was always "why?". Most of the time he is very quiet, and calm. Osbern found that unsettling, I admit. He disliked his lack of interest in fighting, even wenching, but most of all his lack of interest in the land, this land. He felt that was a failing. He saw that the cloister might be best but was adamant that

61

Hamo could not go to the Benedictines until Baldwin was wed, had an heir.' She laughed, suddenly. 'The next morning Hamo came before him and spouted a list of all the lords he could think of in the hundred with daughters unwed, with comments such as "she is fat" or "she has lank hair". I thought Osbern would be angered, but he laughed and said that Hamo was like an arrow, his flight was straight. It was the laughing that upset Hamo, threw him into temper. He did not see it as funny, just sense.' She paused, this time for so long the silence felt teased out. 'Frustrated anger he has at times, but Hamo cannot hate. He does not feel enough to hate. It makes him hard to understand, but also for him to understand others. He did not love his sire but knew that the Commandment said he should honour him, so he did what he was expected to do. Father Matthias says he likes to write out the Commandments. They please him in their simplicity. He says they are not hard to follow. He would make a bad priest but a good monk, I am sure, though he would miss his hawks.'

There was not much to say to that, and undersheriff and serjeant exchanged the briefest of glances. There were no more questions, or rather there was the feeling that there were no more answers to be had.

'Thank you, my lady. The lord Osbern will be buried today, I take it.' This was not really a question. The weather was warm, even though the church good and cool.

'No.' She sounded very displeased. 'Baldwin has said the whole village must be present, and that he will lie where he is until the harvest is in. He said that Osbern would appreciate that. I think it wrong.'

Bradecote, reluctantly, sided with the son over the widow. Baldwin had been quite passionate about his sire's love of the land, the manor as a thing. Bradecote could see that in burying his father with honour at the point when the manor's bounty was gathered in safely, there would be a finality but continuity to it the man would have liked. He therefore made a non-committal sound and said that they would now speak with Hamo, alone.

'He is your child, lady, would be so were he thirty and with sons of his own, but he is not a child whose hand must be held, nor whose words interpreted. Were he a village lad he would be in a tithing by now, and his oath accountable. Green he may be, but no child. You remain here.'

She nodded, accepting. She was used to being commanded. Bradecote turned on his heel, and Catchpoll followed. 'I gets the feeling having words with the lordling Hamo will be like trapping moonbeams,' muttered Catchpoll, as they crossed the hall.

'And if the moonbeams fail us, we look closer at the lordly enemies,' said Bradecote, 'and why their enmity was above mere dislike. At least we have two names.'

Chapter Five

Hamo de Lench was pacing up and down in the confines of Fulk the Steward's dark, low-eaved home, and looking stormy. For a youth who was not meant to have emotions, it was impressive. Walkelin looked as if he had been put in a pit with a bear, however skinny and undersized, and greeted his superiors' arrival with a look of patent relief.

'I am Hugh Bradecote, Undersheriff of Worcestershire,' announced Bradecote. If the lad liked order and simplicity a plain start was best.

'You wanted me to sleep with fowls.' Hamo, who was nearly as fair as his mother but had the thick brows of Baldwin, clearly from his sire, glowered at the undersheriff. 'I do not wish to be here, but your man,' he pointed at Walkelin, 'refuses to let me leave.'

'At my command. I wish to speak to you about the death of your father.'

'We could speak outside. It is dark in here, and I am bored.' The words could have sounded petulant, but they were stated as facts.

'We may speak outside then, if it will ease you, but you cannot try and leave.'

'Run away? I would run away if I had killed my father, but I did not do that, so I have no need to run away.' He looked at Bradecote as if he were an idiot not to have understood this.

'Then we speak in the open air. Come.' Bradecote turned, and led the way out into the sunshine. He stood so that Hamo advanced no more than two paces from the doorway, and had the daub and wattle to his rear, and the sheriff's men covering all other directions. 'You were out hawking yesterday forenoon. Were you out long?'

'I saddled my horse after the hour of Matins, as I would think. Father Matthias went to the field to labour and would have said the Office as he worked. There was no groom here then for he would only have returned from the harvest when the sun was high and the hour of my father's trot up the hill was nigh. He liked to be there about noontide.' There was no regret in the voice, no sense of something or someone now lost. 'I took Superba, my best hawk, and we went out towards the northern boundary of the manor, and she took wood pigeon. Two I brought for the pot, and the third I let her devour as her due when I wanted to hunt no more.'

'Did anyone see you when you were out?'

'I do not think so, and I spoke to none but Superba.'

'She listens?' Bradecote gave a wry smile.

'Not to the words. She is a bird.' There was that tone of dealing with someone of slow wits again. 'She listens to the voice, the way I speak. I could recite the *Pater Noster* or tell her she is the Holy Roman Emperor and it would not matter.'

'Do you grieve, messire, for your father?' It was a straight question.

'He is out of this world now. He built the new church. God will like that, and smile upon him. Why should I grieve?'

'Because your brother is now lord?'

'Baldwin.' He shrugged. 'He is lord because he is the firstborn. He will let me go to Evesham. I think he will want me to go soon. I will be with the monks. I can write, and I will work in the scriptorium. I have wanted to go for a long time.'

'And your sire forbad you?' Catchpoll spoke up. Hamo gave him a quizzical frown but addressed his answer to Bradecote.

'He wanted Baldwin to father a son first. I asked Baldwin to choose a maid and beget one soon, but he laughed. And my father laughed when I gave him the names of all the maids hereabouts. I did not like them laughing. They are the fools, not me.'

'Messire, I do not want you to leave Lench.'

'I must stay to see my father buried. It is my duty, I know. It is right.'

'Even after. Until the killer is taken.'

'Why? It is not me. I did not lay a hand upon him.'

'But you could have paid others to do it, in your stead.'

'Why? I must honour my father and my mother. It is the Commandment of God. Sending men to kill him would be

66

no honour.' He paused. 'Baldwin will not have me in the hall. Must I stay in the steward's hovel? I do not like it. I will sleep in God's house. That does not smell of chickens.'

'The burial is not today. It will be when the harvest is in.'

'God is my father. I will sleep in my father's house, since my other father's house is closed to me. What law forbids it, my lord Undersheriff?'

'It would be seen as strange. It would upset people.'

'But not upset me. I do not care what people think. They sleep with the stench of chickens.' He shrugged again. It sounded arrogant, and yet it was not that. Bradecote could not see any signs that Hamo lied, and his religious belief seemed very strong, stronger even than his dislike of chickens. That his manner would drive Baldwin to fury was pretty plain, and so Osbern must have found him as incomprehensible, but there was no anger lingering in the son towards the father. There was actually nothing at all. The void itself was peculiar. Undersheriff looked to serjeant, who raised his eyes Heavenward.

'There is no law, messire. I tell you only how it will seem. Keep away from your brother if you value your skin.' There was nothing more that Bradecote could think of to say. With a jerk of his head he drew Catchpoll and Walkelin to follow him. 'We will walk to the hilltop and see the world as the lord Osbern saw it.'

Ascending the hill, even on foot, did not take very long, although the heat made them sweat and Catchpoll grumble. At the top Bradecote gazed down, and understood Osbern de

Lench, at least in this. Bradecote was not a man with habit ingrained, but he had sometimes ridden to the top of the little scarp that looked down upon Bradecote, manor and fields, and felt that mutual bond. The land was his, but he also belonged to the land, as his sire before him. Osbern had held other manors, as Bradecote did, but the caput of them, that was special, inviolable. It was, though he would not say such a thing out loud, a love.

A skylark rose into the air, its song hanging above them in the breezeless blue, and then the notes dropping like dewfall. Far to the west, looming behind the bold outline of the Malvern Hills, there was dark cloud building, but here there was time still for sickle and bent back, the gathering of sheaves. A poor harvest meant empty bellies next summer, and a bad one starvation among the villeins. Bradecote crossed himself, and prayed that his barn would be full and the field all stubble.

Catchpoll watched his superior and guessed the better part of his feeling. Catchpoll did not own land, had no desire to do so, but he knew that when he looked over Worcester from the battlements of the castle he felt it was where he belonged. It struck him, quite forcibly, that Bradecote was as good as English. He spoke Foreign at need, but from day to day he worked in good English, he had never been across the water to Normandy and had no reason to ever see it. Before the Normans came, there were still lords and ordinary folk, warrior thegns and farmers and traders. There was thegnlic blood in the lord Bradecote from the distaff, no doubt more so than in the lord sheriff. In the end, the man standing looking down to Lench spread below him was an Englishman like Catchpoll himself. Bradecote took a deep breath. The contemplation was at an end.

'Now what, my lord?' the serjeant asked.

'I don't think Hamo killed his father, by his own hand or by silver.' Bradecote shook his head. 'With him there is day and night, but no gloaming, if you see what I mean.'

'Aye, I do. But there was one moment, speaking with him, when he changed. When he said his brother and father had laughed at him, but that they were the fools, then there was a rage in him. I wonder if, when that rage bursts, like a boil, he might not even think of it afterwards. It happens but is not him?' Catchpoll pulled a face. 'I make no sense, but . . .'

'You think if he had killed his father he would hide it in his mind?' Walkelin looked very confused.

'I just don't know, young Walkelin. Years ago, when I was in your place, a young woman was attacked one evening by the river. She was found wandering in the street by a priest called to administer the Last Rites to some soul departing. There was blood on her, some of it her own, her clothes were torn and it was clear she had been raped. In her hand, still held so tight it had to be prised from her grip, was her knife. We found the body of a man down by the wharves, half naked, stabbed many times, and his face clawed. The tale told itself. The weird thing was, the woman denied it was her, denied she had been harmed, and said she had gone to the river to cool her feet after a hot day and then returned home. She had no explanation of her injuries or the knife other than perhaps she had fallen and hurt herself. She was not mad, but everything to do with what happened was gone, utterly. My serjeant and the lord Sheriff agreed that nothing would be said further. There were no witnesses bar the priest finding the woman, and the dead man was some passing sailor from one of the Severn boats with none to mourn or seek wergild or any other justice. In fact, he got what he deserved, and the woman's good name was not torn from her. Fortunately the bastard left no child in her, and she wed the next year. It sounds madness, but it is true as I stand here. I wondered if the lordling Hamo would be like that, if he had snapped and acted.'

'But the young woman you speak of must have been, in every sense, out of her mind with fear and her act self-defence.' Bradecote shook his head. 'I cannot see Hamo going red-mist killing mad when he accidentally met his father upon the track, and besides, he would know as well as anyone the man's habit, so any meeting would have been planned, in cold blood.'

'And he said he went towards the north, my lord,' added Walkelin.

'He did. If he is responsible, then he is both very cunning and very bold. He strikes me as neither. Which leaves us where? Hoping we find some reason in the hatred of two neighbours.'

'Do we make sure everyone here, on the manor, was seen and accounted for, my lord?' Walkelin was always thorough.

'We should, though I doubt they will thank us for interrupting their labours, and Baldwin de Lench will stamp and shout. I know sense says discount them first and then look further afield, but since there is small chance of our killer being out with a sickle today, I think we go to visit the manors of Flavel and Bishampton. At the very least we will give them news they will rejoice at, if they loathed him as the lady said.'

The trio retraced their steps, pausing briefly so that Catchpoll could show the now barely distinguishable traces in the ground where Osbern de Lench was killed. Walkelin and Catchpoll went straight to the stable to make ready the horses, and Bradecote headed into the hall, to inform the lady de Lench that they would be absent until the evening meal, upon the lord sheriff's business. More than that she need not know.

'The thing is,' said Catchpoll, pensively, as they rode north, 'if Walter Pipard and Raoul Parler have been at such odds with the lord of Lench and the breach so open, why did not the lord Baldwin suggest that they had a hand in the death?'

'Because he wants to see his brother hang?' Walkelin frowned. 'But if he is likely to send him to the brothers at Evesham he would be as good as dead anyway.'

'The cowl does not appeal then, Walkelin?' Bradecote laughed. 'As good as dead, eh!'

'I mean no disrespect to the monks, but . . . other than a payment gift as he entered, there need never be anything after between the two brothers. I cannot see Baldwin riding often to Evesham to ask after his health, and the lordling Hamo seems to have no interest in the manor or its folk, even kin. He would put them from his thoughts. Other than the gift there would be no difference between burying him within an abbey and in the earth.'

'And thus avoid damning his immortal soul with the mark of Cain.' Bradecote urged his grey to a trot. 'Makes sense, but I get the feeling Baldwin would like to see the lady de Lench distraught, not least because she is not so over her dead husband, and having her son at a rope's end would do that. Oh well. Let us find out about Parler and Pipard, and forget the strange Hamo de Lench for a while.'

The manor at Flavel was well kept. It had an orderliness to it, as though it was swept daily. As with the other manors in the district, it was almost deserted, with all that could lend a hand out with the harvesting. The palisade about the lord's hall had new wood, a pale block among the aged oak timbers where a second gateway had been filled in, and Bradecote guessed it was a manor where defence had become unimportant over the years until the dispute between King Stephen and the Empress Maud made having two points of ingress one too many for security. The single remaining gateway was shut. He came before it and announced his name and office, loudly. After a few moments he heard a voice, and the sound of a bar lifting. It would be but a short one that a single man might lift, not a major barricade of defence. The first gate opened a few feet. A man stood before them, built well enough to be labouring, but he stared at them with opaque white eyes and saw nothing. Bradecote repeated himself.

'I am come to speak with the lord Raoul Parler.'

'He is not here, my lord.' The man heard the command in the voice, the expectation of obedience.

'He is with the harvesting?'

'No, he is not here. Would you speak with the lady?'

'Yes.'

The blind man let them in, and walked, with a stout stick sweeping before him, to the hall. He entered and called for his lady. A female voice came from the solar, and a woman then emerged, a woman easing her back as she came, for she was some way advanced in pregnancy. From the solar came the noise of squabbling children, several from the voices. Some women, thought Bradecote, flourished with childbearing. In others it drained them as though each life that emerged left less in the mother. This was such a woman. Her whole being looked worn, aged before the years, and though her belly was rounded, her limbs were thin and her face gaunt. She also looked worried.

'I am Hugh Bradecote, Undersheriff of Worcestershire,' began Bradecote, and she turned white and collapsed in a dead faint before them.

'Well, I have never seen that happen before, just because you gave your title,' remarked Catchpoll, as the undersheriff went swiftly to kneel at her side and rub her hands, speaking her name.

'What has happened?' asked the blind man.

'Your lady has fainted. Women carrying can do that,' Catchpoll explained.

'Aye, especially if given a shock. She will have thought you are come to say he is dead, the lord Raoul.' The blind man sighed.

'Why think that?' Bradecote was watching the first trace of colour return to the pale cheeks.

'Because he left without warning, morn of two days since, after hot words, and she does not know where he went or why. She pleaded with him not to go, but he left and at speed.'

'Had he been sent some message?' Bradecote enquired as the lady stirred.

'That I do not know, my lord.'

'Do not be distressed, lady, I bear no ill news, at least not of your husband, I swear it.' Bradecote's voice was all sincerity.

For a moment she stared up at him, uncomprehending, and then she took a deep breath which was exhaled as a sob. Bradecote felt guilty, though he could not have guessed his words would be met with such a reaction. Her eyes, focusing upon him, still held a fear. He tried to help her sit up, but she actually pushed him away as anger took the place of her trepidation.

'Leave me alone.' One hand slid to cradle her swollen form as she sat, paused, and then called to the blind man. 'Come to me, Siward.'

The man crossed the chamber as her voice guided him, and he felt her hand reach up to touch his.

'Help me rise, slowly.'

He bent, his arm strong. She got carefully to her feet, ignoring the sheriff's men, thanked Siward with a soft word and took her seat upon the slight dais that stood proud of the rush-strewn floor.

'If you come not to cast me into despair, why are you here, my lord Undersheriff?' She was mistress of herself now, and guarded.

'I come because Osbern de Lench lies in his church awaiting burial, and he died by the hand of another.'

She crossed herself, though her hand trembled very slightly.

'God have mercy on his soul.'

'Your lord and he have not been good neighbours these last few years. I wanted to ask him why that was so. I find he is not here, and not seen since the day before yesterday. Osbern de Lench was dead about yesterday noontide. You can see why I find that of interest.'

'Then your interest will be short-lived, my lord. My husband can have nothing to do with the death of the lord of Lench, though it will not be sad news to him . . .' her voice wavered for a fraction of a moment, 'when he returns.'

'But if you do not know where he has gone, you cannot know he is not involved, lady. Why were they at odds? Do you know?'

'I know that Osbern de Lench was a betrayer of trust.'

'In what way?' Bradecote watched her face. She was reluctant. 'In what way, lady Parler?' A hint of steel entered his tone. She wavered, crumbled.

'He had sworn to support King Stephen, but after Lincoln he went back on his oath.'

'After Lincoln many did so, thinking all lost.'

'It is true, but . . .'

He could almost read her thoughts. Parler held the manor from William de Beauchamp, whom the Empress Maud had shown favour after Lincoln. Would his undersheriff report back and place her lord at risk?

'Lady, I doubt not that the lord Sheriff knows his tenants

and their allegiances. In these times I think he would ask only that they do not plot against him. After all, he is still the lord Sheriff, and King Stephen still holds the throne.'

'My lord would not waver. He stays true.'

'But there is more.'

'Yes, but I am not privy to it. Truly, my lord.'

'Were they both at the battle, at Lincoln?' There was brave combat that day, lord upon lord and on foot as in the old days of the shield wall, sword and axe. King Stephen himself had wielded a great axe, and cloven helms and flesh with it. Yet there had likely been betrayals also, personal betrayals. When the man at your side steps back to let an enemy strike you, or worse, strikes foul himself, then that is treachery beyond changing allegiance to a king or an empress. That would not be forgiven.

'Yes. My lord was wounded, lost two fingers of his left hand when an axe went through his shield. I do not know anything of the lord of Lench.'

It was only a possibility then, but more likely than simple disloyalty. After all, King Stephen's own brother had changed sides when the King was captured and in chains, and reverted when he was released and the chances of the Empress actually sitting upon the throne had receded. Oaths were not what they once were, or perhaps they had never been as inviolable as was pretended. What it left the sheriff's men with was a lord who had disappeared just before the killing and had not returned home.

'You have no idea why your husband left or where he has gone? None at all?'

She shook her head, and Bradecote glanced at Catchpoll, who looked grim. Leaving Walkelin, or even Catchpoll, to see if the man came home might prove pointless, and if he did, would he attend to them? Not attending to Serjeant Catchpoll was unwise, but . . . Bradecote made the decision.

'My lady Parler, when your husband returns it is most important that I speak with him. Send him to Lench where my men and I are discovering the killer of Osbern de Lench. If that person is taken before he comes, I will send to stand him down. It will go very ill with him if he ignores this command, which comes from me but with the authority of William de Beauchamp, and ultimately, the lord King. You understand?'

'Yes, my lord.'

'Good.' The sound of squabbling was getting more heated, and an infant's cry was added to it.

'How many children do you have?' He smiled, stepping back from the official.

'I . . .' She hesitated a moment, and Bradecote wondered if she was thinking of children shrouded and buried. 'There are five at home and this one to come.' She stroked her swollen figure. She sounded resigned more than proud. 'My daughter was wed year before last, the eldest boy is thirteen years and now with the lord Hugh de Lacy, but the younger ones are here.'

'Then we will not keep you from them, lady. Good day to you.' He made her a polite obeisance, and requested blind Siward to follow them out and close the bailey gate behind them.

77

'Which is worse, Catchpoll, not being able to discount the lord of Flavel, or not being able to ask him the questions we need answering?' Bradecote gave a heavy sigh.

'Not sure, my lord. Having nobody we see as the killer is bad, but so are "if" and "but" as all we have to go on.'

'Then one way or the other, let us pray that we discover more at Bishampton.' Bradecote urged his grey into an easy canter, and Walkelin kicked his lazy beast into a shambling gait that just about kept pace.

Chapter Six

The track south to Bishampton was good and the manor was less than three miles away, so they arrived some time before the sun was at its zenith. It beat down, but there was a change in the air, something oppressive looming. Bradecote could not help watching the sky to the west, where the clouds seemed to be massing like grey, mail-coated cavalry, gathering together and awaiting the charge. When they swept down to the Severn and eastward, the rain would be heavy. Catchpoll followed his gaze.

'Aye, my lord, it's coming right enough. You have no need to be a weather-feeler, just have eyes in your head. It just depends on whether it plods like an ox or gallops like a horse.' Catchpoll sounded fatalistic. Everyone knew a good harvest was important, and in hard years town dwellers felt it in the price of bread, but he had not the direct connection to the land. As long as the majority of manors had a surplus to sell, Worcester bellies would not be empty. His superior worried about a few small manors, and most of all Bradecote itself. It was his home, and he could name every soul within it.

'I pray for the ox, Catchpoll.'

'As will all who look to the Hills today, my lord, for sure.'

Bishampton was held as two manors, and as they passed the first men piling sheaves onto a cart, they asked which was that held by Walter Pipard. The men, sun-browned and sweating, said that he was their lord, and pointed them towards a modest hall with a fence about it that could not be said to count as any defensive structure. The building was thatched and with low eaves, stone to the height of a man's thigh, and thereafter wattle and daub as any villein's dwelling. Within the enclosure a barn stood, doors wide open, and a man, better dressed and clearly in control, stood with folded arms, watching a cart being unloaded. He turned at the sound of approaching horses.

'Walter Pipard?' Bradecote halted his big grey and looked down at the man.

'That is me.' The man was thinning a little on top, broad of chest and increasingly of girth. He assessed the men before him, and recognised authority.

'I am Hugh Bradecote, Undersheriff of Worcestershire. We are come to ask you about Osbern de Lench.'

'Have you indeed . . . my lord?' The courtesy was not given grudgingly, but with a hint that Pipard saw no need to abase himself in any way. He held this manor of the de Lacys, who held in turn from the Church, but he was not clinging to the edges of lordship. 'You should have been asking about him long ago, may he rot in Hell.'

'I don't know about Hell, but he'll be rotting in the earth soon enough. He's dead.' Bradecote was assuredly not the bringer of bad news.

'Then what is there to ask about him now?'

'Who killed him,' growled Catchpoll.

Walter Pipard's eyes darted to the serjeant and then back to Bradecote, and his look became wary.

'I would shake the hand of the man that did it, but I do not know whose hand to shake, God's truth.'

'It is said you told him that if he set foot upon your land you would strike him down.' Bradecote kept his voice very even.

'As good as, but words like that are as much warning to keep away as threat. He did not die on my land, did he? I have heard nothing.'

'No, upon his own, on the path up the hill.'

'Makes sense. He wore its track deep almost on his own.'

'You knew he went up daily?' Bradecote never doubted the affirmative.

'Everyone for miles about knows that.' Pipard's lip curled.

'So where were you yesterday noontide?'

'In my hall. I had a clawing pain in my guts. I get it sometimes.'

'Had you servants attending you?' asked Catchpoll.

'With the harvest coming in and the weather closing? No. Every hand that can work has been in the field.'

'You are recovered today though.' Bradecote looked at the man closely.

'I am. I never know when it will come, nor go, but a day, at worst a couple, and it passes, though I will not eat today.'

81

'So tell us why you and Osbern de Lench were in enmity.'

There was a silence, a silence that was not a void, but something darker and more threatening than the approaching rain clouds. Eventually, Pipard shrugged.

'God will judge him, so what I say matters not at all now.'

'And what do you say?'

'He killed her. I am sure of it. They said she fell from her horse when riding, and broke her neck, but he killed her.'

'Who?'

'His wife. His first wife. Judith, sister to Geoffrey Corbizun of Exhall. Young Geoffrey has never had the fire in his belly of his sire, or his dam, but she did. By the Rood, she was magnificent.' Pipard's eyes lost focus as the image in his mind claimed him. 'All raven hair and flashing eyes she was. She had a temper, but then so did Osbern. She rode as if the Devil were after her when she was not contained to play the dutiful lady, and I saw her once, her coif quite slipped back from her hair, and she cared not. Her eyes dared me to look.' He sighed. 'Submission was not even a good act with her, and he must have found her wilful once too often. I heard she threw a piss-pot at his head once, in her fury. Magnificent.'

'But how do you know it was not the misfortune that was declared?' Catchpoll did not assume every turbulent marriage ended in a killing. 'And why did you not bring it to the lord Sheriff at the time?'

'Why? Because her brother swallowed the lie, and declared it was her boldness killed her.' He snorted. 'Perhaps he had felt her tongue and her claws as a boy, before she wed. If he said nothing, how would I be believed?'

'If you had proofs . . .' Catchpoll persisted.

'They would have been laughed at.'

'Then tell us now, and we will not laugh.' Bradecote looked squarely at Pipard, whose gaze then dropped.

'I . . . she was not happy.'

'You could read her mind?' Catchpoll sounded sceptical, and Bradecote silenced him with a small movement of his hand.

'Did not need to. She had a look about her, in the month before she died, a sort of fear. Her, afraid! It made no sense. She would defy, she would scream and scratch, I doubt not, but there was something . . .'

Catchpoll ground his teeth, very audibly, but kept his mouth shut. Feelings were all very well when bolstered by good honest facts, but here was a man who had clearly been smitten by the lady's fire and beauty, and he could not accept her death as a thing that happened without great cause. He was a fool then, because death needed no reason, no motive. It just took. Sometimes it dragged slowly from life, sometimes it snatched, and it did not need servants. It was when it had them that the sheriff's men became involved, but by far the majority were just simple *wyrd*, what was fated to be, and that could not be avoided.

'That is not a proof of itself, Pipard.' Bradecote hoped against hope for something more.

'A woman from this manor was returning from Evesham market. She saw the lady de Lench upon the road, and her horse on a slack rein. It had a loose shoe. The next day I heard she had broken her neck in a fall. Do you break your neck falling from a horse at walking pace?'

83

'Mayhap the smith made good the shoe, and she rode later.' Catchpoll sniffed, interested but not willing to show it.

'If she did, then I wonder how it was that her lord was the one to find her. Did he ride out also, by chance?'

'Likely he went out to find her if she had not returned home.'

'He killed her.' Pipard would not be dissuaded. 'I would not share words with him thereafter.'

'But you did not seek revenge. That showed wisdom, my lord.' Walkelin had kept silent. He sounded deferential, and yet . . .

'With the law as doubtful as you are now, I would have hanged. I had responsibilities, a wife, a small son. I owed my name more than I owed her memory, may God be merciful to her. And may Osbern de Lench burn in the eternal fires of Hell.' He spat into the dusty earth.

The cart that the sheriff's men had seen being loaded lumbered into the courtyard, with those to unload it trailing behind. The oxen stood, chewing vacantly, and waited, whilst Walter Pipard encouraged and harangued those within to finish the emptying of the earlier cartload. He turned back to Bradecote.

'I have another cartload to bring in, my lord, before the weather breaks. There is nothing more I can tell you. Find Osbern de Lench's killer if you must, but it is not me, and they did the world a service.'

'We will leave you to the harvest, and with luck you will have all safe before the rain, but if needs be, we will return and ask of you again.' Bradecote nodded a dismissal, although it was he who turned his horse about and trotted from the manor, with Catchpoll at his knee and Walkelin urging his slug of a horse to keep up by means of heels and imprecations.

'I do not think Walter Pipard killed the lord of Lench, hate him though he did, my lord,' said Catchpoll.

'No, nor do I, despite the depth of that loathing. If none saw him when he was sick in his hall then we cannot be beyond doubt, but no. Not least because there could be no sense in killing the man so many years after the cause.' Bradecote paused. 'What do you think about the accusation though? Might Osbern de Lench have killed his first wife?'

'He might, my lord, but as the man said, that is down to the judgement of God, who knows all.' Catchpoll crossed himself reverently.

'But your gut instinct?'

'It would help if I had ever met the man alive, but from report and from looking at the son,' Catchpoll screwed up his face, 'I think he probably could have done for her. I am not one to say couples that shout at each other, even throw things, end up one killing the other, not at all, but the word of the woman who saw the horse with the loose shoe means a lot.'

'And mayhap that is why the lord Osbern built his new church, in penance.' Walkelin spoke up, loudly. He felt left out as well as a bit left behind. 'As he got older he might think upon what is to come and seek to make up for his sin.' He paused. 'And to save up the silver, of course.'

'Personally, I cannot see building a church atones for killing one's wife, but . . .' Bradecote shrugged. 'It is a cost in silver, just stone and mortar, not a living being. For killing in battle, as my sire said was imposed upon those before him who fought at the Battle when the Conqueror claimed the crown, yes, perhaps, but not a murder killing.'

The other two men were silent at that, not because they disagreed, but because the mere thought of atoning for a sin in more than prayers and penitence was beyond the imagination of those who would never count their silver wealth in more than could be cupped in their two hands. The sky was growing dark, and Bradecote glanced towards the west. The cavalry of cloud was galloping towards them from the Malvern Hills, which were now lost in a blue-black greyness. A rumble of thunder made his horse twitch its ears.

'The dead man's distant past is not important now.' Catchpoll grimaced. He was going to get wet.

'Unless it is like with poor Ricolde the Whore, and the killer has only recently returned and seen he still lived.' Walkelin was thorough in thought and learnt from his experiences.

'Not easy in the countryside where any newcomer is talked of for a week until all is mulled over like an ox chewing the cud.' Bradecote understood village life as no town dweller could.

'So the man is not of the countryside, my lord. He is, say, in Evesham. He heard that Osbern de Lench lived, and his old hate burned anew.'

'And all these years later he recalls that the man rode up his hill every noontide?' Catchpoll shook his head. 'No, that has to be one leap too far. All we have is a reason to think better men than the lord Osbern de Lench have met a violent death, and that Raoul Parler might be responsible, but Walter Pipard is not.' He urged his horse into a canter, following Bradecote's example, and Walkelin gave up speech to kick his horse.

They would have had to have galloped hard to reach Lench before the rain, and their horses were spooked by the storm breaking close enough for the thunder to have a crack in it that gave it more than just menace. Forked lightning streaked across the heavens, and as they approached the village, heavy gouts of rain pocked the dry earth at their feet. In the couple of minutes it took to reach the bailey their hair was plastered to their heads and rain was running down their necks. They had expected to find it empty, for sense said everyone would have sought cover, but a scene as violent as the weather met them. Half the village seemed gathered in a semicircle. In the middle of the bailey a man was cowering, trying to curl himself into a ball as he was whipped, his cotte already split and showing scarlet where the lash had slashed his skin like a bear's claws. Baldwin de Lench, yelling as if vying with the thunderclaps, raised his arm and struck again, and then began kicking the prostrate form. A flash of lightning came to earth close enough for a woman to scream, and the thunder followed hard upon it. Baldwin looked up as Bradecote himself cried out for him to halt, raising a face white with anger and something strangely akin to fear.

'Sweet Jesu, you'll kill the man,' cried Bradecote, leaping from the saddle to stand in front of the now-twitching heap of humanity.

'He has his hat!' screamed Baldwin. 'And he gives me nought but lies as to how he got it. He killed my father.'

Catchpoll dismounted also, a little more slowly than his superior. He doubted Baldwin de Lench was in any mood to listen to reason, so he did not bother. The man was focused on the undersheriff and the victim of his wrath, not the serjeant, who came close from one side and punched him very hard in the solar plexus. Baldwin doubled up.

'He might listen now, my lord,' suggested Catchpoll, calmly.

'Get him into the hall, and the poor bastard he is trying to kill. Everyone else go home. Now!' Bradecote had no doubt of being obeyed. They went. Walkelin and Bradecote lifted the injured man between them, as Catchpoll prodded the lord of Lench with his sword's point to follow, still bent and gasping for breath.

'Give us more light here!' cried Bradecote, entering the gloom. The lady de Lench emerged with a branch of candles from the solar, her hand trembling, her face pale and her free hand rather pointlessly covering one ear.

'What has happened?' she stared at the wreck of a man laid now upon a trestle table. 'Is he dead? Who is he?'

Bradecote ignored her, reaching to feel if there was a heartbeat still in the chest, for there was little breath in the man.

'There is life, but no senses. Does anyone in the village have a knowledge of physick? Not that it will do much good.'

'Mother Winflaed is our herb woman, our healer.'

'Then get her, and anything she has for bone and bruise, and bleeding flesh.' Bradecote looked grim. 'He is three parts dead.'

'Why did you stop me?' wheezed Baldwin, holding his midriff.

'Because we gets answers to questions without killing a man, and we needs to know what he knows,' Catchpoll growled, and got a look of loathing, but no more.

'How came you by him?' asked Bradecote, without taking his eyes from the broken body.

'As we came from the field with the last wagon. He walked right past me and commended our luck. He had my sire's hat upon his head, though it lacked the copper badge with the amber boss upon it. My father's hat, taken from his corpse.' There was outrage in the voice, and he pulled from within his belt a dark red cloth hat. 'For one moment . . .'

Yes, thought Bradecote, the hat must be so distinctive it was as though the real owner wore it. Baldwin de Lench had seen a ghost, in his own imagining, just for a moment, and that was enough. Anger and bowel-loosening fear had driven him to a fury of violence.

'So you beat him nigh unto death.' Bradecote had no sympathy.

'I grabbed him, shook him, ordered him to tell me how he came by it, and he whimpered like a cur and said he got it from a beggar. How likely is that? Either he killed my father or he traded with the one that did.'

'And you have nothing from him but denial and his blood upon your earth. Had you not wit enough to bind him and hold him for our return, de Lench?' Bradecote snarled at the man, angry at his short-sightedness, and at the fact that he might have near killed a man guilty of nothing more than giving a silver penny or two to a man who needed bread in his belly not a hat on his head.

A great flash illuminated the chamber even through the narrow horn-paned windows and was followed immediately by a crash that sounded as if an oak was falling. The combination made the lady de Lench scream, drop the candles and cover both her ears. Walkelin stamped out the lick of flames among the rushes with his foot and picked up the candles, though one was now rather flat. Catchpoll sighed and took a rush light to the one that would not collapse.

A woman with a piece of sacking held over her head entered the hall, bobbing to lady and lords as one. She was followed by a girl of about thirteen bearing a plank with pots all covered with an oilcloth to keep out the rain. Without a word the woman, a round, comfortable-looking woman nearer her later years than youth, went to the body on the trestle table. She crossed herself, said a swift *Ave Maria*, touched the bruised and battered head and torso, and asked Walkelin, being the one male in the chamber she felt she could command, to turn the man onto his side. She went round the table to see his back and tutted, and then looked at the undersheriff as the one in control.

'His ears do not bleed, nor can I see any place where his skull is caved in, my lord, but I have nothing to waken a man as is jangled of brain. If he wakes, he wakes, but he may not, may never. As for the rest, there is ribs broken, doubtless, but he breathes as one with lungs that work, and his belly is soft so nothing seems burst inside, which would surely mean he dies. I can clean and salve the wounds to his back, anoint his bruises and give a draught that if he does wake will ease his pains a little, but the rest is prayer, my lord, the rest is prayer.'

'Thank you. Do what you can for him.' He gave her a smile, and the elderly dame blushed in the candle glow. She bade the girl assist her, and worked with whispered instructions, except when she needed Walkelin's strength. Bradecote and Catchpoll glared at Baldwin de Lench.

'So, if he never wakens there is a death to be answered for,' said Catchpoll, soberly.

'But he—' began Baldwin, before being interrupted by Bradecote.

'He might have a connection, or he might not. What he said might be true. You never even considered that, did you.' It was not a question. 'We do not even know where he was going.'

'Flavel. That is where he was going, my lord,' piped up the healing woman's youthful aide, and dipped in obeisance.

'You heard him?'

'Aye, my lord. He was in good humour and hoped all was safely got in back in Flavel, he said, so I am thinking that is where he was going, for the direction was right.'

'He was not on a horse?' For one terrible moment Bradecote feared this might be Raoul Parler. He had no recall of the look of the man although he and Parler both held of William de Beauchamp.

'Oh no, my lord, but he was striding fast, knowing the storm was coming in swift.'

'Did you ask him his name, de Lench?' Bradecote looked back at the now-silent Baldwin.

'No.' He sounded sulky.

'Well, at least if he dies we can take the corpse to Flavel and see who mourns him, and get his name,' sighed Bradecote. 'Tell me exactly what he told you.'

'He just said he got the hat from a beggar upon the road, and commented upon it, for the hat was good and the beggar crippled and ragged. The beggar said he had found it, and so the man offered him a penny ha'penny for it, thinking a hat was less use to him than food. He handed it over and went on his way.'

'Which way?' growled Catchpoll, and the growl deepened when de Lench said he had not asked.

'He can only have come from the south or east, since he was going through Lench and heading to Flavel,' noted Walkelin, reasonably, 'so chances are the beggar is heading in one of the two directions.'

'And there would be alms at the abbey at Evesham. Walkelin, you are to ride there first thing to ask of the Guest Master and Almoner if any beggar arrived this night,' ordered Bradecote. 'If he is there, find out how and when he came by the hat, and any other belongings.'

Walkelin looked pessimistic. 'You think I will get there before noon, my lord, on the beast I ride?'

'True. Take the horse the lord Sheriff sent back here. It is his animal, and we can have the groom come back with us on it to Worcester and collect the lord de Lench's own beast then. Serjeant Catchpoll and I will speak to the Flavel man if he wakes, and,' he was about to say exactly what they would do, but thought better of it, 'look into other things.' He heard Catchpoll's exhalation of relief. 'But now, and if this man can be lifted to a palliasse on the floor, I hope to eat. I am hungry.'

Chapter Seven

Hugh Bradecote did not know if it was down to his prayers or the good work of Winflaed the Healer, but the injured man was not cold and lifeless when dawn came, though he showed no sign of waking. His breathing seemed stronger, however, and the girl who had assisted the healer was set to watch him and report any sign of his regaining consciousness to the lord undersheriff. She clearly felt the importance of her task and watched the sleeping form with determination writ large upon her face. If he as much as moved a muscle, she would see it. Bradecote felt a little jaded, having not slept well and woken with a crick in his neck. He rubbed the back of his neck and winced, for the third time. Catchpoll grunted.

'If you wants sympathy go elsewhere. I'm getting too old for sleeping on floors, and it takes me an age to get up off 'em.' He sounded grumpy, and hunched his shoulders as they went out into a morning that had a freshness in the air after the storm which had lasted several hours into the night. The ground was damp, the earth darker, and within the bailey a scattering of straw from the cartloads coming into the barn had a randomness as though it had fallen from the skies as pale golden rods.

'Now the harvest is in, they will bury the lord Osbern, which is good and proper, but makes it easier for them to put it behind them and forget things, sort of intentional. Life is for the living so . . .' Catchpoll shrugged expressively, and Bradecote wished that today he could do the same without grimacing in pain.

'But Baldwin will not forget. In fact, the more he thinks on it, the more he will need to find someone to wreak his revenge upon. I doubt yesterday assuaged that,'

'Which leads me to the beggar, my lord.' Catchpoll pulled a thoughtful face. 'It would be good to find him, and I wishes Walkelin good hunting in Evesham. A beggar would not take a hat and leave other good clothing, since the hat is least useful in summer, leastways the sort of hat a lord might wear. So we has to think that he is wearing the rest or the hat was all that he found. If so, then why was it on its own? Was it tossed into a bush, and where are the other things?'

'Very true. Unless it was the thing that was distinctive, and they, one or several, decided it was too great a danger to keep. What happened thereafter sort of proves that as true.'

'Now that is a good thought, my lord. Should have thought of that myself.'

Walkelin emerged in the wake of Fulk the Steward, yawned, and came to his superiors.

'The lordling was less trouble now the smell of chickens is not as strong, and he is afraid of thunder, but nothing else to report, my lord. I am ready to ride to Evesham.' He looked quite eager.

'The excitement of riding a horse that won't wear you out kicking it, young Walkelin?' Catchpoll's mouth lengthened in a smile.

'Yes, Serjeant. I don't think the animal I usually get is a horse at all, just a cow in disguise.'

'Well, remember you are about the lord Sheriff's business, not riding for pleasure, and bring us good news if you wants a warm welcome back. Off you go.'

'Yes, Serjeant.' Walkelin could not help grinning as he disappeared into the stable.

'The simple pleasures of youth, eh, Catchpoll?' Bradecote gave a wry smile, and his eyebrows rose, creasing his forehead.

'One of 'em, my lord. In his case the other is that wench Eluned, who is assuredly now a maid by her work but otherwise a maid no more. The castle knows all about it, but I wonders if his mother does. I am not sure whether she'll tan his arse with her broom or welcome the girl to her bosom as a daughter.' The smile in his eyes faded, and he said, more solemnly, 'Do we go and look at the body one last time, my lord? If there is none else by.'

'Will it profit us anything?' Bradecote wondered how it had fared over two days, even in the cool of the church, for the weather had been so close before the storm broke.

'Couldn't say, but we cannot be about asking questions of the villagers while they are rising, or as they files into the

95

church and pays their respects, however little they mean it.'

'Fair enough.'

The pair went to the church. Father Matthias was not present, and there was a stillness in the very air itself, as though not one mote of dust had moved since sunset. The priest had brought in bunches of lavender and wild garlic, clearly as a precaution. Mortality was not a good smell, and one best avoided, since it lingered almost as a foul taste in the mouth. They genuflected before the altar and then turned to unwrap part of the shroud from the now-coffined corpse of Osbern de Lench. It made things more difficult, but Catchpoll seemed to be able to reveal the face and upper torso without making it obvious that the body had been disturbed. Bradecote thought, not for the first time, that the dead soon looked as though they had never drawn breath at all. Catchpoll touched the fatal knife wound, pale lips of parted flesh where no lips should be.

'The death wound is simple enough, but one meant to kill, not injure so that the man might be robbed and left to die. The killer wanted the life from him, and got it. We must hold that in mind, my lord. They truly wanted him dead, which means a strong reason to kill him. Then they struck twice to make it seem less planned, but without a killing madness, no vengeful strike.' He sighed. 'Reminds us that talk of robbers is just talk, or a trick to keep us from the real reason for the death.'

'Yes, the theft of the clothing was indeed a false trail laid for us, but does it make the question of the hat more interesting?' Bradecote rubbed his hand about his chin. 'Of course it might just be the colour was thought to draw the eye too much.'

'We cannot be certain of whether it was thrown away on its own until Walkelin returns, my lord, and only then if he comes with a smile upon his face.' Catchpoll rearranged the cloth with such care that even the priest would not have seen that they had been there, and then looked directly at Bradecote. 'So after the burial we speaks to the villagers. Do you come the high and mighty and let me act the willing vessel into which they pours their rememberings?'

'Well, that way the easily overawed will speak with me, and the others you catch when they are less wary. I want to come into church when all are assembled, and we watch from the rear. I doubt Father Matthias would welcome us stood like acolytes at his shoulders, and though we cannot see faces for the service, we shall see them as they depart.'

'Fair enough, my lord. Where would you have us go till then?'

'Back to where the body was found, I think, though it will gain us nothing but thinking time.' Bradecote sighed. 'I hope we glean something from a villager.'

'Well, I will leave Winflaed the Healer to you, my lord. You have a way with older women. The way she looked at you last night you would think she was about to get more 'n a smile off you.' Catchpoll chortled at his superior's horrified expression. 'No?'

'No.'

With the harvest in, there was a sense of relief in Lench that even the presence of their lord's corpse in the church could not diminish. In the end, who had power over them was of less interest to the villagers than knowing they would not starve next summer. They would pray dutifully for the man's soul, but none would have their heart in it. The lord Baldwin, wanting things to be done properly, but with an eye to keeping the villagers at work, wanted the funeral rite administered without them all standing dusty and coughing from threshing in the barn, so the service and burial were early. As undersheriff and serjeant came back onto the Evesham track the church bell began to toll, slowly, though it was a small bell and its note was bright. They arrived in time to follow Fulk the Steward and be before the family. Baldwin de Lench looked solemn, almost haunted, and walked first. Behind him by several paces came the widow and her son. The lady was veiled, and Bradecote thought it must be concealing not grief but a mixture of relief and uncertainty. Hamo de Lench looked as unconcerned as he would simply attending Mass.

The sheriff's men stood at the back, observing rather than taking part beyond the required responses. Speaking with the villagers was for afterwards, but watching them, even without seeing their faces, gave an overview. There was quite a lot of shuffling of feet, and women looking sidelong at other women. Father Matthias made much of the lord Osbern's piety and ignored the less appealing aspects of his character, as funeral orations were wont to do. He did mention, briefly, that whilst man was mortal and death a part of the cycle of life, this death had been the result of an act of evil, and God would punish the offenders whether they faced earthly justice or not.

'So is he hinting we will fail, or saying it does not matter if we do?' whispered Catchpoll, out of the side of his mouth.

'Could be either, or both.'

'Well, my prayers are we succeed, my lord.'

'Amen.'

Walkelin was enjoying his ride back to Lench, and not only because for once he felt he was doing less work than the horse beneath him. Serjeant Catchpoll had said that if he wanted to be greeted with favour he should return with good news, and he therefore hoped to be met with commendations.

He had gone first to Abbot Reginald, thinking it polite to seek permission for his questions, though as he opened his mouth he realised that should he be denied he would find himself in a difficult position. Returning to Lench to tell the lord Bradecote and, far worse, Serjeant Catchpoll, that 'the lord Abbot would not see me' would earn him a clip about the ear and days of disfavour. However, the abbot had been amicable when the sheriff's men had been in Evesham in the spring and was happy enough now for his obedientaries to assist the law, though he shook his head over the need of it.

'The lord Osbern was a man who found piety in the middle of his life, though I could not say it tempered his nature. A man of impulse, he was, and alas, of anger within his heart, though he was generous enough to us and spared no cost in the renewal of his parish church.' Abbot Reginald sighed. 'I am inclined to think both were his attempts to make up for that character, which he knew fell short of what God would wish. His repentance was real, but he continued upon a path where it was much needed. "A soft answer turneth away wrath" was not a message that he understood, but soft answers are less used than hard swords in the realm these days. Ask your questions, my son, and may the answers aid justice.'

Walkelin had found the Guest Master in the Almoner's little room, for the giving of shelter and alms were often intertwined. Both expressed shock at the news of the violent death of the lord of Lench. The Almoner went quite pale as he crossed himself.

'Such an end to a life. Thanks be to Heaven he saw his church finished. I will pray for his eternal soul.'

'As will we all,' added Brother Jerome, the Guest Master, piously. 'Now, you came not to bring just the sad news I take it?'

'No, Brother, I have questions also, about those who took shelter here last night, of your charity.'

'Then I shall leave you and be about my duties,' murmured the Almoner, and left, brows knit together.

'Brother Theodosius is a soul who feels the pain of others most acutely,' explained Brother Jerome, when he and Walkelin were alone. 'He even rescued an injured crow from boys who were stoning it, some years back, and cared for it until it recovered, so well that it would linger about the enclave and if he came outside would land upon his shoulder. Some objected, saying that since we have no possessions a pet should not be allowed, but Father Abbot decreed that the bird was not being kept, and that if alms of food were given to one of God's creatures, there was no harm in it. The novices still call him

Brother Corvus behind his back.' The Benedictine smiled, but had to explain the Latin.

'Ah, I understand. But now, Brother, what of your guests?'

The Benedictine had reported that there had been three guests the previous night from whom he had asked nothing but attendance at the Mass in the morning, and one had come, he knew, from Stow-on-the-Wold to the south-east. Of the other two one was known by name, as he passed through quite often. He was Alnoth the Handless, and his name told all. Some men lost hands for crimes committed, but he had been born with one forearm tapering to nothing and the other bearing but two misshapen fingers. The Guest Master said he was a 'gift from God' because there were some midwives who would have ensured he never drew breath, mortal sin though it would be. Walkelin had not thought this man sounded likely as the one he sought, until the Guest Master added that he had been in a good humour, and even offered a halfpenny for his bed and board, having come into silver, and being blessed with new garments and good boots, though he said it would take more wool gatherings in them to make them fit without rubbing raw.

'You know, he had a leather tunic, open and sleeveless, and made a jest of it, saying he who was somewhat lacking in arm was better off than a poor tunic that lacked any sleeve at all, and would care for it. Mind you, I said no to his offer of coin, for his wealth was but a penny ha'penny, and that will not last him long if he wants to eat on his travels. He is a godly soul, and I think the Almighty listens to his prayers.'

'Is he here still, Brother?' Walkelin had tried not to sound too eager.

'No, but he had hopes of earning a little by guarding baskets of produce at the market today and will no doubt return this evening. He often stays with us for a day or so if there is the market.' The good brother smiled at Walkelin's consternation. 'Yes, I can see you wonder how a handless man can guard anything, but he is known, and none would steal from the goods he protects. It happened once, a few years back, and he called down the Curse of Heaven upon the culprit, who fell as he ran and broke his arm. No, none would take from the baskets under his eye.'

'So I shall find him in Evesham still.'

'Assuredly, but surely the Law does not seek Alnoth for a wicked killing?'

'No, merely seeks to know what his eyes may have noted on his way here. Thank you, Brother. Er, I came quick this morning and have not so much as taken a beaker of beer. Might your kitchens be generous to one in the service of justice?' Walkelin had smiled, looking virtuous but hungry. The Guest Master sent him to Brother Cellarer with his blessing. It had been a contented Walkelin who set off among the buyers and sellers in Evesham that morning.

Identifying Alnoth the Handless was not a problem, so Walkelin did not have to advertise his interest in the man by asking after him. He was beside a stall of fruit, bowls displaying the first picked blackberries from the hedgerows, and jewel-like currants in blood red and pearly white. The stallholder was a girl of about twelve, who clearly had little faith in her ability to prevent the filching of her laboriously gathered produce. She actually begged Alnoth not to desert

102

her when Walkelin began to speak with him.

'I am not here to take him from you, maid,' Walkelin had assured her, and had given the girl a small smile.

'Then what is it you seek of me, friend?' enquired Alnoth, sounding curious but not wary.

'I am Walkelin, Sheriff's Man, and I need to know about the hat you sold to a man of Flavel yesterday, and how you came by it and the boots upon your feet.'

'By no thievery or wickedness, I swear oath.'

'No oath is needed, for the man who owned them before, left this world the day before yesterday, right by Lench, which is not two days' walk from here.'

'But it is two days since I came upon the things, Master Walkelin.'

Walkelin had been momentarily taken aback, for nobody had ever addressed him so respectfully. Had the term been used it had been laced with irony and accompanied by a sneer.

'Er, it is?'

'It is.' The man clearly had no thought to dissimulate. 'I was on my way from Worcester. I takes it at an easy pace, though my legs are as good as any man's, and had spent the night at Aston, on a way as gives me fair lodging, not the swiftest, for I knows when the markets are held and need only to be in the towns for them. The God Houses are always generous and kind, but townsfolk can be harsher than their country brethren, and I like the walking. The lord of Aston is none so particular welcoming, but his man as is steward has always seen there is room in a dry stable for me and a meal in the kitchen. In exchange I bring the news of the shire as I

103

hears it. Amazin' how many thinks a man without hands is also without ears or wits.' Alnoth chuckled. 'I gave the manor the news when the lord King was freed from chains, afore it came to the lord himself, and knows the gossip of the markets, where there have been thieving bands upon the roads, even the sins of the lords, though none would let that reach their master's ear. The lord of Flavel, now, he has a woman in Worcester, fine skin she has and a fair figure. Not a patch on the poor Mistress Ricolde, God have mercy on her soul,' Alnoth crossed himself, 'but she was of as beautiful of heart as body, and generous. Never failed to give me a ha'penny if she passed me. The lord Raoul's woman has him in her bed out of need, for her husband died and her stepson took the trade and cast her out.' He sighed. ''Tis an unfair world.'

Whilst interested in Alnoth's rambling discourse, Walkelin needed him to return to the matter of the clothing, but he first asked one question.

'What is the name of the fine-skinned woman?'

'Her name be Leofeva, widow of Will Brook, the coppersmith. Now—'

'I thank you, but we must speak of the hat and the clothes you found.'

'Ah yes. Well, as I said, I was on my way from Aston, and was a bit short of Lench. Came a time I needed to step off the way, you might say, my innards being something urgent.'

For a moment Walkelin had been completely distracted by how a man with but two fingers like talons might drop his breeches, and his face made Alnoth laugh. He was a surprisingly happy fellow.

'O' course, you being a man as questions things would wonder. I has a piece of wood with a hole bored through it, and the cord is tight through that and long enough so as I can hold the end with my teeth and move the wood with my fingers. Ways and means, master, ways and means is how such as I get by. It takes a little longer, but I found an old tree stump and—'

'You found the hat there.'

'No, no, you gallop when you should walk. I was there, a-doin' what was natural, and I heard a voice, a man's voice, and twigs breaking. Well, I supposed it to be a man with mine own intent, and kept quiet, or mayhap it was a man with a maid, but there came no woman's words. The voice muttered for a moment, and then it was quiet, and I waited for the sound of him leaving and the branches telling me so, but there was nothing. When I came from my tree stump behind the bushes I was curious, and went towards where the sound had been, and there they were, a hat of fine, dark red, felted wool and a short cloak, well used and the bottom edge given a new binding, but sound. It was not so thick as to keep out rain and winter, but another layer is always of use to me. Since they had been cast into the wood I took them, and no thieving was it, for I do not steal, God's oath.' Alnoth repeated his avowal.

'Be easy, friend, but did you not question why someone had cast them away?'

'Ah.' Alnoth nodded. 'Had I found some poor soul upon the road, robbed, I would have given him help, and the hat and cloak also, but I saw none.'

'And what about the other clothes?'

'I had but hat and cloak, then.'

Walkelin frowned. It was not what he was expecting.

'What time of the day was it?'

'Sun was right high, so a mite after noontide, near enough.'

'And then you went through Lench and found the boots after that? Did you see anyone?'

'I did not go through Lench but skirted about it.'

'Had the lord Osbern been heavy of boot to you?' Walkelin had decided Osbern and Baldwin de Lench were very alike in use of the lordly boot.

'No, though I recall him as a man of temper, years back. He has a son, a strange son. The lordling followed me once, when I passed by, and stopped me. He was full of questions, not like yours though. He wanted to know how I did this and that, whether I felt hands that were not there, how did it feel to be "of no use". It was like he was interested but not seeing me. Fair made the hair stand up on the back of my neck it did, and I vowed never to go through Lench again, lest I see him and he see me. So I went around the place, west side, and rejoined the Evesham road a ways beyond, as it rises and where the horse path leads off the road and up the little hill. Then I saw something, lying at the edge of the horse path, just before it bends to follow the hill slope proper-like, and it was a boot. For a moment I surely felt as I would see a body. I went to look, cautious though, and the other boot was in a bush, and the tunic, but there was no body. It made me wonder, for if there had been a man killed, who would take the body and leave the good clothes? Makes no sense. I did not go further up the hill, for I heard a horse's hooves on the path. That would be the lord of Lench, for everyone for half the hundred knows it is his hill and he sits upon it every day when the sun is high. I had no wish to meet with him and be accused of wrong, so I gathered the clothes and ran, and it was a warm day to run. I spent the night at an assart on the Evesham road where an old man gives me a fair pottage in exchange for company at his board, and then came here to Evesham yesterday mid morning. There was no need for speed. It was just after I had set off that I met a man heading north. He admired the hat, and in truth it was so hot upon my head in that heat afore the storm, I said, in jest, I would sell it to him for tuppence. He offered me a penny ha'penny and I agreed, right there. That was it. Then I carried on to Evesham.'

The sheriff's man was silent, thinking, then he asked a sober question. Alnoth's cheeriness diminished in the face of it.

'When did you discover the clothing had blood upon it and was cut?'

'Not until I was with the old man. I had bundled everything together and not looked close.'

'And it was not odd that almost all that might clothe a man was found together? You must have thought the reason unlawful.'

'I have to live as best I can, Master Walkelin, and as I said before, there was none to whom I could give aid, nor report upon neither. What good would come of reporting not finding a body? Who would look for something that was not there?'

In Walkelin's mind the answer was instantly 'Serjeant Catchpoll', but he did not voice it.

'You saw no body, but body there was, and up the path to the hill. The lord Osbern of Lench was taken by a knife and stripped.'

'Sweet Jesu, but . . . I heard his horse.'

'You heard a horse, aye, but he was not upon its back. Now, let me see the marks upon the tunic.'

The tunic was of soft leather, open down the front, designed to be held together with a belt and a clasp at the neck. Alnoth said he had seen no belt, but that such a thing might easily have been cast further and lost to view in the undergrowth. The jerkin was dark brown, and the stain where the knife had entered under the ribs was not as large as he expected, nor the slit wide. Walkelin measured it with his finger. There were no other cuts in the leather, so he surmised that either the lord of Lench had ridden with the tunic loose, because of the heat of the day, or it had been removed before the other wounds were made after death. He grunted.

'The boots and tunic can stay with me?' Alnoth was now being practical.

'They are of no use to him. Both Abbot Reginald and the lady of Lench say the man was pious in his way, though of an evil temper. Best to think he would see such charity, even unintended, as aiding the passing of his soul, yes?'

'That be a good thought, master, and I shall be sure to say a prayer for his soul every night right until . . .' Alnoth thought of a distant date, 'the Feast of St Luke.'

'That seems fair. You do that, and safe travels.'

'I would say none steals from a man with nothing, but,' the man laughed again, 'I am now the proud owner of good boots. I take your good wishes, master. And may you find him as took the lord Osbern's life.'

'We shall.' Walkelin spoke confidently, as he thought Serjeant Catchpoll would answer, and then left Alnoth the Handless to his guarding duties.

Chapter Eight

Bradecote had no wish to speak with the villagers of Lench under the eye of the new lord, since they would undoubtedly be casting a wary eye to him and be more concerned about upsetting the lord of their manor than the lord Undersheriff of Worcestershire, who would be among them but briefly. Fortunately, it would be impractical to speak quietly with anyone with the threshing going on about them. Baldwin de Lench might not like it, but he decided to call the workers out in twos and threes, and send back swiftly all who looked blankly at him or shook their heads. This turned out to be the majority, though Catchpoll was watching them to see if any were overawed by rank and keeping their mouths shut on the principle that saying anything was dangerous. The boy who had espied his lord, and said as much to Baldwin, was neither shy nor overawed. He felt a certain importance, knowing something that powerful people wanted to know themselves, and it overcame any natural diffidence before such an august personage as the undersheriff of the shire.

'You are sure that it was him you saw?' Bradecote asked, without sounding as though a wavering would bring down curses upon his youthful head.

'Sure as I sees you, my lord. Couldn't see his face, o' course, but it was him as sure as the sun rises in the east. I saw the grey mare, pale on the hilltop, and the whole shape of him was right, from head to toe. I would swear oath to it, my lord, that it was the lord Osbern.'

Since the boy was being perfectly open, Bradecote questioned him further, upon who was present in the field.

'You seem a lad who takes notice of things.' A little flattery would do no harm.

'Whole village was there, and the lord Baldwin came to oversee things. Our lady was not, o' course. Fine thing it would be if she had to labour in the field. Oh, and the lord Osbern's groom came back later, after the lord Osbern went riding.'

'Was the groom expecting him to ride back to the field on his return then?'

'No.' The boy frowned. 'I doubt that. But he had no need to worry, cos Fulk the Steward was there to see to the horse afterwards.'

'Fulk the Steward was not with the harvesters?'

'He was, but not all the while, my lord. He went back to the village late in the morning, but I would not know why. Mayhap it was something about the loads already in the barn?'

111

With this nugget, Bradecote was content to let the boy return to the threshing. He looked at Catchpoll.

'Well, that gives us something new, and of interest. You would have thought Baldwin de Lench would have said something, but for the fact he sees only what he has decided he will see.'

'Best if we speak with the groom afore we corners the steward, my lord. If he was dismissed to the field it must have been by Fulk, and he might have had good reason to be away from the work.' Catchpoll did not make this sound very likely.

Kenelm the Groom was, however, far less willing to talk than the boy, thinking several steps ahead and fearful of what retribution might descend upon him. He said he had seen nothing, which made Catchpoll smile. That smile alone had opened mouths more oyster-shut than Kenelm's. He stepped forward and stood next to his superior.

'You see, that is where you goes and makes my lord Undersheriff upset. He doesn't look upset, I grant that, but he is. And if he is, then so am I, and you won't like that.'

Kenelm shook his head without even thinking, and Catchpoll continued, while Bradecote stood, arms folded, and looked what he hoped would be 'upset but not showing it'.

'You says you saw nothing, but you are the lord's groom. You have got to be the last person as saw him alive, except for his killer.'

'I never killed him,' gasped Kenelm, paling.

'Of course you didn't, but you can tell us everything that happened when the lord Osbern called for you.' The serjeant sounded very reasonable, even soothing, which was peculiarly unnerving, and with even the merest hint of suspicion hanging over him, Kenelm nearly fell over his words trying to get them out.

'He was in a foul mood, but that was none so rare, not with him,' he confided. 'He had been shouting at his lady, but that too was just as always. I thought, though, that the day was a bad one,' the small man frowned, 'a day of ill-fortune.'

'So he went off on his horse, and you waited for him to come back and swear at you.' Catchpoll knew this was wrong but wanted to get a full account.

'Oh no. Fulk came round from behind the barn, where the middens are, and asked if there was reason for the lord Osbern being so angry. Then he said as I could go back to the Great Field and he would see to the grey on its return.'

'Did he often offer to do that?' interjected Bradecote, sharply enough for Kenelm to flinch.

'Sometimes, when the whole village is busy and the labour long. I think he must like a little idleness and taking the weight off his feet to show he is a bit above the rest of us.'

'You would think he would be more keen to oversee the work and show his presence,' mused Bradecote. 'How did the lord Osbern take that?'

'Doubt he ever knew, my lord. It is . . . was nearly always when he went up the hill, which is why I was given leave to go back to other work.'

Undersheriff and serjeant exchanged a glance so fleeting that Kenelm did not notice it in the least.

'So you went back to the harvesting. Did you too see

the lord Osbern up on the hill?' Catchpoll ensured the man thought any positive answer was just corroborating a fact already learnt.

'Aye, I did. He always just sat there, looking. Then he would ride back, nice and easy, on a loose rein, and in better humour too, mostly.'

'You've good sight then, for I am sure I could not make out one man from another up there.' Catchpoll sounded regretful about his own eyes rather than doubting.

'You don't need the eyes of a hawk to spot the lord Osbern. The grey mare is always pale, and even in summer the lord Osbern rarely left off his short cloak and his hat.'

'Would you have expected him to come to see the harvesting, when he returned?' Something was niggling Hugh Bradecote, but he was not sure what it was.

'I suppose so, but I was working hard after and did not think. The lord Baldwin was with us, so I may have just thought he had been sent instead.'

'Been sent? He arrived after you were back in the field?' Bradecote's brows drew together.

'Yes, for he tied his bay to the branch of an oak and came to watch the women gathering the sheaves.'

'Not the men cutting them?'

'Not sure he would enjoy the view as much, my lord.' Kenelm could not help but grin. 'When they bends over, you see.'

'Yes, I see. Does he . . . does he do more than look?'

'If he does, who's to stop him?' The groom shrugged. 'Many's the wench as goes to the marriage bed having learnt its secrets

114

from the one man she could not refuse, and it would be the foolish husband as blamed her for it.' He sounded resigned.

Bradecote looked genuinely shocked. Never having wanted a fumble with a girl on his own manor, and with lascivious thoughts about maidservants limited to gazing dry-mouthed and breathless as a girl stripped to the waist and washed in a courtyard when he was an adolescent squire, he was stunned to think not that it happened, but that it was simply accepted as quite ordinary.

'And is he like his father in that?' Catchpoll could have laughed at his superior's innocence but kept to the task in hand. 'Old stags don't just bellow.'

'Mostly he was bellow.' Kenelm looked less comfortable.

'Only mostly?'

'Her husband says as the babe will be his, but there's whisperings.' The man looked at his feet.

'The woman who came from the village to tell of the riderless horse. Why was she not working?' Bradecote, focusing back on what was being said, posed it more as a question to himself.

'Too far gone to bend, she is, and likely to have it within the week, according to Mother Winflaed,' Kenelm gave the answer anyway.

'And it is her you meant?' Catchpoll did not want them asking awkward questions of every pregnant woman in Lench.

'Gytha, wife of Edmund.' He nodded.

'And when she came to the field you went back to the hall, after the lord Baldwin?' Catchpoll wanted everything in one line of time in his head. It was easier to file it away that way.

'I did, as we all did. Harvest was clean forgotten. The grey was before the stable, tied to the ring as if waiting, except that the lord Baldwin was ranting so it was getting upset. I calmed her though, and could assure him and our lady, when she came out after Fulk, that at least the horse had not fallen, for it was clean and pretty sound, though she had been a little less willing than usual. She is none so young and had a bruised frog the beginning of last week, and how the lord Osbern berated me, as if I could have prevented her stepping on some sharp stone.'

Bradecote opened his mouth and then shut it. The state of the horse was barely a confirmation, but the casual mention of the steward was another matter. However, it was one best kept between the sheriff's men. The man before them could not have been the killer, and he was dismissed back to work.

'So we have a possible motive, though dismissing this Edmund will be easy enough if he is vouched for as in the field, and Fulk the Steward came out of the hall, which is actually far more interesting,' murmured Bradecote, pensively.

'It makes you think, for sure, my lord. We discounted the lady herself, and that still stands, but if those bruises we saw were inflicted by her husband and she was angry enough, then she might have been able to persuade the steward to do what she could not. We had not considered her arranging the killing.'

'No, we had not, and there was no affection, it would seem, in the marriage. In fact, the reverse, and Osbern came out to his horse having had angry words with the lady. The only trouble is that this was not unusual, from what the groom said, so why would this one thing have pushed her so far?'

'Well, be fair, my lord. We only saw the bruises on her wrist. Who is to say what else happened besides?'

'Yes, but the steward would not have known that when he came back and sent the groom to the field. It would have had to be a chance, and would a man go off and kill another because a woman told him to do so when in a temper?' Bradecote could not quite see it working. Every man knew that women could fly into a blind rage one minute and as likely be meek and loving as brittle and sharp-tongued the next. At least every married man knew it. He had made the assumption that Fulk the Steward was wifeless now but had been married. Could it be that he had never taken a wife at all?

'Depends on the woman,' responded Catchpoll, but did not elaborate, as the girl set to watch in the hall came to them and made a deep obeisance to the undersheriff.

'My lord, the man stirs. I cannot say he speaks as yet, but he stirs for sure, and when I touched him he moaned.' Her voice held awe, but Catchpoll thought it more the act of speaking to someone as illustrious as the lord undersheriff of her shire than the fact that the sick man showed signs of returning to the land of the living.

'Good. We shall come and see him, whether he speaks or not. Go and fetch the healer to him also. We would have her views.'

'Yes, my lord.' The girl dipped again, but then grabbed the hem of her skirts and raced, swift as if she were chased by wolves, to fulfil his command. The sheriff's men walked towards the hall.

'If everyone was that obedient with you, we would solve our problems so much faster,' remarked Catchpoll, with a grin.

'Sadly, too many take your path though, Catchpoll, and are tight-lipped, stubborn and downright disobedient.' Bradecote sighed, but his eyes were screwed up with unvoiced merriment.

'Yes, there is that. Mind you, most are not such crafty bastards, which is a relief.'

Bradecote laughed then, and was still laughing as they entered the dimly lit hall, but the laughter died instantly as he saw Baldwin de Lench standing next to the sick man. His back was towards them, but his fists were clenched.

'De Lench.' The undersheriff's voice was very calm, though he wondered if he might have to spring forward. The lord of Lench turned, showing them a grim visage.

'I do not see why you want to hear his lies,' he growled through gritted teeth.

'Your trouble, de Lench, is that you make a decision based on thin air, and then hold to it as if a holy vow. You decided this man was guilty of your sire's killing because he wore his hat and refused to believe what he told you about paying for it. Do you think only you are able to speak true? Are you so wondrous in your own eyes?' Bradecote could not keep the sarcasm from his voice.

'And are you?' returned Baldwin de Lench, in no way abashed. 'You want things to be some sort of tangle that you have to be so clever to work to its end, when plain truth stares you in the face.'

'What's staring my lord Bradecote in the face this moment is a man who does not know when to hold his tongue.' Catchpoll felt the slur was upon the whole process of discovering truth,

118

and it flicked him on the raw. Baldwin de Lench's eyes turned to the serjeant, and his lip curled.

'Are you his bark?'

'No, but I can bite,' snarled Catchpoll, stiffening, though Bradecote raised his hand slightly to keep him from any escalation in the antipathy. How well it might have succeeded was debatable, but at that moment Winflaed the Healer entered, with her youthful aide behind her.

'Heaven be praised, my lord, if the man stirs, yes?' She bustled forward without waiting for an answer, and almost barged past Baldwin de Lench to place her hand against the man's cheek. She patted it gently, and he moaned. His eyes remained closed, but the undersheriff came close and spoke to him anyway.

'Can you give us your name, friend? Your name?'

There was silence, but just as Bradecote stepped back, thinking nothing would be said, the man's lips parted, and he breathed a word. It was half groan, but discernible.

'Edgar.'

'And where do you live?'

'F'avel.' This came more upon a sigh. 'Where . . . is . . . this?'

'Lench.' Bradecote wondered if the man might have no recall of the previous day's events. It would be a blow if he had no memory of any of it at all.

Edgar, the man from Flavel, ran his tongue slowly over his lips. Old Winflaed the Healer watched him closely.

'Let be a while, my lord. You has his name and the poor soul will be better for a draught of warmed ale and herbs, and mayhap then can answer more to you. God be thanked he has his wits and breath in his body.' She crossed herself, but Baldwin de Lench made a derisive snorting sound. She glanced sideways at him and shook her head. 'There now, my lord, you'll be getting yourself into a fever if you let that anger boil away inside of you. I dare swear you have not slept well these last nights. 'Twas ever thus, and no fault of yours, of course, with sire and dam both of so hot a temper, and neither ever happy to let a thought, once in the head, creep away if 'twas wrong, though it cost them dear. Let me brew you a calming draught and weave a cross of lavender you can take to your bed this night and thus sleep sound. It will soothe your mind.'

'My mind does not need soothing, and I am not an infant to be dosed with whatever witches' brew you stir up.' He stared at her malevolently and turned on his heel, stamping his way to the door. 'I will be atop the hill,' he threw back over his shoulder, as if daring the undersheriff to forbid him. The woman stood very still, and then turned to Bradecote.

'He speaks in heat, my lord, for he is a man of heat. He has never understood the *laececraeft*, though he has been grateful at times for the treatments. I learnt it from my mother, and she was the fifth generation in this place, healing the folk beneath the hill and in the manors about. Good Father Matthias would surely shun my salve that he rubs in to ease his hipbone ache if it came of evilness.' The woman was clearly aggrieved. 'God sees all, right enough, and is pleased that we who are able to ease the pains and ills of this life do so, and give Him thanks for the plants and our knowledge. Never have I harmed a soul, nor a beast neither, and if some has stepped beyond life then it was their time and the Will of God. I can but do my best.'

'And it is appreciated.' Bradecote let his face relax into the hint of a smile but paused before he spoke again. 'Your salves for broken skin and bruises, have you often had cause to use them within this hall?' He waited, for the old woman was staring at him intently, gauging what she might say and what he might do with the knowledge. Eventually she nodded.

'My lady is one who bruises easy, mind. There's some as does and some as has thick skin. The lord Baldwin, like his sire, has thick skin in so many ways, excepting where it comes to taking offence. The lady is the opposite. Long-suffering she is.' There was something in the way she said it that intimated at more than just her character. 'There now, my tongue outruns my wits.' She turned to the girl, who was frowning, not quite understanding the undercurrents but aware they existed. 'Be a good girl and go and set a pot of ale over the hearth to start warming, and bind me sage and yarrow, wrapped about with ash bark.'

Dismissed, the girl went upon her errand, and Winflaed the Healer sighed. 'Not for young ears. The lord Osbern had always a heavy hand. Now, as a husband he had his rights, and I deny them not, but from almost the dawn of the marriage he lashed her with his tongue, and with hand and rod also, like he felt he was breaking a horse. Or mayhap it was that he was used to shouting but that his first lady wife had given as good as she got. In my view he wanted obedience but despised those who gave it with a whimper. My lady has never made complaint against him, nor said anything but that she had been clumsy, but I can tell a knock bump from a hard blow or a tight grip. Course I can.'

121

'You sees things. A trained eye.' Catchpoll gave her her due. 'Which makes me think you a good soul to ask if any who ought to have been labouring in the field were not there, at the hour the lord Osbern met his death?'

'You think one of us could have killed our lord? Would have dared to try?' She shook her head. 'No, though I was with the older folk gathering the sheaves to be placed on the cart, and my back was bent and aching, I tell you that. It had been a long day already, for we was out at dawn and feeling the tiredness in our bodies by noon. However, 'tis that or risk knowing hunger next summer.'

'The lord Baldwin, when did he come?' Bradecote did not want her straying into the effects of famine.

'Not so very long before young Gytha came, all breathless, with the news of the riderless horse. He was making sure everyone put their backs into the work. He tied his horse's rein to a low bough so it could crop a little grass and then he strutted about.' It was evident that the woman did not think that this meant son could have killed father, but Bradecote sensed more than heard the small grunt that Catchpoll gave.

'Fulk the Steward was not there.' The undersheriff did not make this a question.

'No, he was not, my lord, not then.' The healing woman's lips compressed slightly, and Bradecote thought he detected a hint of disapproval.

'Not a time to be idle,' commented Catchpoll, innocently.

'I doubt he was idle,' responded Winflaed, cryptically, but then said that she ought to go and tell Hild, her apprentice, not to heat the ale too much and destroy the goodness of the herbs. She was eager to be gone, and the sheriff's men did not press her. In the doorway, she nearly collided with Fulk, who looked agitated.

'Messire Hamo, my lord Undersheriff, he has ridden off with his hawk, say what I would to stop him.'

Catchpoll swore under his breath, but Bradecote remained impassive.

'He rode out, though he knew he was meant to remain?' The undersheriff was not going to show any emotion.

'I told him again, my lord, but he said he was not leaving, just going hawking, and you had not said he might not do that.' Fulk looked perplexed. 'I suppose that might be so but . . . what could I do, short of pull him from his horse? And he is the lord's brother.' The steward ended on a pleading note.

'Then we are going to have to wait for him to return. If he had meant to go to Evesham and remain with the monks, which is where he has declared he would like to be, he would not have taken his hawk.'

Fulk heaved a sigh of what might have been relief, and the comatose Edgar stirred again, perhaps being aware of the raised and worried voice.

'E'gar . . . F'avel,' he mumbled, moving his head in agitation.

'Why did you not come to us when he asked for his horse?' grumbled Catchpoll. He did not think the youth had saddled the animal himself. He was too much aware of what was for him to do and what was 'for others', though the serjeant would be hard-pressed to call it arrogance.

'I . . . I did not think to it. He just upped and said, "I shall go hawking now," and it fair left me witless.'

'Doesn't take much then.' Catchpoll was not in forgiving mood. Fulk looked both shamefaced and aggrieved at the same time.

'If my son says that he will do something, it is pointless to gainsay him.' The lady de Lench stood in the solar doorway, one hand upon the oak frame. She looked calm, in command of herself and the situation, and Bradecote had not seen that before. 'He does not see reasoning, not our sort. You would only have kept him here by force.'

'That could be achieved.' Catchpoll folded his arms across his chest.

'But you have not seen how he is when thwarted. He loses himself to the frustration, the anger. I have never seen anyone like that not even my hu—' She halted. Was it because she would not speak ill of the dead, or feared incriminating the living? It might even be both.

Footfalls sounded in the passage, and Walkelin, slightly pink of cheek where he had spurred his mount to a fair turn of speed for the last few miles, entered like a hound with two tails, as Catchpoll remarked afterwards.

'My lord, I have news, news that aids us,' he announced, with relish, and looked likely to launch into it forthwith, except that the serjeant interrupted him.

'Oh good,' said Catchpoll, but without any enthusiasm whatsoever. 'You can tell us outside.'

Chapter Nine

Bradecote had the forethought to request that the lady remain in the hall to report if any words were spoken by the sick man, though he was aware that what he might say ought only to corroborate what Walkelin was about to tell them. He was also not quite easy about leaving lady and steward together, when they might formulate some plan, should Fulk prove to be the man they sought. There was little else that he could do, however, without directly accusing Fulk of the sin of adultery and the betrayal of his lord, which was as bad in its own way. All they had was a suspicion, and one which both parties might refute with ease. The trio went out into the bailey, serjeant and undersheriff blinking in the brightness. There was nobody in view.

'So, you think you have discovered things that will aid us, Walkelin?' Bradecote could have smiled at the puppyish eagerness of the serjeanting apprentice, but it might be seen as patronising, so he schooled his features into mere interest.

'I think so, my lord. I spoke with Alnoth the Handless, and—'

'Who?' Catchpoll frowned. 'Best you take this steady lad, and give us all, not skip about. From the start, now. You ought to know better after all this time.'

'Yes, Serjeant. Sorry, Serjeant.' A slightly chastened Walkelin began again, telling them how he had gained the lord abbot's permission to speak with his monks, and had found out that the beggar with new clothes was one Alnoth the Handless, and that the man was considered of good word.

'Fair enough,' conceded Catchpoll. 'And what did this Alnoth tell you?'

'More than I hoped, Serjeant, for he actually heard the hat and cloak being thrown into bushes at the wayside.'

'Too much to hope he saw also?'

'Alas, yes, but it was definitely a man.'

'There now, and I had the healing woman as our likely killer,' sighed Catchpoll, but his eyes danced.

'Do not put him off, Serjeant.' Bradecote's rebuke was delivered with a wry smile, and Walkelin, after a breath, continued.

'The thing is, the hat and cloak were found to the north of Lench, but then Alnoth discovered the other clothes near the point where the hill track and road to Evesham meet.'

'Now that, young Walkelin, is very interesting.' Catchpoll pulled a thinking face.

'He came through Lench then,' mused Bradecote, fastening upon that fact first. 'He saw nothing of use?'

'He skirted by the village, my lord, lest he meet the messire Hamo, who he said was very strange and had asked him odd questions in the past. So he left the road and rejoined a little ways up the hill. He saw a boot on the track, and found its mate cast into a bush, then the clothes. He then heard a horse coming down the hill and made his best pace away, lest he be accused of thieving.'

'That cannot have been the killer upon the horse if the clothes were already found, so it was most likely the grey coming home to its stable. I know you speak to the dead and get good information, Catchpoll, but pity it is you do not speak horse also. That grey could solve all our problems.' Bradecote's mild jest covered him thinking, processing the information into time and order.

'True enough, my lord, but since I do not, we plough on. Did the beggar give an hour, Walkelin?'

'About the noontide, Serjeant. He met the man who was beaten upon the way next day and sold the hat for a penny ha'penny. He kept the cloak, boots, though they needed padding, a shirt and sleeveless tunic, but gave the shirt to Brother Almoner in the abbey, since its sleeves were far too long and the tunic ideal. I told him he might keep them, as I did the good brother, who used to know Lench well, he said, and was very upset to think of the killing and hoped the lord Osbern had died shriven. I did right, leaving them all?' Walkelin looked to the undersheriff.

'You did right, Walkelin. Osbern de Lench has no need of them, and I hardly think Baldwin would wish to wear his father's garb, bloodstains and all. This means the killer was heading northwards and makes me wonder even more if that points to Raoul Parler.'

'But why did he keep hat and cloak until after Lench and then discard them, my lord? He could not have been mistaken for the lord Osbern in them, not to the man's own folk, and indeed might have had the hue and cry raised after him if any had been in the village and seen him.' Catchpoll shook his head. 'That makes no sense.'

'Does it have to? Sometimes men do things that show no sense. He thought to keep them and then realised they linked him to the crime and so hid them.' Bradecote shrugged, though he was not convinced by his own argument.

'And if it was the lord Parler, why would he want a hat and cloak?' Walkelin was a practical young man. 'Though I already have a possible answer as to where he—' What the red-haired serjeanting apprentice was going to say next was not voiced, for sounds of an altercation came from outside the bailey.

'Sweet Jesu, has Baldwin de Lench found another man to harangue and assault?' Bradecote strode towards the gateway, followed closely by his companions. Out among the scattering of dwellings a man with high cheekbones and an aquiline nose was sat upon a nervous chestnut, trying to look haughty whilst controlling his jittery horse and being threatened by Baldwin de Lench, who was waving his arms about.

'What is going on?' yelled Bradecote, over the sound of de Lench's ire.

'He dare come here, now my sire is dead, when he knows that he swore he would strike him dead if he as much as set foot upon our land.' Baldwin was incensed. It was not that hard to work out which 'he' was which in the complaint.

'I am here at the lord Undersheriff's command, or else I would not sully my horse's shoes with this earth,' declared the rider, whom Bradecote realised must be Raoul Parler. He therefore addressed him by name and thanked him courteously enough for coming.

'It was not, as I heard it, a request.' The lord of Flavel still sounded aloof, even slightly bored, but his eyes were watchful. 'If you need speech with me, let us have it, but not with him close by.' He pointed at Baldwin, now grinding his teeth.

'This is my manor, my hall and—'

'For the love of Heaven, be silent.' Bradecote had had enough. 'Come to the church, my lord Parler, and we will speak there. You,' he addressed Baldwin de Lench, 'will not follow.'

Baldwin de Lench opened his mouth, and then shut it again. The undersheriff led the way towards the little church, and all he could do was clench his fists and feel the nails dig into his flesh.

Bradecote strode purposefully towards the church, consciously controlling the irritation that had built in him. It would not help matters. In its cool silence he turned to face Raoul Parler.

'So, you have returned to lady and manor, and can now give an account of yourself.'

'You demanded that I come, so I have done so, but I am wasting both your time and mine own.' Parler sounded bored.

'I am the undersheriff of the shire with a killer to discover. I have the right.' Bradecote remained assertive. 'Tell me why, despite the pleading of your lady, and without telling her where you were going in haste, you abandoned Flavel in the forenoon three days past.'

'I have a woman in Worcester.' Raoul shrugged. He sounded sullen.

Bradecote raised an eyebrow.

'I keep her. Is it so uncommon a thing to have a leman? Besides, my wife seems always to be with child, and a man has needs.' He sounded as if he blamed her for being so fecund and frequently pregnant. Bradecote, who had accepted prolonged abstinence as the duty of the husband when his first wife was increasing, gave up a silent thanksgiving that his union with Christina was one of love not duty, and also that other than during the weeks of sickness she still, to his surprise, seemed to welcome his attentions. It was an added blessing in the marriage.

'And you went off, suddenly, at harvest time, to visit her, leaving your wife in worry? Are your loins so very insistent, Parler?' Bradecote did not conceal his disgust.

'No interest of the Law if they are, but no. It was not that. She sent word with a carter on his way to Bidford that her landlord was pressing her to pay more at Michaelmas and threatening her with . . . dire unpleasantness.'

'Would the landlord's name be Mercet?' asked Catchpoll.

'Yes. Nasty bastard. I went to confront him. He mewled and made excuses, but I told him if he raised her rent then I would complain to William de Beauchamp and have all his taxes doubled.'

'I would have loved to see that,' murmured Catchpoll, with a sigh.

'He backed off then, of course, and I told him also if anything happened to my woman I would cut off his pintle.'

The serjeant actually beamed at Raoul Parler. He could sympathise with that desire to do Mercet violence, and often regretted the law held him back.

Bradecote could also understand wishing violence upon Robert Mercet, but still disliked Parler's dereliction of duty to his manor and family.

'So you visited Mercet. That could be done in a day with ease. You were away for three full days. Keeping your whore safe, or keeping your lust assuaged? By the Rood, Parler, have you so little care to what is yours by right and duty, your wife and your land?'

'You tell me my duty and preach like a priest.' Parler's lip curled in disdain. 'I have an excellent steward, whom I trust, and as for my wife . . . she does her duty well enough.' He shrugged. 'Too well.'

Bradecote opened his mouth to speak but decided against it. What could be said to a man who blamed his wife for producing children that he got upon her with such regularity that it was perfectly clear that it was literally wearing her to death? What was amazing was the devotion of that lady to her lord in such a case, so strong that she had fainted at the thought that harm had come to him. He was unworthy of such regard.

'You were at odds with Osbern de Lench, as we have heard proof from his heir.'

'Half the hundred was at odds with him, and the other half did not know him, so were unaware of their good fortune.'

'Your lady said that your hatred of each other came to a head at Lincoln, at the time of the battle. Why was that?'

'She would have been better to keep my affairs private.' Parler did not look pleased.

'Why were you such enemies?' Bradecote would not let the question be ignored.

'He wanted my eldest daughter for his whelp. He came to me, full of the "advantages" of the match. I saw none. Lench is just . . .' Parler spread out his hands, 'this, and I had already a far better marriage planned for the girl. Besides, I had doubts the church would sanction it. Some of the rules on blood are not obvious.'

'Why?' Bradecote was genuinely puzzled, and his brows drew together.

'My first wife was his younger sister. I had had enough of the family. She proved sharp of tongue, unwilling and as good as barren. When she did eventually fulfil her duty, she died in childbed and took the babe, a son too, with her. I could almost say that was spite. I wasted four years with her.'

The undersheriff stood very, very still, so tense that Catchpoll thought he might reverberate like a bowstring. Hugh Bradecote disliked Baldwin de Lench, but this man appalled him in his callousness. Yes, a wife was expected to produce an heir, but he had seen what the cost could be. He had come to the stage where the memories of Ela were no longer as bright as the blood as her life faded, though he conscientiously prayed for her soul. He had not loved her, but he had cared about her, his wife. This man blamed his first wife for not giving him living children, and his second for giving too many. There was a long silence before Catchpoll spoke, filling the emptiness.

'I can see as how you might refuse the bond, my lord, but not how it would lead to such as we saw when you arrived. Nigh on a blood feud, that was, from the manner of the lord Baldwin.'

'He is like his sire,' sneered Parler. 'He thinks roaring and stamping impress. You want to know why we were at each other's throats? Well, Osbern discovered the union I had planned, and went and told the man Baldwin had been before him with my daughter. Sullied her name enough that it came to naught. I could have had an alliance with a lord who holds manors in six shires but for that. In the end I married her off to a lesser lord down below Oxford. It is fair enough, but not what I wanted. So I paid him back.'

'How?' Bradecote had power of speech again.

'Well, his first wife died. Fell when riding, as I recall. I just made it clear, in front of many, that she died in an accident and he was with her, alone. He went white of cheek when he heard that.' Parler smiled, but it turned to a grimace. 'Then bad luck would have it that we were in the line alongside each other in the battle. I had to watch my back. As it was, he ought to have stood firm but stepped back when we clashed with the Empress Maud's men, just enough to leave me open on the blind side. I tried to parry a blow but lost these.' He held up his left hand, missing the fourth and fifth finger. 'I heard Osbern laugh. He laughed, I tell you.' Parler ground his teeth.

'And did you have any reason for thinking the death of the wife was not an accident?' Catchpoll made the question almost casual.

'That? Why should I? It was the only way I could pay him back in words, and it worked better than I expected. He was not made as welcome by several important men.'

'Did Baldwin de Lench fight also that day?' Bradecote asked the question, which had not occurred to him before. Baldwin was certainly of man's years and ought to have been at his father's side.

'No. He had broken a bone, as Osbern gave it out, a bone in the forearm. His sword arm was useless.'

'And you and Osbern de Lench never came nigh unto each other after the battle?'

'No. He turned, offered his sword to the Empress, when he thought the crown hers. Much good it did him. We did service once, afterwards, at the same time, but we neither spoke nor ate near each other. The lord Sheriff decided we would not be called upon the same duties. He sent a servant, Osbern did, with his threat that if ever I was found upon his land, I would not leave it living. I returned the compliment. It meant that we both had longer rides, he to Worcester and me to Evesham, but it matters not.'

'Why did Osbern want the match with your daughter at all?' Something did not sound quite right to Bradecote, hidden in the detail.

'That is easy enough. That fat toad Pipard, as holds the half of Bishampton, the half, mind you, had married off his son too well. With his new relatives at his back he might have caused both of us trouble. Untrustworthy he is and no mistake.'

The description of Pipard did not match the undersheriff's first estimation of the man, but the reason was sound enough in dangerous times when petty rivalries hid beneath greater ones.

Perhaps, just perhaps, Osbern would have thought it safer to be on better terms with Raoul Parler than find him even going to support Pipard and his powerful ally. It did make sense, and Bradecote was aware his bias against Parler's character was not based upon any lawbreaking.

'Very well, my lord Parler, you have given your account. Should there be any other reason to speak with you, I, or my serjeant, will come and have words.' Saying that he might delegate to Serjeant Catchpoll was a nice insult, and he saw Parler's eyes narrow for a moment. 'You may go.' Adding a dismissal doubled it. Raoul Parler glared at Bradecote, then turned away and walked out in silence.

'Now I had not thought to see you find a man you disliked more than Baldwin de Lench on this trail, but so it is, my lord.' Catchpoll rarely saw his superior more than tetchy, and lords were often that, as if it proved their lordliness.

'And neither looks likely to be more than just a bastard. You saw the wife, Catchpoll, and you heard him.'

'Aye, but it seems he cannot have taken a knife to Osbern de Lench.'

'No, but . . . Walkelin, since you have enjoyed galloping about the shire today, you can ride again. I want you to go to Worcester and speak with the coppersmith's widow he uses. Find out exactly what happened and when. It might be possible to have ridden south and killed Osbern and then gone back on himself and to Worcester.'

'But why, my lord?'

'Because I say so,' declared Bradecote, sharply, venting the bubble of wrath inside him.

'No, no, my lord. I meant not that, but why would the lord Raoul suddenly think "I shall kill Osbern de Lench today" when he was called to Worcester.'

Bradecote ran his long fingers through his hair. What Walkelin said made good sense, and he was thinking in anger. He sighed.

'You are right, Walkelin. There is no good can come of sending you to Worcester. Like Walter Pipard, Parler is glad Osbern de Lench is dead, but did not kill him, for there was no reason at this time and old hatred was just that – old. So we have to look here, and here alone, and as the chance of it being a field-working villager is almost none at all, we are left with the most likely knife-wielder being the manor steward, and we have not yet spoken to Fulk, not properly.'

'My lord, I think what the lord Raoul said may be true enough, for among the things Alnoth told me was that he, the lord of Flavel, keeps a widow in Worcester.'

'Oh aye, and who would that be?' enquired Catchpoll, with interest.

'The widow of Will Brook, the coppersmith.'

'Well now, I suppose that would fit. Will's son by his first wife has no love of the second, who is but a handful of years his senior. Comely woman she is, and no doubt had hopes of another craftsman taking her to wife, but her luck was out, for the son cast her off before it was seemly to wed again. Without kinfolk it is not easy and I thought she must be taking in more than washing, but whoever it is, he is not from within the walls of Worcester.'

'Which all means it is very unlikely that Raoul Parler had

anything to do with the death of Osbern de Lench. You stay here, Walkelin, after all.' Bradecote rubbed his chin, thoughtfully. 'The best thing to do now is to speak with Fulk the Steward, and away from the lady.'

'You think he would say anything to protect her, my lord?' Walkelin asked. 'But it was a man as left the—'

'We have heard that Fulk was not only in the hall when the body was brought back but has been known to be there at other times, times when his lord was upon the hill.'

'But . . . he wouldn't dare . . . I mean . . .' Walkelin was shocked, not so much by the thought of the sin, for he was learning to see the world through a serjeant's eyes, but at the risk.

'Oh aye, Osbern would have flayed him alive no doubt, if had known of it,' Catchpoll folded his arms, 'but sometimes folk take risks that go against sense. The lady is the sort of woman many men feel protective over. Mayhap it began like that, and him seeing her treated harsh like, well he might get ideas if she showed him kindness. From there it would be but human nature.' He sniffed, as if he was not too admiring of the idea.

Bradecote kept silent. To betray one's lord was akin to a mortal sin before one even added the obvious sin of adultery. He could understand why even a lord less bellicose than Osbern de Lench would show no mercy to one of his men who betrayed him in such a way. Since they had already been given the hearsay that Osbern had killed his first wife for a perceived betrayal, it must mean there was no thought of that in Lench itself, for Fulk would not have risked not only his own neck but the lady's also if the man had shown such violence before, would he?

137

'If we do get Fulk to tell us the truth, it will come out slowly, if at all, and if the lady was involved, he may deny it to the end.'

'We can only find out by asking him, my lord. I will fetch him from the hall.' Catchpoll saw no need to dither.

'Not here. I think admitting adultery, murder or both would be hard in the church, unless to a priest. We will go to his dwelling and await you there. With young Hamo absent it will be empty enough.'

The trio left the church as Father Matthias came to say the Office. The priest gave a slight smile and an acknowledgement to the sheriff's men.

'Let us hope that all will be peaceful now,' he said, with a strong overtone of hope over expectation in his voice. As if to prove he was to be sorely disappointed there came yelling from the hall. Ignoring the priest, the three men ran to see what was happening within.

Chapter Ten

Hamo de Lench was sprawled upon the floor of the hall, his mother leaning over him, both solicitous and protective at the same time. Baldwin was staring at him, breathing hard. Even as Bradecote entered the chamber, the youth scrambled to his feet again, shouting incoherently, pushing his mother away, and launched himself at his brother, who sidestepped and kicked him hard in the backside as he stumbled past him.

'What is—?' The undersheriff got no further, for Hamo, wild-eyed, whipped round, drawing his knife from its hanger at his belt. There was a madness in the eyes that was a battle-rage, a determination to spill blood and a recklessness about his own. 'Put it down, messire.' Bradecote spoke firmly but without heat. Hamo ignored him, his eyes upon his half-brother.

'You had no right. Nobody touches it, nobody,' Hamo panted.

'Hardly relics, were they. Just useless scribbles,' Baldwin goaded, fanning flames of anger that were already a conflagration.

Serjeant Catchpoll did what was best in cases of fire; he threw water on it. There was a shallow dish set upon a trestle, with a damp cloth hanging over the rim. It had been used to bathe the brow of the injured Edgar. He picked it up and dashed the contents over Hamo de Lench. It did not calm him, but it did stop him in his tracks. Catchpoll then stepped smartly forward and, grabbing the spluttering lordling by the scruff of the neck, pulled him backwards and off balance. Baldwin, seeing his chance, advanced, but found his way blocked by Bradecote.

'No.' The single word of command was as curt as if to a hound. The undersheriff stared him down, and Baldwin reluctantly lowered fists and gaze. He was at least silent. Hamo was, by contrast, voluble in the extreme.

'You had no right. It was my box, my treasure!' he cried.

'Treasure.' Baldwin spat the word derisively. 'I never heard of bits of old skin with marks upon them being treasure. They held no value.'

'They are God's words,' the youth cried, piously. 'God's word is to be treasured.'

Whilst not disagreeing with the theological argument, Bradecote was yet again surprised by Hamo de Lench's very literal attitude.

'What did you do, de Lench?' He thought asking the older brother would at least get an answer that he understood.

'Nothing worth all this. I found his box of so-called treasure. He has always been so secretive about it I wondered if he held anything precious after all. In many ways I was wrong, for it was full of scraps with writing upon it, but there was one thing of great value, at least to me.' He opened his palm and in it, the pin drawing drops of blood where he gripped it so tightly, was a copper badge, wrought with indented crosses and with a large amber boss in the middle. 'Ask the worm where he got my father's badge. Ask him, my lord Undersheriff.' He ground his teeth.

Bradecote looked at the squirming young man in Catchpoll's grasp, and his eyes rose for a moment to the serjeant's. What he saw was a reflection of his own surprise.

'It is a fair question, messire. How came you by your sire's hat badge?' The undersheriff at least sounded as though the revelation was not unexpected.

'I did not. I have not seen it, not since last it was upon his hat.'

'Which could have been the moment you took the life from him,' remarked Bradecote, knowing the exactitude of Hamo's speech.

'I saw him last in the morning, when he was shouting at my mother. It was too loud and so I went hawking. I never saw his hat or badge again. It was not in my box.'

'Yet that is where I found it. Did elves place it there?' sneered Baldwin.

'And where did you find the box, de Lench?' Bradecote was still watching the youth.

'Does it matter?'

'Answer me.'

'It was with the priest. Oh, I knew he kept it there, long ago, but . . .' Baldwin hunched a shoulder. 'It seemed unimportant then. But you see, unlike you, my lord Undersheriff, I have been wondering about this badge. A good thing too that I did.'

'Tell me, messire, did you think your box secret from everyone?' Bradecote was not prepared to see the finding as proof of guilt in an instant.

'Father Matthias has always known, since I left it with him.'

'That is understood. Any other?'

'Not unless Father Matthias told, and why would he? He knew it was my private thing.' Hamo could not see why anyone would be other than straightforward.

'Walkelin, go and fetch the priest.' There was more command than usual in Bradecote's voice but Walkelin guessed aright that showing it was important in this hall.

'At once, my lord,' he responded, as one who would jump to his lord's command in an instant. Walkelin caught Catchpoll's eye for a brief moment, and saw approval. He bowed and went straight to the door, leaving a chamber silent but for Hamo's still-heavy breathing and made oppressive by the atmosphere of anger and loathing. Hamo stared at Baldwin, who stared back. The lady, her hands clasped together, and pale of cheek, watched them both, and looked unsure as to whether she would cast herself between them, or simply swoon. Bradecote's authority lay over everything, maintaining the peace that was not peaceful at all.

Walkelin returned with a slightly breathless Father Matthias in tow, the hem of his habit held up to reveal pale shins.

'Here he is, my lord,' declared Walkelin, seemingly eager to prove he had obeyed. A muscle twitched, very slightly, at the corner of Catchpoll's mouth. Overdoing the obedient servant was young Walkelin, but his acting could not be faulted.

In response, the undersheriff, who would normally have indicated at least a nod of thanks, ignored Walkelin and spoke to the priest.

'Father, the box belonging to the messire Hamo. Did anyone know where it lay other than yourself?'

'It was not something I spoke of, my lord, and the only person who might know of it otherwise is Mother Winflaed, who not only provides me with good pottage but comes to change the rushes upon the floor when she says my home is less tidy than a swine pen.' He smiled gently. 'I am not a tidy person, and thank the Lord untidiness is not a mortal sin. But she is an honest and godly soul, and if she has seen the box she has never said anything, even to me. She keeps what she knows better than most women, though a little gossip has been known to pass her lips. Her girl has come in her place if she has been ailing, but she would only then set the pot and stir the pottage every so often.'

'Thank you, Father.' Bradecote turned his gaze back to Baldwin de Lench. 'So, you entered Father Matthias's dwelling and searched for the box. You knew what it looked like.'

'How many boxes would the place have in it? A small box is none so common.' Baldwin ignored the look of mild reproach from the parish priest. 'Besides, I recall the fuss the boy made about having it just so when it was put together. Almost stood over the man in Evesham as he constructed it, but he had to have what he wanted. All he had to do was ask. If I asked for what I wanted I got a short answer.'

'Well, I but wanted a box, not a tradesman's daughter to wife.' Hamo was still trembling with anger, but this was less a jibe than a stated fact.

'Keep your tongue between your teeth, or I will remove the teeth,' growled Baldwin, colouring, 'and she is a lord's widow.'

'And still the daughter of a man who sold cloth. She may have been good enough for Robert FitzBernard, but not us, and his family were swift enough to send her back to her sire.' Hamo was not going to be halted.

'Us? Since when have you been one of us? You are scarce part of the world, let alone this family.' Baldwin's lip curled in disdain, but rather than fuelling Hamo's wrath, it seemed to puzzle him.

'I am the son of Osbern de Lench, son of William Herce, son of—'

'I know the bloodline, dolt.'

'Then you know I am of this family and your question is no question at all.' Hamo, rather to the surprise of the sheriff's men, sounded suddenly his usual self, as though the rage had never existed.

'As long as your mother did not—'

'Stop!' Bradecote held up a hand, though his voice alone would have been sufficient. 'Squabbling may please you, de Lench, but we have better things to do than listen to it. I would speak with each of you, but not together. Lady, take your son into the solar and remain there.' He looked to the pale widow, who nodded, and went to lay a hand upon Hamo's arm. He looked at it, but said, quite matter-of-factly, that he did not need support and was not in any way hurt. As the solar door closed,

Bradecote folded his arms and addressed Baldwin de Lench.

'So your sire forbad the match with the widow whose blood he did not think worthy. Was he going to disown you?'

'For him?' Baldwin pointed to the shut door and laughed, mirthlessly. 'No. He had more care to his lands than that. He had another match in mind for me, but Jesu, the woman is a cold, silent piece. As well lie with a corpse as her. I told him nay. We argued, but then we have argued often enough before. It was our way.'

'And after this argument, the lord Osbern relented, did he, my lord?' Catchpoll was in no doubt of the answer.

'No, he did not. He said that just as his brother, Roger, is master of the manor that came with his wife, I could live in whatever came with her, which is nothing, or bide my time in the mercer's house. He would not let her set foot in his hall in his lifetime.'

'A lifetime now cut short,' commented Bradecote.

'Not by me. Had I wished that, surely I would have done it then, when he said it, and that was months ago.'

'So why did he send you to Tredington? Was it not to cool your heels?'

'No. Well, in part. I kept quiet about Emma, but I remained resolute that I would not wed the woman of his choice. Finally, I told him I would rather not sire a son at all than with her, and he told me I would do as he bid, and to go to Tredington, oversee the harvest and think upon the foolishness of my words.'

'You obeyed him in that, then.' Bradecote noted.

'It was easier, and besides, the steward there is as dithering as an old woman and always sending messages to ask this or that. The man cannot make a decision about wiping his own backside without consulting someone else. We ought to have got rid of him ages past, but his sons died and his grandson is still learning the duties. By next harvest I will have someone there who can think and can obey without knowing every last detail.' Baldwin sounded perfectly reasonable. He sighed. 'Emma was available to me, since I can pay for her, and I could afford to wait until my time came as lord. My sire was not a young man, and of late seemed to dwell increasingly upon his own mortality. Whether I had the running of the manors or not, they were mine by blood inheritance and were not going anywhere. I am Baldwin de Lench.' He shrugged. 'I doubted he had many more summers, and Emma is but seventeen. We have time on our side.'

'If you can pay for her, why hold out to have her as your wife?' It was cynical but practical, and Bradecote saw Baldwin as fundamentally practical when his anger did not cloud him.

'I pay as much to keep her money-grabbing father from selling her off to another man as anything, and to keep her as she has been used to live. It is her and no other, for me.'

Bradecote could not quite conceal the astonishment he felt at this admission. Baldwin de Lench had not seemed in any way a man who would have such an attachment. He looked more the sort to take his pleasure and move on. Nor, importantly, had he shown any sign of being a patient man. It gave the undersheriff doubts.

'If you have no other cause to keep me, I will be about my business, my lord Undersheriff.' Baldwin did not sound as if he intended to remain, unless physically constrained, and half turned before Bradecote gave the nod of agreement. Walkelin, who had been by the doorway, stepped aside, and the lord of Lench passed him with a grunt. Father Matthias, feeling his was an unwanted presence, begged to be excused in far more emollient terms, and departed with an obeisance to the undersheriff.

'And how much of that was true, I wonder?' mused Catchpoll.

'Well, he may have his aim set only upon the widow now, but will he be constant? I have no idea. I think he believes what he says about her though.' Bradecote rubbed his chin. 'Not a side I had expected, Baldwin the lovelorn swain.'

'More important, my lord, was he as accepting of his father's command as he said?' Catchpoll sounded doubtful.

'It seemed to me,' offered Walkelin, 'that he respected his father, on the one hand, and railed against him on the other. Two peas from the same pod in character, so they would be bound to rub each other the wrong way, but the lord Baldwin sort of understood how his father viewed life.'

'I can see Baldwin being hot-headed and violent. Holy Virgin, we have seen that ourselves, but if this forbidding of his wedding the love of his life is not of very recent date, would he plan a killing in cold blood? Both sons seem to be prone to a sudden killing-anger, and they got that from the siring side, no doubt. Of course we also have to consider that the finding of the copper badge must mean one of the two is the killer. Either Baldwin had the badge and broke into the box to make it seem hidden by his brother, or he did discover it there.'

'Fair enough, my lord, but not quite as clear as it seems. There is always the chance that someone else put the badge in the box, and . . .' Catchpoll still frowned.

'But only the priest and the healing woman knew of it, and you do not suspect either of them, do you, Serjeant?' Walkelin sounded incredulous.

'No, that I do not, but I am never totally sure that those who claim to have spoken nary a word about somethin' are speaking true. They might think they have been silent, but it is very easy to let slip a detail and not know of it. It is just possible there was someone who knew. We have to bear it in mind, even though just that.'

'You are right, Catchpoll. We must consider, but nothing more, and now we speak with young Hamo, who appears to have calmed as quickly as he rose to fury.' He strode to the solar door with Catchpoll right behind him and Walkelin several paces to the rear, not totally sure if he was included or not.

Within the solar, Hamo de Lench was sat upon a stool, leaning forward and with his hands clasped together loosely, his shoulders hunched. His mother fussed over him, and the youth's expression was one of put-upon adolescence, resentful and yet still obedient.

'So you have never possessed the badge from your sire's hat, messire?' Bradecote saw being direct as the best, if not only, way of dealing with Hamo.

'Oh, I have, but that was years past. My father pinned it to my cap once, when I was a small child. It made holes in the cap, for it was too heavy.' Hamo sounded as though he felt his father ought to have foreseen that eventuality.

'But not since.'

'No, my lord. It was his badge, for his hat.' This was a conclusive reason to the youth.

'And your box?'

'That is mine, and none see within it. None, not my father, nor mother, nor Baldwin, nor—'

'Yes, we understand. Nobody looks in your box.' Bradecote interrupted, lest every member of the community should be named. 'How came you to be in the lodging of Father Matthias? You had gone hawking, so I was told, against my instructions.'

'You did not say I might not go hawking.'

'Not specifically.' Bradecote sighed. This was becoming tiresome. 'But I said that you should not leave the manor.'

'And I did not. I had nothing to do, so I went hawking. Superba was restless also.' Hamo looked a little confused. Why was he being asked this? Bradecote wondered why he was bothering also.

'So it was to exercise yourself and the hawk. Yet you did not say that you were going.'

'I did not see you. If I had seen you I would have said.' Hamo sighed.

'But you did not enjoy your sport for long, did you.' It was not put as a question. 'You returned to find your box and contents strewn about.'

'My hawk was unwilling, and there was nothing to be gained, so I came back. Then I found out what Baldwin had done.'

'And had we not come in when you and your brother were fighting, would you have killed him, if you could?'

'Baldwin is stronger than I am, but . . . we do not get on.'

'Yes, we gathered that. But you do not answer me, messire.'

'Killing is wrong, murder killing.'

'But you were blood-angry in the hall.'

'Was I? I did lose my temper I think.' Hamo shrugged, and looked to his mother. 'Was I very angry?'

'Yes, my son, you were.' She sounded exhausted by the altercation.

'Baldwin should not have opened my box, and indeed he damaged the lid.' Hamo's sense of injustice was strong, but the sheriff's men were not looking into the damage of a box, and Bradecote picked up on something else the lordling had said.

'The last time you saw the badge it was upon your father's hat, on his head, the morning he was killed.'

'No.'

'But you said—'

'It was on his hat, but his hat was in his hand, in his fist, all crumpled.'

'Ah.' Bradecote gave a half sigh of relief. 'You saw him here in the hall, and he was shouting at your lady mother. Do you know why?' Having heard Hamo's brief but straightforward answers to other questions Bradecote did not think that he would lie over such a thing.

'I . . . he often shouted. He shouted at me, at Baldwin, at . . . but I think he was angry because . . .' Hamo frowned.

'My son does not understand the relationship betwixt a husband and wife,' murmured the lady and coloured a little.

'Osbern treated any refusal of . . . even when I could not help . . . it made him angry. His rights were not to be denied.' The blush now turned her pale cheeks crimson. 'My lord, I would not care to discuss the matter here, this moment.' Her eyes moved to her son, softened, but her mouth formed a twisted smile. 'You will permit—'

She got no further, for a boy of about eleven burst in without even knocking. His chest was heaving, his ears, which stuck out from the side of his head and parted a tangle of sandy hair, were red, as were his eyes, which were round with horror.

'She's dead!' he cried, in anguish, his voice tear-heavy.

'Who is, lad?' Catchpoll's was the voice that calmed.

'Mother Winflaed. I found 'er in the Far Coppice. The pigs was rooting there today.'

'Fair enough. Now, you take us to see where she lies.'

'It was not me.' The boy seemed to feel that the weight of the law would fall upon him.

'We knows that. Now, lead us.'

'I will speak with you, alone, later, my lady.' Bradecote, grim-faced, nodded to the lady de Lench, whose mouth was agape, and the trio of sheriff's men followed the small discoverer of the body of Winflaed the Healer into the hall and thence into the sunlight, where they were accosted by the healer's girl, wringing her hands and weeping.

'Say it is not true, oh, say it is not. I can't do it all, not right I can't, and there's the birthing for Gytha, and all I have done is help and watch, not been a-catching of the babe myself. Holy Virgin aid me!' The girl Hild was clearly as distressed at the

151

burden laid suddenly upon her as at the loss of her mentor. She looked to authority, to the undersheriff.

'Wait here.' It was a command, but not harshly given. A panicking girl was the last thing they needed at the scene. He sensed more than saw the lady of the manor behind him and turned. 'Will you keep her with you, my lady, until we return?'

She nodded, and the swine boy and the three men left the woman and girl together.

Chapter Eleven

The coppice was mostly hazel with a little holly scattered amongst it like prickly green sentinels and the odd legacy of a greater wood, an occasional oak or ash. The body lay in a small clearing, where one of the great trees had fallen, not at its end of years, but lightning-struck and split. Such a 'ghost tree', accounted cursed by many, had not fed the village hearths, and its parts lay supine, the saplings that would fight to replace it merely supple mourners about the skeletal remains. The clearing was perhaps fifteen paces from the trackway, behind a wall of hazels and green shrubbery. A shaft of slightly dappled light played over the corpse like shimmers upon water, creating an illusion of movement, though Winflaed the Healer would never move again. She lay with one cheek upon the earth as if listening to its heartbeat, one arm still outstretched towards a sprouting of mushrooms against the pale roots of the ghost tree. Another of the tree's roots, ripped from the earth and pointing skywards, seemed to be drawing the attention of Heaven to the evil that had been perpetrated. Her other arm was still beneath her, and the fact that it was not flung out suggested to Bradecote that she had been insensate even as she toppled forward. He did not need Catchpoll's skills to work that out. The pale cloth of her coif was pale no longer, but heavily stained scarlet, and the ground was damp-dark.

Catchpoll skirted to the side of the body and knelt down. He touched the flesh of her cheek.

'Only warmth in the skin is the little from the sunlight.' He closed the sightless eyes. 'No real death-stiffening as yet, but then we knows she was alive a couple of hours ago, so that is no surprise at all.'

'And the basket for her foraging is almost empty,' noted Walkelin, picking up a shallow basket that the woman had evidently set down out of the way before her death. It had but half a dozen mushrooms and a sprig of some plant, its leaves slightly wilted. 'So she was killed not long after setting out.' He cast about the edge of the clearing and added that a horse had been there. 'We are not far from the track, but no rider would bring their horse among the trees and bushes by mistake.'

Catchpoll nodded his agreement and approval, though he was still looking at the body. 'Leastways it was quick.' His fingers touched the red stain upon the neck of her gown and soaked into the folds of her coif. 'Blade went in behind the left collarbone and straight down to the heart, I reckon.'

Catchpoll looked up and caught the movement of the swine boy wiping his sleeve across his nose. He looked pinched and rather green-tinged. 'You go back and fetch two men and a strong blanket or a hurdle, boy. Be swift.' The boy just nodded, turned and ran. 'Should've thought of him before. Doubt he will say anything but we doesn't want gossip, and we doesn't want the truth spread neither.'

'Agreed.' Bradecote was pondering the wound. 'That is clearly not a woman's strike, nor that of one who has not borne arms. It was a man, with a dagger or as good as, and one who knew what he was doing.' The undersheriff frowned. 'So if we discount a wild coincidence that had her killed for no good reason by a passing stranger, it leaves us with Baldwin de Lench, who left us just before she did, and whom we did not see again between the confronting of Raoul Parler and the fight over the treasure box, and his brother, Hamo, who was out hawking until the same time. The angry lord Baldwin stamped out of the hall saying he was going up the hill, but I doubt he went.' He shook his head. 'This seems very cold-blooded for both, who are quite capable in hot blood but . . .' The undersheriff did not look happy.

'And that messire is no warrior, my lord. You can see as how he would make a monk, but I doubt his sword arm.' Catchpoll sniffed.

'My lord, what about the lord of Flavel?' Walkelin encountered a look of some surprise but continued. 'I do not say it is likely, but is it not possible? He left from the church before we did, but what if he had seen the healing woman as he mounted his horse?'

'But what reason could he have to kill her, lad?' Catchpoll's face screwed into an expression of strong doubt. 'Good that you consider it as an idea, but . . .' He was gently rolling the body over. The right hand had been pressed over her chest, but once released fell sideways.

'What reason had anyone to kill her, though? None we can see, and yet there she lies.' Walkelin pointed at the corpse and sounded almost angry, affronted. In truth, he found the murder of this woman who did nothing but good far more of an outrage than the killing of her lord. Lying on her back made her look less at one with the earth, more dishonoured by death. The cheek that had been to the ground had little fragments of leaf and soil dirtying it, and stuck where blood had, dried them to the skin.

'Look you here, my lord. The wound that killed was swift, but she was threatened first, I would say. There is a small mark here, a knife's tip, no more.' Catchpoll had moved the sodden coif to reveal the throat, and touched a mark that scarcely deserved the name of a wound, being just a nick in her neck, under the chin, and a thin line of blood that could easily be overlooked when there was so much more soaked about it. 'He placed the point there, and either she did not give him what he wanted, or he's just a callous bastard and did for her anyways.'

'So it was one of the two lords,' murmured Walkelin, 'since we can discount the steward, we—'

'Why do we discount him?' Bradecote's question was asked of himself as much as his companions.

'He's no soldier neither, my lord.' Walkelin shook his head.

'Not now, not perhaps for many years, but he is a strong-looking man, and who is to say he was always the steward. Even if he followed his father, well, as a young man he might have taken years as one of his lord's men-at-arms. We have not looked at them in a different way to any other, because everyone at this season is a farmer, getting in the harvest, and I can say for sure that my men-at-arms turn their hands to what is needed, not just practice with sword or bow. Who is to say Fulk was not more soldier than steward in his young manhood?'

'A fair point, my lord,' conceded Catchpoll, 'and we have not seen him since we went to the church with the lord of Flavel, though why would he bring a horse this short step of a way?'

'To be swifter than any would think otherwise? He might have come bareback and with the animal merely haltered.' Bradecote shrugged. 'All I say is he is not cast out of our net.'

'It would have been a risk, someone seeing him with a horse and wondering why he needed it. But if we say it could be so, then that means all four of 'em, the men we have as even possible killers of the lord Osbern de Lench, had the chance to kill this good woman, and if other than the lord Raoul, you would have to ask why now? The others saw her every day of their lives, near enough.'

'Then it has to be something done, or said, this morning, and I doubt collecting mushrooms and plants for her potions would drive a man to killing. So let us think what she said.' Bradecote's brow furrowed.

'We cannot know if she met the lord of Flavel though, my lord, or what she said if she did.' Walkelin frowned.

'No, but of the others . . . can we be sure that anything that passed her lips was not heard by one of the three?' Bradecote ticked them off on his long fingers. 'Baldwin de Lench was in the hall, and when he left might have stood in the cross passage and listened, rather than go up the hill as he said. Young Hamo went hawking, but might have only gone shortly before it was reported to us, though if so he was not keen on his sport today. Fulk came with that news, but might have been listening before he came in. So what could they have heard?'

Walkelin sat upon the ground and waited silently. He had not been present, so could be of no use in this.

'I cannot see why the lord Baldwin would kill her for her desire to make him a potion,' grunted Catchpoll.

'No, nor I, but think on it, she did give quite a broad hint that the lady of Lench has suffered physical harm from her lord in the past.'

'But what of it if she did, my lord? The man is dead, and Baldwin would not see a heavy hand as something shameful.'

'I know, Catchpoll, but if there was more she could say, or he feared she might say . . . the lady could be persuaded to say nothing through threats to her beloved son, but the healing woman . . .' Bradecote sighed, and ran his fingers through his hair. 'No, I agree, it is seeking what is not there. Nor is there anything that might have concerned Hamo, and I do not think he killed his father or this poor woman unless in red-mist anger as we saw. Coming across her foraging would not anger him. He would scarcely notice her. That leaves us with Fulk the Steward, and he might just have had more cause. When we asked her about him she said he was not in the field, and that alone is not damning since everyone saw it, but the way she said "I doubt he was idle" was full of meaning, even if you could not see her expression. Even if she did not reveal more to us, it is possible Fulk feared she might do so to the lord Baldwin, and what would you give for his life then?'

'Not as much as a grain from the threshing, and it would not be an easy death, neither.'

'But are you saying he also killed the lord Osbern?' enquired Walkelin.

'I would like to say yes, Walkelin, because two different killers in so few days seems beyond thought, but we have not discovered more than that it is likely he was betraying his lord, so he did have motive.'

'We might also press the lady on the argument that the messire heard and which sent him off hawking the day of his father's death. She lied, and lied scared, my lord. She wanted time to make up some yarn for us, and did not want her son blurting out truths.'

'Very true, Catchpoll. We will see Winflaed the Healer carried home, speak with her girl to know a little better when she left, and then we speak, at last, with the perhaps none-so-loyal steward.'

'He might be loyal, my lord, but not to his lord.'

'Which we will discover shortly.'

'My lord.' Walkelin had been staring towards the mushrooms, thinking, but was now looking. 'I think I may also have a reason for the Healer's death. Look here.' He got up and went to kneel a foot or so from the fungi. There was a tangling of undergrowth bowing down to the ground, but Walkelin moved it. 'Someone has dug, and dug straight, and then tried to hide it with the branches. I saw the edge of the mark.' There was a line of fresh earth less than a foot and a half long, and although it had been stamped flat it was a little darker.

'Now that,' commended Catchpoll, 'is using your eyes.'

'Osbern de Lench had a dagger, and it was not abandoned with the clothes,' murmured Bradecote. 'We just assumed it was worth the taking, and kept, but if easily recognised . . .'

'We cannot be sure that this was not the place that Alnoth the Handless did not step aside and then find the cap and cloak, my lord.'

'Scrabbling about to bury it would have taken longer, as I see it,' said Bradecote, thoughtfully. 'Whoever killed her would have removed it, yes? There would be bound to be a hunt for her when she did not return.'

Walkelin clawed at the earth where it was loose, and shook his head.

'Nothing remains, my lord.'

'Yet something narrow was there, and if whoever buried it even heard this poor soul so close, then she was doomed.'

'But there's the thing, my lord.' Catchpoll got up, slowly. 'It would have to be the greatest of mischances for him to be close enough just when she was here, unless he followed her. So we have the slim possibility that it was the lord of Flavel as that mischance, or we have one of the other three who already had a reason to follow her to silence her, and then found even her

160

death would point to him the more. If that be so, you would have to think he is now wondering if he is destined for the noose whatever he does.'

'If we succeed, Catchpoll, he is.' Bradecote looked grim.

The final return of the healing woman was met with much genuine grief, and no small degree of concern in some minds, as they wondered if the girl Hild knew enough of her craft to keep any from pain, let alone death. She had less than three years as the healer's aide, and, as was noted in sob-laden whisper by the heavily pregnant Gytha, was not even woman enough to bear a child as yet, let alone deliver one. The healer's body was taken to the church, where it was tended by priest for the soul, and Hild's oldmother, who was Winflaed the Healer's sister, for the body. Catchpoll was confident that he did not need to look upon the body further. The girl was kept from the washing and shrouding, and so Hugh Bradecote took her to one side and gently asked what had happened when she had gone to prepare the sick man's warmed ale and herbs.

'I did what Mother Winflaed told me, my lord. I bound the herbs and had them in the pot warming up gradual, and then she came in and said as she might add more sage, and that a pottage with a little of the healer's mushrooms in it might be good for the poor man. I can recognise them, every time, and offered to go, but she said it was a fair day and she had thoughts to think, and . . . and . . . and that was the last I saw of her.' The girl wiped her eyes and sniffed, dolorously. Bradecote was about to dismiss her when he thought of something.

'Tell me, when you have gone in Mother Winflaed's place to Father Matthias, to cook and such, have you ever seen a box, a small box?'

The girl shook her head and denied the presence of any box that she knew about. Bradecote sent her to minister to the injured man in the hall, thinking it neither too difficult and yet something for her to do other than worry about her own competence.

'So those that knew of the box leaves Baldwin, young Hamo and the priest, who is much used to keeping secrets,' Bradecote declared to his subordinates.

'No wait, my lord. Fulk knew, for it was him as told me about the box with vellum writings in it.' Walkelin spoke up, urgently.

Bradecote swore at his own forgetfulness, low but long, and Serjeant Catchpoll sucked his teeth in a hiss of self-disgust.

'Trouble is, my lord, this has new things tumbling upon us like rocks in a defile, and we is so busy dealing with the current one we loses sight of what lies behind. We was all set to speak with the steward Fulk when the girl came and called us to the injured man of Flavel, and we no sooner tried to have words with him than we had the messire going off hawking, the lord of Flavel turning up, then the fight between the brothers and the death. All in all, it is not a surprise we forgot Fulk, and forgot he knew of the box.'

'Perhaps not a surprise, but Heaven help us, Catchpoll, we need to keep everything in mind, and it is not as though we have a large number of people who could be the killer. There are four men, and that is all.'

'Aye, my lord, but the answer is not leaping out at us because of time.'

'We are short of it?' Bradecote frowned.

'No, my lord, because there is no sense to either death being now, at this time, unless something we do not know has set it all going. If we had that we would have our man quicker than you could say a *Pater Noster*.'

'As it stands, my lord, surely now the steward must look most likely our man?' Walkelin preferred optimism. 'We know he was not in the field with the harvesters, so he could have killed the lord Osbern. If he was angered by the lord's treatment of the lady, then he had a reason to do it, or she asked him to do it. He also knew about the box of writing so could have placed the badge in it, and he could have overheard the healing woman, and been afeard of what she might say to you or the lord Baldwin. Makes it seem good sense it was him.'

'Yes, and yet . . .' The undersheriff rubbed his chin. 'Something is there, something we cannot yet see, and I am not sure it lies with Fulk the Steward.'

'Best we goes and speaks with him, nice and firm like,' muttered Catchpoll. 'Things may be clearer then.'

'And I still want to speak with the lady and hear just what Edgar of Flavel has to say also,' added Bradecote. 'He might have a clearer head after taking the brew that was prescribed for him.'

Fulk the Steward was a flustered man. The lord Baldwin wanted everyone back to their work and much as if nothing had happened, and every other man, woman and child in Lench could think and speak of nothing else but the killing. If the death of their lord had been unexpected and shocking, it was as nothing to the grief and a blossoming sense of fear that now showed upon every visage. Osbern of Lench had been killed, but it had not made the villagers feel particularly threatened. If someone had killed Mother Winflaed, who had never harmed a soul, who was next? Baldwin reviled them for looking like bleating sheep afraid of a wolf, but Fulk had heard a mumbled male voice saying that sheep had every right to be afraid of wolves. So the villagers wanted reassurance he could not give and the lord wanted industrious labour they were in no state to provide. Life was not being kind to Fulk the Steward.

'Ah, there you are, Master Steward.' Catchpoll's voice was jarringly cheery, as though he were seeking Fulk to sit and have a beaker of ale with him in the shade. Fulk tensed, and turned to see the three sheriff's men walking towards him. He muttered under his breath, and it was not a prayer of thanksgiving.

'I am here, but am set about with tasks.' It was the nearest he dare come to telling them to go away.

'Well, while you are talking with us you can not be set about with 'em but set 'em aside.' Catchpoll was now, if possible, even more cheery. His death's head grin slashed across his grizzled jaw, and Fulk the Steward found it extremely unnerving, just as the serjeant intended it should.

'You have need of me?' The steward managed to sound as if he desired to be of service to the sheriff's men, but only just.

'We do, and would prefer to speak with you in private.' Bradecote felt Serjeant Catchpoll had achieved a lot with few words but sought to keep the steward aware that it was shrieval power from higher up the scale that was in command of the situation.

'You can be sure as I will help all I can, my lord, but . . . well, this last terrible thing has set all in uproar and no mistake. I cannot find it in me to blame them, the folk here, for their fears. Who would do such a thing to a woman as never did aught but good all her life?'

'It is indeed a mystery, and one we intend to solve. But we have other questions for you first. The church is still being used by priest and kin, so I think we will speak by your own hearth. It will be quiet enough.'

'Quiet enough for what, my lord?' Fulk was still caught off balance, and that was not a situation he was used to in any way. It was bad enough having to get used to a new lord, as likely to be wrathful as the last one, but with the added eagerness of one upon whose shoulders the mantle of lordship lay new and just a little heavily withal. Baldwin de Lench clearly wanted to make his mark, and that might yet be upon the body of the manor steward.

'To discuss your absence from the harvest at the time of the death of your lord, for a start.'

'I was in the barn, preparing for a cartload to come in.'

'The hall is not, as far as I can see, a barn.' Bradecote noted, eyebrows raised, and not in the tone of one merely making an observation. He did not usually sound supercilious, but he was not going to be played for a fool. He began to walk towards the

165

steward's cott, and let Catchpoll and Walkelin herd, more than push, the steward in his wake.

'Ah, that was just afore everyone came to see the lord Osbern's horse had come back empty. I wanted to see there was wine set ready for his return,' Fulk admitted, reluctantly.

'So you went from the barn to the hall just a short time before?' Bradecote did not look back but asked his questions commandingly.

'Yes, my lord.'

'Yet you did not see the grey without its rider in the bailey. How . . . strange.'

Catchpoll grinned. This was going to be entertaining. He felt that the lord Bradecote could keep Fulk off balance with words very cunningly, letting the man trip over his own mistakes. The tall undersheriff opened the door and ducked into the dark chamber, letting his eyes adjust to the gloom. Then he turned and faced the steward, his arms folded and awaiting the response.

'When I said it was just afore I meant not a long time, my lord, but the horse was not there when I entered the hall, or indeed I would have seen it and raised the alarm.'

'There was time for a woman so heavily with child she could not work in the field to see the horse, tie it, get to the field, and then the rest of the Lench folk to return. I do not call that short. Shall we try again? What were you doing in the village when the lord Osbern went up the hill?'

'I . . .' Fulk's denial crumbled. 'I went to the hall, to see how my lady did. Kenelm said as how there had been loud words and the lord Osbern was in a foul temper, not that such a thing

166

was rare. He was not a gentle man.' Fulk sighed. 'He would raise his hand to her, for little reason or none. I feared one day he would leave her as dead as his first wife.'

'But she died in an accident.' Catchpoll spoke up.

'Aye, so it was said.'

'But you knew different, did you?' The serjeant pressed.

'Not knew, but . . . the lady Judith, I remember she rode so well. The lord Osbern brought her home across his horse, before him, her body I mean, and he wept, but . . . I always asked myself how he came to find her as they did not ride out together and it was not that her horse returned as his did, riderless. He asked Mother Winflaed to try and save her, but a broken neck is beyond any healer, as we all told her. There was nothing she could do.'

'So you thought he might harm his lady, to her death?' Bradecote took over once more.

'I did, my lord.'

'And so you have spent time alone with her as often as you could when the lord Osbern was upon his daily ride up the hill. That seems devotion of a very high degree.'

'I . . .'

'You see that it might look as though you were not simply finding out that she had not been hurt. It occurred to me, and I am not a suspicious man, am I, Serjeant Catchpoll?'

'Many a time I have thought you was not nearly suspicious enough, my lord, not nearly enough.'

'So you see, steward, I do not think it unreasonable to ask – were you betraying him, with her?'

'No. No, my lord, I was not.' Fulk looked affronted, and

blustered, which might have accounted for his reddened face.

'A comely woman, a woman needing the protection of a good, strong man, and you a good, strong man? It looks almost certain. In fact, I wonder that it did not occur to the lord Osbern. Did it? Is that the suspicion that made him angry that morning, and did you simply take a horse from the stable, ride up the hill and end the threat to her, and to you?' Bradecote posed the questions very calmly.

'No, my lord. I swear oath I did not kill the lord Osbern. I never left the hall.'

'Just stood there looking at 'er, were you, seeing she could move her arms and legs?' Catchpoll joined in, sounding equally doubting. 'That would not take long.'

'We talked.' Fulk looked somewhere between sulky and guilty.

''Bout what? You'll never tell me she was asking how many sheaves had been cut that morning.'

'No. Other things.'

'But not killing her husband.'

'No, not that.' Fulk looked beseechingly at Bradecote. 'Whatever you thinks, my lord, I never killed the lord Osbern.'

'And where were you after you came and told us that the lordling Hamo had gone off hawking?' Bradecote did not want the man to regain any sense of balance.

'This morning? I was here putting the pebbles in the bag.'

'What?' Catchpoll stared at him, but Bradecote did not look confused in the least.

'So you were accounting all the sheaves that had been brought in.'

'Aye, my lord. It is a good sign, though of course you can have a poor yield from plenty of stalks. It gives an idea of what we would expect to thresh.'

'My steward does it thus, but it does not take him so long, I think. And it is not so far to where Mother Winflaed was found dead.'

This time Fulk went pale and his response was stammered. He crossed himself.

'No, no . . . m-m-my lord, I would not, could not do such a thing. Why would I?'

'Because I think she was of my mind, and thought you and the lady were lovers, and if you thought that either she would tell the lord Baldwin or let it slip even by accident, your life and the lady's would not be worth one of those pebbles you count.'

'I had no idea of that, and secrets were safe with her, always. That is the healer's way, bit like the priest. No, my lord, I did not kill Mother Winflaed, and would take up my hatchet to him that did. Seek her killer elsewhere.'

Undersheriff looked at serjeant, who shrugged. What had begun as lies, easy to see, had become as good truth, and if he was lying now, it was an amazingly swiftly learnt ability.

'Very well, but I suggest you be very careful in when you see the lady and what you say before the lord Baldwin. Until the killer is caught I am minded, for all your swearing, that you had good reason to see both dead.'

With which Bradecote gave a jerk of his head and led his men out into the open air.

'Did he do it, Catchpoll?'

'Wish I knew, my lord. It fits together like a nut in its shell, but yet I do not feel he took a knife to either.'

'Nor me. Oh well, let us speak with our battered man, not that it will aid us. There is something, somewhere, that will make all plain, but either we have not found it or we have missed it, and I hate both options.'

Chapter Twelve

The man Edgar was sat up, his legs still stretched out before him, leaning forwards with his hands on his knees. He looked beaten and he looked in discomfort, but he no longer looked a man addled of wits. How much was down to the efficacy of the draught prepared by the girl Hild and how much to his own constitution was impossible to tell. He looked far more aware of his surroundings and could hardly fail to be aware of his carer, who was dabbing some preparation on his bare back, which made him wince at even her most delicate touch. Hild looked torn between knowing she was looked upon as a mere slip of a girl and that she held the position of Healer, which commanded respect and gave her authority. Having been nearly silent when she was the mere attendant, she was now voluble, using the phrases that her mentor had used. Hearing motherly advice issuing from such youthful lips was remarkably disconcerting, and Edgar looked ill-at-ease as well as aching of body as he was admonished and cosseted in equal measure.

'If you feel pain, my friend, it is a good thing, for it shows you are fully in this world.' Bradecote sounded cheering. 'I am Hugh Bradecote, Undersheriff of Worcestershire, and I would ask questions of you, but know the answers will give you no blame. We need truth, that is all.'

'And truth is what you will get from me, my lord, as best I can give it,' the voice was stronger, 'but I could not tell you sure if today was Tuesday or Friday, and that's a fact.'

'All we need is information about yesterday and your journey here to Lench. We know that you bought a red woollen hat from a beggar on the Evesham road. Can you tell me about that meeting?'

'I did that, my lord. I knew him, o' course, for all in Evesham know Alnoth the Handless who comes regular to the town. It was not that many a mile out of Evesham. He had that red hat and a cloak too.' Edgar gave a small laugh that became a groan as his ribs hurt, and Hild shushed at him. 'The sun shone bright, and there was sweat running down from his brow and I offered to buy the hat to give him ease. He asked tuppence for it and I gave him a penny ha'penny, which was a fair price to us both.'

'There was nothing on the hat?' enquired Catchpoll.

'Only Alnoth's sweat.' Edgar swivelled his eyes towards him, keeping his body as still as possible.

'Hmm.' Something was niggling the serjeant, whose face was ruminative. He ignored the mild jest. 'It's an odd time to leave the manor, when harvest is coming in,' he remarked.

'Ah, I left it long ago, not days past, and was hoping to reach it afore the harvest were all gathered.' Edgar sighed. 'I left Flavel years back and was apprenticed to a wheelwright in Evesham as had married my aunt. The wheelwright in Flavel was young and strong and had no wish to take on a lad then. I served three years and then the pair of 'em upped and died one winter, of the green cough. I was newly a father, and thus a husband also, but thanks be that Evesham has a fair few wheelwrights and another took me on. Then, when I was a journeyman, the child died and my wife followed soon after. Took the spirit from me, that did, for a while. Eventually, well, I became full partner, but there was a fire, end of last month, and it is all gone and old Wulfram with it. No other wheelwright, nor craftsman of any sort, will work with me, for they say as I am cursed with misfortune. True enough that Evesham has brought me no joy for long. Mind you, after what has happened here, I wonders if I am not cursed wherever I go and ought to take up a pilgrim's staff.' He looked disconsolate. 'I never liked the river much, so I doubt I dare cross a big water like sea, but there is St David's, I suppose.'

'I'd as soon take the sea,' mumbled Catchpoll, who had never seen more than the estuary of the Severn above Gloucester. 'There's an awful lot of Wales to St David's.' He shook his head. 'An awful lot.'

Nothing, thought Bradecote, would ever rid Catchpoll of his dislike of Wales, but this was not the time to dwell upon Edgar's future plans. He opened his mouth to speak, but Edgar was before him.

'Well, we shall see. Mayhap my path ends in Flavel, since I was given such a sign.'

173

'A sign?' Catchpoll snorted. He was largely dismissive of signs.

'Aye, but to see my lord, and just when I was wondering if I ought to return, it being a time when all are of use, that made me sure.'

There was a silence, and the sheriff's men stared at Edgar in stupefaction.

'You met with the lord Raoul Parler? When?' Bradecote spoke slowly, deliberately.

'Why, but the day before . . . what day is this? No matter . . . well, the day before I met Alnoth on the road. I would not say as I met with him, not to speak to nor even make my bow to, but I saw him right enough. He was not cold sober, and the woman on his arm is known to half the shire, if you get me, but I had not seen him in Evesham these two years past. I took it as a sign.'

'You are sure of this?'

'Of course, my lord.'

'And when in the day?'

'The early eventide, my lord.'

'Walkelin.' Bradecote turned urgently to the serjeanting apprentice. 'I know we said we did not need you to go to Worcester, but go now and do not dawdle. Find his woman, and find out when and for how long he was with her, if at all. How much of what he told us was lie or half-truth I do not know, but by the Saints of Heaven I will have the truth from him. Return here, for he will have no cause to think we are interested any more in him and will sit secure in his manor, and I do not wish to confront him without the news you bring.'

'Yes, my lord, at once.' Walkelin looked to Catchpoll. 'Can you tell me where to find the Widow Brook, serjeant?'

'Aye, I can that. I will come with you to saddle up, if my lord gives leave.'

Bradecote nodded, told him to return to the solar, where he would be speaking with the lady, and belatedly wondered why Catchpoll was being so deferential. Then he saw Baldwin de Lench in the doorway. Catchpoll was wily, insubordinate and sometimes outright disobedient, but he knew the value of everyone respecting the office of undersheriff, and he would play the game to accentuate the idea that his superior must be obeyed. No doubt he also had other instructions for Walkelin on how to conduct his meeting with the leman.

'Need this man remain in my hall?' Baldwin pointed at the injured man. He sounded as if Edgar were an unpleasant smell. To annoy him, Bradecote looked at the girl.

'What would you say, Healer?' He could give her the title but calling her Mistress would sound as if he spoke in jest and also feel foolish. She would need some years yet to earn that.

'I . . .' She wavered, but found that the lord undersheriff's gaze, and his addressing her with a title, could give a girl courage. 'I would say, my lord, that he could be brought to Mo . . . the Healer's house, and I would care for him there. In a day or two, why then he might go on to Flavel, if he finds a cart going there, or walks slowly, and with a stick. The legs are strong, and 'tis but the breathing that will be hard at first.'

'Then there is your answer, de Lench. Your Healer says he can be moved, so move him, but gently and under her guidance.'

Bradecote hid a smile. Baldwin de Lench would not like that, not one bit. Without looking at the lord, however, he thanked the girl and went to the solar door, opening it as one with the right.

The lady de Lench was sat upon her chair, and from the size of it Bradecote thought it had always been the lady's seat. Hamo was on his knees upon the floor, which made the undersheriff's brows rise, but then he saw that he was taking his pieces of vellum and arranging them in some order which was meaningful to him. He glanced up at Bradecote, hunched a shoulder and resumed his task.

'Perhaps you should take those to the priest, messire.' Bradecote wanted him gone, for it was hardly likely that he would find out anything about the mother and her relationship with the steward when the son was in the chamber.

'Father Matthias does not need to read them. He knows the words. I am missing one, missing the commandment of the Lord Christ, the one to love one another. It is very hard to do. I do not love Baldwin. I try to do so, but I fail and so I ask forgiveness for it.'

'It might be still in the priest's house, fallen upon the floor and in a corner. You ought to look for it.' Bradecote was all helpfulness.

'Yes, but if he had found it, the good father would have brought it to me.'

'Indeed, but remember he has been looking only to the body of Winflaed the Healer and praying for her soul, as we will also.' Countering logic with logic looked most likely to have an effect, and Hamo certainly looked more pensive than aggrieved.

'Yes. The potions she made were often foul to the taste, but she intended nothing but good. Murder is against God's commandment, but some seem most specially wicked. I will pray for her too.'

'I suggest that if you go and look for your missing vellum and then go to the church, your prayers and those of Father Matthias will ascend together.'

Hamo wavered, sat back upon his haunches, and then, gathering his neat piles together, he rose.

'Mother, you will keep these for me? The box is broken but if you place a pebble upon the top they will not become disordered, and Baldwin does not come in here.'

'I will keep them.' She smiled at the youth, who returned the smile, but as though mirroring it rather than feeling it within himself. He left, and she sighed, turning to the undersheriff. 'You cannot think he would harm his sire, nor poor Winflaed, my lord.'

'I think it unlikely, I grant, but I have seen also how he can be killing-mad upon a cause most would think should merely give rise to shouting or a raised fist. You cannot deny that he would have killed Baldwin in the hall, had he been able.'

'But . . .'

'He would not kill in cold blood, I am sure of it, but if he snaps as he did over the box, nothing is beyond him.' Bradecote realised he was making an even better case for Hamo's innocence. Neither killing bore any sign of rage in the attack, nor an attempt at defence, which being advanced upon by a man behaving like a crazed fiend would have made certain. 'I am not here now to talk of your son but of your steward.'

'He is a good man.'

Her words were guarded, and Bradecote noted she did not give him his name. Was that intentionally stepping back? He did not challenge her but decided to seek at least some of his answers by a different path. He heard Catchpoll enter behind him but did not turn round.

'Tell me about him. Is he the steward by inheritance, following his father?'

'Yes, this I know for sure, since he was not steward when I came here to wed. He was learning, had learnt from boyhood, but his father was steward then.'

'And was learning the sum of all he did? I cannot believe the lord Osbern would see that as a day-long task.'

'Mostly, by then, for his father was stiff of joints and sometimes unable to stand all day, so Fulk gave up his hours with . . .' Her eyes widened a little, as she saw a trap looming. 'His hours with those labouring.' It was not the real answer.

'How many men-at-arms did your lord keep?' Bradecote asked, softly, and she reddened to the roots of her hair.

Catchpoll gave a faint sigh of pleasure. This was serjeanting craft.

'The marks upon your arm, lady, came from being held, held hard.' Bradecote suddenly lunged forward and took her by the wrist, not too tightly, but watching the instinctive cringing and pulling back, and the fear in her eyes. 'Yes, you are not unused to such treatment.' He let her go. 'Osbern had a temper, as we see in Baldwin, and you say he was not a man as was liked. He was a man who hit and held, wasn't he.' It was a statement, and she merely nodded, and rubbed at her wrist as if also from habit.

'I failed him,' she whispered. 'I failed him in sons, and I failed him in spirit. He wanted what I could not provide and what I could not be. I think . . . I think he wanted the wife he had lost, though it was a tempestuous marriage, from what I gathered. Yet when he selected me it was, my mother told me, because I would cause no trouble and be biddable.' She sighed. 'Perhaps he did not know what he wanted. Sometimes he was angry because I was quiet, sometimes because I made some mild comment. It was never right.'

'You must have felt very alone.'

'Yes, I suppose so. I did not question it.'

'And Fulk the Steward tried to protect you?'

'Protect me?' She gave a shrill laugh. 'If he had he would have been dead years ago. Osbern had his rights and would brook no interference with them.'

'So if he did not protect, did he solace?' There was no judgement in the question.

'He was there. That is what meant something. It was as though there was something at my back so that I would not fall backwards into an abyss.'

'Strange. I had not seen Fulk in the light of a listener.' Bradecote raised a brow.

'Listener? Not really, but listening to him, just him saying that what had happened was wrong . . . it made it easier. If it had been right, normal, natural, then I could not have borne it for all these years.'

'Fulk must have been angered at times, not being able to protect you as he wished, being only able to speak freely with you when your lord, and his, was up the hill. At least it was at the same time, almost every day. It was your time, yes? To do with as you willed.' There was no implication that what they willed involved adultery, for if it had been there, she would have heard his disapproval. It was not just a morality about adultery, but about lordship, and the trust within it. For some men it was one way, as with Osbern and the women in his manor, but Hugh Bradecote saw it as a mutual bond. Breaking it broke more than a commandment.

The lady de Lench lowered her gaze anyway, and her hands found each other for support.

'When you last saw your lord alive, there were hot words, even from you, words that sent young Hamo away to avoid them, and more than words. Your skin tells us that. What was it that caused such heat on both sides?'

'I suggested to my lord that it would be better that Baldwin married and sired sons than did not wed at all.'

'You would have had him bring the tradesman's daughter as lady?' The undersheriff was surprised. 'Even your son thinks that would be demeaning the name of the lords of Lench.'

'Yes. I have not so great a feeling for the name, since it was imposed upon me by my marriage, yet is strange that Hamo has found within himself that much blood. But he is thinking one way only. If he thought more then he would see the advantage to himself. Baldwin has but to sire a son and he can go to the monks and be safe.'

'You thought he was not?'

'No. Yes. I mean the bad feeling between Hamo and Baldwin has been greater of late. What you saw over the box, well, it might have happened at any time, and had you not been there,

Baldwin would have killed him and been able to say he was but defending himself against a man gone mad with rage.'

Bradecote was a little surprised. He had not thought the lady had much beyond a sad and pretty face. She saw more than expected. It was a sound enough conclusion to reach.

'So you would see Baldwin happy to save your son.'

'Hamo is the only child I will ever bear. I would give my life itself for him, however so strange he may be.'

'And Osbern saw it as what? Betrayal?'

'Yes.' She nodded. 'He said I was disobedient and disloyal. Said I betrayed him and there was no greater sin in a wife. Then he held me, hard, and said it again, very deliberately. I thought he . . .' She looked frightened, the ghost of the fear Osbern must have seen. There was a silence, and then, slowly, Bradecote asked the question at long last.

'Had he cause, lady?'

'He had cause. God in Heaven forgive me, he had cause.' She bowed her head in shame and began to weep, softly. 'It was comfort and meaning something to someone.'

'And so when Fulk came you told him what had passed between you.' She nodded her answer. 'And was it he or you who decided that the only way to protect you both was to kill Osbern de Lench?'

'No!' Her head rose instantly, and her answer was vehement. 'It was not like that at all. Fulk is not a man who would stand back, seeing me hurt, would give his life for me, but I did not want his life given. I made him promise he would do nothing and said that we must cease our . . . meetings.'

'And he agreed?' The undersheriff's disbelief was obvious.

'I am the lady de Lench and he is the manor steward.'

Bradecote was surprised to hear the assurance in her voice. Would a woman who was surely far more like Ela than Christina, and had brought out the protector in Fulk, assert her rank?

'But if your husband had strong suspicions, ending the disloyalty would not be enough. He would make you pay for past deceit, as he would the steward. His life would still be forfeit, as might yours be.'

'I was not entirely certain, and Fulk said his life was here or nowhere. What would a steward who had run from his lord do? Heave flour sacks on the Evesham wharf? Not that Evesham would be far enough away. No, Fulk would not leave Lench, and my life is not so much to forfeit.'

Bradecote felt he understood, at least in part. Just as Osbern de Lench had a powerful connection with this land as his, so did also the folk whose ancestors had been working it for generations. A few left, girls to marry, youths to crafts, as Edgar of Flavel had left his home, but the tie was strong, a tie of blood and earth. Fulk would rather die here in Lench than live elsewhere.

'And would you swear Holy Oath that Fulk did not leave you until the riderless horse returned and those from the harvest arrived?'

'I would swear, my lord.'

Bradecote gave a small nod, and turned to Catchpoll, grimacing a little. It had seemed so likely, was still possible, but only just. The lady was not a good liar, so when she had spoken true it was equally clear. They left her, drying her eyes.

'Are we much the better for that, Catchpoll?' grumbled the

undersheriff, clearly not thinking to receive an affirmative answer.

'Every little thing that makes the path clearer is worth the effort, my lord, and I thinks that does. The steward is not some innocent lamb, but nor is he the killing wolf in this. He had the chance, but he has the lady who would swear oath for him, and it would be a good one.'

'So now we await Walkelin, and what comes from Worcester. I dislike Parler, but that just means I find it the easier to believe the man guilty without solid reason, and if it is not him we still have no reason, no reason at all.' Bradecote shook his head. Much now depended upon Walkelin. 'Is there anything we might do while we wait? Let me see. I suppose we might speak with the woman Gytha, to be sure what she saw of the riderless horse, and if any other horse passed through the village. It will not give us much, I am sure, but I do not want us to be sat here, kicking our heels. I want to gather every loose end of the tangle so that nothing else might surprise us.'

'Fair enough, my lord. We can do that.'

That they had not as yet spoken with the mother-to-be Gytha had not been a matter for concern, since it was unlikely that she would reveal anything if the father of her child was a man now dead and not her husband. She seemed preoccupied, but then with a belly as round as hers and no experience of childbirth, it was reasonable that she did not give all her attention to them. They sought her out in her home, since the only labour she was fit for was the bringing forth of new life. At least they might speak in private.

'I am sorry we are asking questions now, but they must be asked.' Bradecote did not want to sound the bully, though Catchpoll felt that he was too apologetic. 'You and your husband must be eager to see the child and hear its cries.' A whisper of sorrowful remembrance passed through his consciousness. Ela had heard cries, but dimly, and for so short a time.

'Aye.' It was a guarded confirmation.

'After all, a man is always proud to be a father, see his line continue.'

'Aye.' She looked to the ground.

'And your husband, Edmund,' there was a very small pause, 'he is the father?' Bradecote hated himself for asking, for she looked honest, and what gain could a village woman have made from giving herself freely to her lord?

'Aye.' There was doubt in the voice, and then she took a deep breath, almost a gasp. 'I hopes and prays so.'

So that was it. The poor woman did not know if she bore her husband's babe or one foisted upon her by a commanding lord.

'And Edmund, does he know of . . . the doubt?'

'Aye.' She frowned. 'I am an honest wife, in all I can be.'

'We understand, mistress. Now, the day the lord Osbern was killed, you saw his horse return and raised the alarm.'

'I did, my lord.' She was glad to speak of other things.

'And you saw or heard no other?'

'No, my lord. It was very hot, indoors and out, and my back ached and I was not comfortable anywheres. I was coming outside and the lord's grey mare came trotting in, just as always. I suppose I thought to see him on her back, but when I turned my head I saw the saddle empty. Fair shook me it did. I . . . part of me hoped . . . but it was a sinful thought and I have confessed it to Father Matthias.' She winced. 'Then I went to the Great Field, to tell the others, tell our steward.'

'You did not know he was here, not in the field?' There was a pause, and he repeated the question.

'No, my lord. I must have been inside when the lord went off up the hill. My Edmund, he has made a cradle, to show he . . . I was thinking of the babe in it and had fallen asleep upon the bed . . . then I woke and needed the pail and when I came out I saw the horse. I saw nobody and heard nothing afore that, 'cept a horse passing through, a bit before.' Her frown became one of a deep concentration and she held her breath. 'Might have been the lord Baldwin but . . .' The words were forced and ended with a moan. 'My lord . . . I can't . . . not now . . .' The 'now' was more a cry of pain.

'You mean . . . ?' Bradecote turned in horror to look at his serjeant.

'We leaves this to women,' declared Catchpoll, evenly, and turned to leave, the sound of Gytha's groan following them.

In the open air the undersheriff took a deep breath.

'I'll get the girl Hild and whoever else would be with her.' Catchpoll did not look in the least perturbed, though Bradecote had paled a little. Having lost a wife to travail almost exactly a year past, and with the prospect of his new lady passing through that particular ordeal in but a few months to come, well, he might just be forgiven a pale cheek.

Catchpoll did as he said, and Hugh Bradecote leant back against the warm daub of the wall of the cott. Another cry of pain came from within, louder now the woman felt able to express her agony. He offered up a prayer, heartfelt, for this woman in her time and for his Christina, when hers came.

Hild appeared, as pale as he was himself, and with her oldmother, who looked a little like her sister in shape but not in features. Hild carried a basket covered with a cloth and did not acknowledge his presence in any way but moved on past him. He was not affronted. The girl had far more urgent things in her head than politeness. Behind them came Catchpoll.

'Right, my lord, I do not see more can be learnt from Gytha, and I saw her husband. He looked confused, to be honest. Did not know whether to be eager, worried or miserable. As of now I suppose the middle one. I never saw him as dangerous and he was in full view with the harvesters. It does mean she could have heard the lord Raoul's horse, not the lord Baldwin's, but that is not much use to us either way.'

The oldmother emerged from the cott and did remember to dip in obeisance to the undersheriff.

'Sorry, my lord, she forgot the vinegar. My sister swore by it.'

Bradecote was wondering if the labouring woman had to drink vinegar, and why. His curiosity made him ask the question, and the old woman laughed.

'Bless me, no, my lord. It is to rub the end of the cord when the babe be born. Winflaed, God rest her,' she crossed herself and sighed, 'said it helped it shrivel clean.'

'I pray it all goes well.'

'Aye, as do I, my lord. Poor girl, she will have a hard time of it.'

'It is likely to be a difficult travail?'

'Ah no, my lord, I meant my Hild. It is her first.'

'And the woman Gytha's also.'

'Yes, but . . . she has good broad hips and is strong. I just hopes as her size does not mean there is two. For the both of 'em.' The oldmother tutted and went to find the missing vinegar. Another tortured cry came from within, and the undersheriff moved away. It was a distraction he did not want.

Chapter Thirteen

Riding back to Worcester, and being depended upon yet again to make discoveries and decisions on his own, filled Walkelin with a bubbling excitement. He would go directly to the castle stables and return the horse, and give orders that the animal belonging to the lord of Lench be ready for him upon his return. He smiled to himself. Yes, this was Walkelin, erstwhile just a man-at-arms, going to give orders to others. He felt he had somehow achieved a rank, not that of serjeant of course, but above his previous station. It was also good that the information which gave the name and location of the lord Raoul Parler's woman had come through him. This was his part of the tangle to unravel and make plain. He did not gallop as if the Devil were on his tail, but he made a good pace, and the horse, which he silently blessed, was willing and fleet of foot.

As he approached the castle from the Sutheberi gate he could see the gates were open, and could not resist urging his mount back into a canter and entering with a degree of speed and purpose. He dismounted with urgency, and called to a man engaged in no more than picking his nose to have the horse rubbed down and stabled, and to have the animal from Lench held ready.

'I am on my lord Bradecote's orders, and to be swift,' he announced, in a confident voice. It was, he felt, the spirit of truth even if the lord undersheriff had not actually spoken the words. He was pleasantly surprised by the man's obeying without a word. This was command, and he must now look like a man who commanded. Alnoth the Handless called him Master Walkelin, and although being looked up to by a beggar was not much, it was a start. As he turned to go out into the streets, he glimpsed a shapely figure emerging from the kitchens. It was not, he decided, wasting the lord Bradecote's time if he smiled and raised his hand at his own favoured maid. Eluned gave him a saucy look, and, having checked nobody else was watching, Walkelin blew her a kiss and winked.

Serjeant Catchpoll had told him where Leofeva, the Widow Brook, was living, and it was not long before he was knocking upon the door. It was not much of a place, and nothing compared to that of her late husband, the coppersmith, which was a fine burgage plot. No answer came to his knocking, however, and he was cursing his misfortune when a neighbour emerged, shaking out her besom and making a hissing sound as if shooing the dust from it.

'If it's her you're wanting, she is down by the river with the washing today.' The woman gave Walkelin a sideways glance and her eyes narrowed for a moment. 'I know you, don't I?'

'I am Walkelin, the sheriff's man,' he declared, in his new-found voice of authority.

'Are you indeed. I was just thinking you are the nephew of poor Mildreth Hedger as was sent from life on a knife's blade.' The woman did not sound very impressed.

Walkelin frowned. He did not much like being reminded of his aunt's fate, nor that him being a sheriff's man had not enabled him to save her from her *wyrd*. The woman, having made her point, moved on from the fate of Widow Hedger.

'Report him, did she?' She gave a nod towards her neighbour's door. 'Well, I doubt anything will be done, not when he is so high and mighty. Fine lords like him can do as they please and no notice taken.' The woman sniffed. Walkelin had the idea she was a woman that sniffed a lot.

'There was no . . .' Walkelin was going to deny any reporting, but caught himself in time, 'mention that she would not be at home this morning.' He paused. 'Did you see anything of what happened?' It was worth a try.

'Not saw, but half the street heard, if not half of Worcester. She screamed as if he were tearing her limb from limb, but there, if she takes to selling what she has been selling, it happens, and it is not my fault, whatever Dunstan over the way says. If she was honest there would be none of it.' The woman looked suddenly guilty. The Walkelin of less than a year ago would have looked blankly at her, but now a more knowing Walkelin made an educated guess.

'Took in more than one man's washing, did she?' The accompanying leer would have made Catchpoll proud, though it sat a little oddly on the fresh and slightly freckled face, and the woman looked momentarily taken aback before answering.

'Foolish thing to do, dealing with two of the lordly sort, and neither of 'em the charitable kind, and I would have said nothing, not one word, if him with the nose and the sneer had not been rude and dismissive of me. So pleased with himself, he was, he needed that smile wiped from his proud face.' The woman, whose own nose was turned up and narrow, giving her a very nasal sound, clearly bore the lord Raoul ill will. Walkelin also wondered if she resented her neighbour's previous more comfortable existence, or whether the Widow Brook, however low she had come, still had the airs of a burgess's wife.

'So you told him he was not her only visitor, did you? If neither looked charitable you were setting her up for trouble. You call that neighbourly?' Walkelin could not quite disguise his disapproval, much as he tried.

'I could not have thought she would end up like she has though.' The woman was defensive again. 'I did not wish it upon her, I swear oath I did not.'

'And her other lord, what is he like?' Walkelin was not very interested, but it sounded a good serjeanting question to ask.

'Shorter, fatter, a bit older. Always wears a red hat with a smart badge on it, leastways till he gets in her bed. I doubt he wears it then.' The accompanying smile was not a pleasant one, but the young sheriff's man did not even register it.

'A badge?' Walkelin felt his heart thump. 'What was it like?'

'Just a badge, copper, which is funny when you think what her late husband was, and with an amber stone set in the middle.'

Walkelin actually felt sick with the rush of excitement, but kept his voice calm and asked where upon the riverbank Widow Brook generally did her washing. She was not the only one at the chosen spot, but she was easily identifiable, for no other woman looked as she did, and they all seemed to be keeping apart from her as if she carried some disease. She was stood, slowly wringing out some sodden clothing.

'Widow Brook?' Walkelin did at least make it sound a question, though the answer was obvious. The woman turned to him and merely nodded, looking cowed and wary. The slow and reluctant way that she moved made him think she had been kicked, or beaten with something heavy about the body. Her face was a mess.

Both eyes had dark circles about them that made them seem as if sunken into her skull, and far more than the sort of black eye he might see when two men took a swing at each other to settle an argument. Her right cheek was puffed up, shiny purple and red where it was not sloe-black, and swollen from lower lid to halfway down her face, distorting it so that he could not imagine her as the good-looking woman Catchpoll had described. Her coif hung a little loosely at the neck where she had been bending forwards, and he could just see blue marks. He thought very harsh thoughts about Raoul Parler.

Walkelin had lived a simple life in a household where his mother's word held sway, even back in the days when his father lived. Until he had been taken under the wing of the sheriff's serjeant he was in blissful ignorance of just what happened to women in some other dwellings. Serjeant Catchpoll had taught him about the beating of women, women who then denied all but a 'foolish slip'. Men in drink, men in blind rage, they might lash out at a wife, a daughter, a whore, grab her by the throat, perhaps shake her, bang her head against wall or floor. If the woman did not die, little was done by the law, especially if the woman had children about her skirts, for a breadwinner was a breadwinner, however rough. If he learnt about it, however, the serjeant had a way of 'having words' which made men think twice, at least when sober. As Catchpoll said, a breathing, beaten woman might be a corpse another month, and he would rather it was not so. He had added that at least, if it came to pass, it was a lot easier if all the sheriff's men need do was bring in a guilty husband.

'I am Walkelin, Sheriff's Man, sent by the lord Undersheriff of the Shire, to ask you if the lord Raoul Parler was with you three days past.' He spoke firmly, but not loudly. If the other women did not know the widow's trade then he would not add to her dishonour.

'He . . .' She licked lips that had been split, and sniffed, for her nose was running. 'He came as you say, but he left the morning after.' Her diction was impeded, and her voice barely a whisper, but clear enough to be understood.

'He left next morning. Was that late or early?'

'Early.'

'Do you know where he went?'

She nodded but said nothing.

'He did this.' It was not a question, and Walkelin looked grim. She just looked at him, and then shrugged, wincing a little.

'What's done is done.' She sounded utterly defeated.

'Does not make it right.'

'Right? Does that exist? Not in my world, not now.'

'I am sorry,' Walkelin apologised, but even as he said the words he realised how foolish and pointless that was. 'Did he, the lord Parler, seek out a man with a red hat? The lord Osbern de Lench?'

'Yes.' She nodded, and sniffed again, wiping her forefinger beneath her runny nose.

'The lord Osbern is dead, but by whose hand is not yet known.'

'If it was him as did it, he may return and . . .'

'If it was him, mistress, he will not return, except bound, and if not, well, the lord Undersheriff will not permit him to harm you again.'

It was small comfort to the woman, he thought, for now both her providers were lost to her, and washing alone would not keep her in bread and the payment of her rent come quarter day. If her injuries healed but left her disfigured, there would be small hope of another man to keep her and she would exist from one encounter to the next. Walkelin thanked her and returned to the castle in a far less exultant mood than the new information should have led him to enjoy.

Serjeant Catchpoll was idly rubbing the remnants of a broken wheat ear between his fingers and watching his superior, who was leaning back against the outer wall of the hall, and now rubbed his hand across his furrowed brow.

The lord Bradecote had become quite good at the acting of being an undersheriff, playing up to what was expected of the role, just as Catchpoll had honed his 'sheriff's serjeant' to perfection over the years. Yet the man had eyes that could give glimpses within, if you looked, and his weakness, if you could call it that, was his wife. He feared for her future and was impotently outraged at her past, the suffering that could not be undone. Well, that was foolish, in Catchpoll's eyes, because he could not alter what had been, and what would be, would be. He might be better, of course, once she had safely presented him with the babe she carried. Catchpoll tried to recall if he himself had lived with dread when his wife had been carrying, and he thought not, but then, he had never lost a wife to childbed.

'Well, we are still at the point where, in spite of our working out that everything fitted if the steward killed his lord, it looks very unlikely that he did it, and if he did not kill Osbern de Lench he did not kill Winflaed the Healer.' Bradecote sighed. 'The two deaths have to be linked.'

'They do that, my lord, especially since there is that burying of the dagger, and it could be nothing else in that little grave, empty as it now is. And as for the steward I don't see he did it and the lordling looks about as unlikely, for all that pointed to him is just possibility. That leaves us with the lord of Flavel and our new lord of Lench, unpleasant bastards both, but if only unpleasant bastards did murder our lives would be the much easier. So far we have nothing known about the first one, barring he did not tell us a full tale, which makes us suspicious, and no cause for the second.'

'Raoul Parler will remain an unknown at least until we hear from Walkelin, so we look yet again at Baldwin de Lench. We see no reason, nothing that gave him cause now, rather than in general, so perhaps we should limit ourselves to whether it was possible – could he have done it from the facts we know. Firstly, he had been in Tredington, which lies by Shipston. Unless he came in haste, and nobody said his horse looked sweated up when he reached the field, he must have taken three or four hours, whether he came the northern way through Stratford or the southern through Evesham.'

'My penny would be on Evesham, my lord, and him leaving the manor the day before. That would give him a night's fumble with his woman there, and he would take what opportunity he could. I doubt he sought to leave early either. Now, it might be that he left her late to be upon the track to meet his father as he came from his daily stand upon the hill, which means he planned it cold, and the trouble there is he is a man who acts, not thinks first. Also, you would wonder how he got to the village, then the field, and had been there a while afore the near-her-time Gytha reached the harvesting.'

'It was not a long time, and the woman might well have come slowly, in her state.' Bradecote did not sound convinced by his own idea.

'Both true enough, my lord, but it is not far from where the lord Osbern fell, and if the son did for him and jumped upon his horse again to rush and be seen, then the grey mare would have been trying to follow.'

'He could have secured the reins to a bough?'

'And risked the animal pulling away faster than he expected, or not at all, and some cry would be raised if the lord had not returned after a while, for there would be someone waiting to take his horse. It would have looked very strange indeed if he was found as if robbed, yet his horse was neatly tethered by the body. We have also that there had to be time to cast away the clothes, and, mark you, there is the burying of the dagger and hiding the hat and cloak, which would mean going through the village, or round it to be safe, and adding more time.'

'Yes, though the dagger might have been buried the day after. We were not looking for it in particular, nor was Baldwin watched every hour of the day following. Had we taken up his loathed brother, Hamo, he would not have needed to hide it, and could simply claim to have discovered it sometime in the future, if he wished to wear it.'

'Fair thought, my lord, but you still have to ask why he would leave the clothing in two places.'

'Because Hamo had gone to the north when he went hawking? No, I am a fool. He could not have known that Hamo had gone hawking. If he had planned it all and wanted to remove the unwanted Hamo, his argument that Hamo paid cut-throats to do the deed did not need the lad to be out of the manor. That was just chance, a good one for him, and he was always keen to advance the idea of killers doing it for silver.'

'But no thieving killer stuck that knife up under the lord Osbern's ribs, and nor would they have been allowed so close.'

'I know, Catchpoll. So if it has to be Baldwin or Raoul Parler that makes Baldwin the more likely, but . . . he is likely and unlikely in the same breath.' Bradecote shook his head. 'Everything he has done since has honoured his sire in memory, the acts of a devoted and grieving son, and I would swear he means them too.' He shook his head. 'You know what, I think I am getting some of your serjeanting sense, and that definitely tells me there is something we are not seeing, or not seeing the right way.' The last word was said slowly, and a look of intense concentration furrowed the undersheriff's brow. 'Catchpoll—'

At which point Walkelin galloped into the bailey and pulled his horse up short. It was an impressive entrance, though his serjeant was not going to look impressed at all.

'Not here to tell us there was nothing of interest then, young Walkelin,' murmured Catchpoll, as Walkelin almost threw himself from the saddle. He was a little breathless, not that he had galloped all the way from Worcester, but that the Lench horse was not as eager as the animal from the castle stables and had needed a lot more urging to move at speed.

'No, Serjeant, and that Raoul Parler is a nasty bastard, real nasty.' Walkelin looked at Bradecote. 'Even though he is a lord, my lord,' he added, a little apologetically.

'Rank does not come into it, and I happen to agree with you. Now, get your breath, and tell us what you found out.' Bradecote sounded calm but was keen to hear what Walkelin had discovered. The serjeanting apprentice did as ordered but spoke before he had all the breath he needed.

'He went to Worcester sure enough . . .' Walkelin took another gulp of air, 'but he did not stay, and left the morn of the day the lord Osbern was struck down, my lord. What is more, he was in killing temper and was seeking him out most particular.'

Walkelin had the satisfaction of seeing both his superiors look taken aback.

'Why was that?' asked Catchpoll, simply.

'Well, I went to find the Widow Brook, but she was not at home, and I spoke with a neighbour, the sort as looks and gossips. She told me that the widow had been visited by the lord who looked down his nose at folk, but also said as she, the neighbour that is, had told him he need not look so pleased with himself, since there was another lord who came to the widow's door and stayed within. She described that lord as one shorter, fatter, with a red hat and a badge upon it, amber bossed.' Walkelin delivered this nugget with some triumph.

Catchpoll gave a low whistle through his uneven teeth.

'And then?' Bradecote felt everything they had learnt so far had been in half-tales and had confused them.

'I went down to the riverbank, where the widow was doing washing. Easy it was to pick her out. What he had done to her, the lord Parler . . .' Walkelin shook his head. 'Her face was a right mess, all huge bruises and deep black eyes, and I glimpsed blue marks at her throat, Serjeant, the sort you have told me about in the past, when a man shakes a woman and half strangles her. She moved as the man Edgar will move now, in pain. He half killed her, and that's a fact, and her unable to defend herself.'

Bradecote's face was grim, though Catchpoll just nodded.

'So the lord Raoul was killing-mad and wanted the lord Osbern's blood. Seems a good chance he got it,' the serjeant remarked, 'and then went on to celebrate in Evesham with beakers of ale and an armful of woman.'

'Even if he did not, Catchpoll, Parler needs to know he is marked. If ever anything untoward happens to the Widow Brook, or we hear of a lordly man in connection with a Worcester woman's death, I will be upon his threshold, and he will have to do much to prove his innocence.' Bradecote was beyond shouting anger, and spoke slowly and deliberately. 'Let us go to Flavel and hear what he has to say about his actions and his lies.'

Chapter Fourteen

It was an unsmiling trio that rode into the manor of Flavel, and a scene in marked contrast to their last visit, when it had been near deserted. It was a hive of activity, and a man who was directing other men beginning a rick of straw, turned at their arrival. He was short and stocky of build, but had authority. Bradecote guessed him to be the steward.

'I am the lord Undersheriff of Worcestershire, come to speak with your lord. He is within his hall?' Bradecote's voice was cold.

'Aye, my lord, he is.' The steward sounded guarded. 'I will take you to him.'

'No need. Your duties are many at this season. Just see that our horses are tethered.'

The man looked almost relieved, and gave a nod that was both agreement and obeisance in one. He called to a youth to follow the lord undersheriff and his men into the bailey and see to their mounts. Bradecote trotted the grey into the enclosure and dismounted, Catchpoll and Walkelin right behind him. The lad ran to keep up.

Bradecote nodded to Catchpoll, and the serjeant opened the hall door, stepping inside and holding it open for his superior. It lacked a cross passage and Bradecote could see Raoul Parler, leaning back in the lord's seat, his booted feet upon a bench, and a pitcher and beaker resting there also. He did not move as the sheriff's men approached.

'Forgive me if I do not offer you hospitality,' muttered Parler, with just the merest hint of a slur to his speech. 'This,' he kicked the pitcher so that it fell upon the floor and cracked into three pieces, 'is empty.'

Bradecote said nothing, but crossed the floor in a few long strides and kicked the bench from beneath Parler's feet so that it landed with a heavy crash, and the man had to hold hard onto the arms of his chair to prevent himself sliding onto the floor in a heap. The noise brought an opening of the solar door, and the lady Parler stood in the doorway, hand to breast, and wide-eyed.

'No need to fear, my lady. There is no threat to you or your children. Just shut the door.' The undersheriff spoke with calm deliberation and did not take his gaze from Parler. She did shut it, but behind her, and leant back against it, breathing a little fast, and at that he did spare her a swift glance before returning his cold gaze to her husband.

'So be it.' He paused for a moment, and then gave a sharp command. 'Stand up!' It was so unexpected that Walkelin actually jumped.

'You do not yell at me in mine own hall,' growled Parler. 'I am the lord of Flavel and—'

'You have seisin of it, yes, but lord? You shame the title, and you shame the name of a man also. What sort of lord, what sort of man, beats a woman half to death?' Bradecote regretted saying it before the man's wife, but realistically, if the lady Parler did not know of her husband's tendency to violence by now it would be as well she heard and was warned.

'I do not share whores,' Parler sneered. 'Do you? What is mine is mine alone. I do not share, and I will not be betrayed.' His lip curled. 'You would cry shame upon me for a woman like her?'

'Women like her exist because of men like you, Parler; lechers, bullies, and liars.' He spat the insult, goading the man to stand, which was just what Bradecote wanted him to do, for it meant the undersheriff could simply lean a little forward and grab him by the throat so that the man choked and flailed ineffectually at him. 'None so pleasant, being on the receiving end, is it? And be thankful there is not a wall so close I could bang your head into it as you did, no doubt, with hers.'

Catchpoll watched, his face seemingly impassive, but his eyes held a smile. The lord undersheriff was not a man who approved of heavy-handedness in the pursuit of justice, but just occasionally he stepped across that line himself. The serjeant did not think he was changing his view, which would have been better, but he would he hard-pushed to repeat his original instruction that violence was never to be used. In fairness also, this was more a show of control and power than harming the man, but the threat was there, and a believable one at that.

'So,' Bradecote let Parler struggle for another moment, then thrust him back down into the seat, 'having lied to us once about where you were when Osbern de Lench was killed, you had better not try it a second time.' His voice was measured again. 'You left the woman in Worcester, beaten and bloodied, and departed in the early morning of the day de Lench died. You were not yet here when we came the next day. Where were you all that time?'

There was silence. Raoul Parler stared at the undersheriff with a mixture of insolence and wariness.

'He was here.' The lady spoke up, suddenly, and all three sheriff's men stared at her.

'He was not when we came, lady. Your servant said so and—'

'Siward is blind. He does not know all, and if I had asked, he would have lied anyway. He is loyal. No, my lord was here, in the solar.'

'But you fainted when I asked after him.' Bradecote was certain that her unconsciousness had been real.

'I . . . I knew about the woman in Worcester. My lord said she had . . . had tried to kill him as he slept and he had lashed out. When you came asking after him I thought . . . I thought he must have killed her and . . .' The woman was desperately trying to make up reasons. 'I did faint, but because I thought you would take him away, and I did not want you to find him.'

'So he was in the solar, was he?'

'Yes, my lord.'

'I see. And remained there until he came to us in Lench that morning?'

204

'Yes, my lord.'

'You are a loyal wife, my lady, and a weak liar. Your lord was seen and recognised in Evesham, the day of the killing.'

'It is impossible.'

'No, he was seen, and the person who saw him had no cause to lie to us.' Bradecote turned his attention back to Raoul Parler. 'You did not come here at all. You left Worcester with spilt blood on your hands and the spilling of blood in your mind. You and Osbern de Lench loathed each other, and then you found out he was bedding your leman, whether by accident or gaining pleasure from knowing he usurped you. Do not lie to me again and say you did not seek him out.'

'All right, so I did, but I did not kill him.'

'And why would you not?'

'Because I did not see him.' Parler sounded both relieved and yet still annoyed at this, and it held the ring of truth because of it.

'What do you mean?' Bradecote regarded the man suspiciously.

'Just what I say. I rode to Lench, or leastways near to it. I did not seek him out in his hall, for if he had his men there I could have been overpowered. I knew, as all knew, that he sat upon that little hill as though he were God Almighty, every noontide, so I kept on the Alcester road instead of cutting south on the Evesham road to the village and went up the hill from the north-east, thinking to confront him there.'

'And?'

'And nothing. He did not come. I assumed I must have been too late, or for some reason not gone there that day. I waited, but in the end it was stupid to remain. So I went to Evesham.'

'And did you or did you not come down the hill and join the Evesham road where the track joins it?'

There was a silence. Parler stared stonily at the undersheriff.

'Answer the question, my lord.' It was the first time Catchpoll had spoken, and he did so quietly but firmly.

'I did.'

'And did you see the corpse of Osbern de Lench?'

'I did, and spat upon it.' A slow smile grew on Raoul Parler's face. 'It was something worth celebrating in Evesham, I can tell you.'

'And what exactly did you see?'

'I saw him lying there, on his back, eyes shut as if sleeping, and had he been fully clothed I would have thought him but unconscious after a fall.'

'You did not touch the body?'

'No, why should I have?'

'You did not perhaps add to his wounds?'

'What possible use was that?' Parler snorted. 'The work was done for me. My only sorrow was I suppose he died swiftly. There was a knife wound that would surely have killed him in moments, though I still hope he felt the other I saw first.'

'You saw but one other?'

'Yes, but I was not counting or looking. I was just plain rejoicing.' Parler gave sharp crack of laughter. 'It did me good to see it, and I thank God I was in that place and at that time.'

'Was his horse there also?'

'No. It was just him, and the sound of the skylarks

rejoicing with me. Even the birds were happy he was dead.'

'And did you find his hat and cloak?'

'That hat! No, I did not, though I was not seeking it. Worn that hat he has since but a few weeks after his first wife died. That badge was hers, I heard, some brooch for a cloak. I would not have called the bastard sentimental, not in the slightest.' He shook his head, but the smile, which had not faded, lengthened the more. 'I suppose it was him wearing it at Lincoln gave me the idea of suggesting he killed her. Must have hurt the more, eh?'

'You really did hate him, didn't you.' It was not a question.

'Oh yes. Never liked him, even when there was his sister as link between us. Lincoln was just when it all came to a head. Well, the boil is lanced for good now, though I have to put up with that blustering pale imitation that is his son in his place. I never suggested he was not lawful, however good the jest, because there is no doubting his siring, though he takes in character as much after his mother.' Parler sighed. 'Now, since you have it all, get out of my hall.'

'Not yet, Parler. You lied to us before. How do we know you are not lying to us again? Nothing you say can be proved. Your explanation sounds sensible, but could as easily cover the deed, so why should be believe you?'

'Bu . . .' Walkelin opened his mouth, and shut it again, even before Catchpoll growled at him.

'Why would I lie?' bemoaned Parler.

'To keep your neck from a rope would be a good reason. You left Worcester intent if not upon killing Osbern de Lench then at least harming him as much as you did the woman.'

'Yes, but I did not actually kill him. I never saw him until he was already dead. You have to believe me.'

'No, we don't,' Bradecote responded, instantly.

Catchpoll very nearly sighed with pleasure. This was just how serjeanting worked.

'Even if we do, eventually, and only by finding a killer who confesses to it, you are still facing the ire of William de Beauchamp.' Bradecote, though he felt that it was unlikely Parler had slain Osbern de Lench, did not want the man to feel he was free of either blame or shrieval disapprobation. 'You knew a man had been killed, not by accident, but by intent, and did not seek to make it known.' The undersheriff was dubious as to whether concealing the killing was against anything in the laws, but it felt wrong. 'Thus whoever did it had more chance to escape punishment. I will ask the lord de Beauchamp if you can be amerced for that. If lords do not see the laws kept and wrongdoers taken, what can be expected of the ordinary man?'

Catchpoll hid a smile at that, for from what he had seen of lords they would get away with whatever lawbreaking they could and claim it as some right of their rank.

'Also,' continued Bradecote, 'if ever a hand is laid upon the widow in Worcester I will come first knocking upon your door, and will need very good proofs it was not you, or if any man of your description is ever declared where a woman has suffered injury, there or . . . here. Your name and reputation will be remembered, by me, by the lord Sheriff and by Serjeant Catchpoll here. We have long memories.' The undersheriff turned to the lady Parler, who did not look, he thought, entirely shocked or surprised by her husband or his attitudes. He wondered, yet again, why she had been so desperate to see him return safely, why she had been prepared to lie for him today. He stepped towards her and saw her press herself a little more against the oak. He made her a small obeisance.

'I have disturbed your hall, lady, and am sorry for that. Few men have such loyal wives or are as undeserving of them.' He could not help but voice the question, 'Why would you—?'

'Some women are strong. I am not. There has to be a man, and they seem little different, one from another.' It was barely even a whisper and sounded resigned, tired. It occurred to Hugh Bradecote that in some ways she was little better off than the Widow Brook in Worcester.

'I wish you well for the babe to be born. Perhaps, with so many sons, you will be blessed with another daughter for company.' He smiled, but she gave no echo of it.

'Why would I wish that? Daughters are not valued.' He had the idea that she was assuredly not valued now, but nor had she been before she was wed to Parler. There was nothing else to say, but he vowed to make it quite clear to his Christina that a daughter would be a blessing if a daughter it was, and that she would be as loved as Gilbert, or any other son. He bowed again, and turned to Catchpoll and Walkelin with a small nod. Walkelin opened the door and they passed out into the sunlight, their eyes narrowing in its glare. None of them said a word until they had ridden from the village.

'I said he was a nasty bastard,' commented Walkelin. 'Why did you not say we would bring him before the justices for what he did to the Widow Brook, my lord?'

'No right o'yours to know,' chastised the serjeant.

'Tell him, Catchpoll.' Bradecote felt suddenly tired of Parler and beaten and defeated women.

'Well then, young Walkelin. If we was to take him up before the justices, two things would happen.'

'Yes, Serjeant?'

'Yes. The first is that the Widow Brook would deny anything ever happened, and the second is that the justices would say they were very sorry to that nasty bastard and make our lives a misery, through the lord Sheriff, for upsetting him.'

'I knows that, sort of.' He did, but he wanted to believe someone more senior might be able to change things. 'But I saw her face, Serjeant.'

'And what has that to say to anything?'

'It's not . . . fair.'

'Fair? Life's not fair. If it was, the godly and innocent would live long and happy lives and those like him would die young and badly. You may have noticed that it is not the way things happen. So we makes the most of what we can. The lord Bradecote did the best we could for Widow Brook, aye, and for the lady also. They threaten, men like that one, but we out-threatens 'em. He won't get within a mile of Worcester for months and will for sure never get within speaking distance of the widow.'

'You know, Serjeant. I am glad I am not a woman,' remarked Walkelin, thoughtfully.

'So are we. You would never run fast enough in skirts.' Catchpoll grinned, but Bradecote merely gave a small smile.

'It seems very unlikely that Raoul Parler stuck a knife in

the lord Osbern, not least because he did not meet him, and since a man had been seen on the hilltop, he had obviously already been and gone. So the answer lies in what I thought back in Lench, before we set out here, and that is that we have the thing back to front.'

'My lord?' Walkelin look puzzled, but Catchpoll groaned.

'Should've thought of that.' The serjeant swore.

Walkelin looked from one to the other.

'But does it fit for Parler, my lord?' asked Catchpoll.

'Not sure it does. We need to work this through very, very carefully, and if truth be known, my head is too full of today. We have had Parler, the box and the badge, the man Edgar and the death of Winflaed the Healer, and now all this. I am sure it is important, and it will get us to the end, but . . . I do not want to make any mistake, and it would be too easy.'

'Ah.' Walkelin had come, he thought, to the right conclusion. 'I suppose it works, but does it not make it more strange that the Healer was killed?'

'Yes, a little, which is why we sleep upon it, and why we will keep a very good eye upon Baldwin de Lench, just in case we are right.'

Any hopes Hugh Bradecote had of an early night and time to rest his brain rather than just his body were dashed upon their arrival back in Lench. He swore under his breath even as he urged his horse into a canter, hearing the many raised voices. For one desperate moment he wondered if there was a hanging, but the villagers were before the hall, in a circle.

'Holy Mary, has the man found someone else upon whose

211

body he can vent his ire?' complained the undersheriff, and then he saw what was happening. 'Halt there!' he cried, in so loud and peremptory a voice that obedience would be instinctive. The lady de Lench, her wrists bound, her head bare and her hair in disorder, was tied to the ring in the wall where her late husband's mare had been tied upon its return. The gown had been stripped from her back and hung in tatters to her waist. She was screaming, pulling in vain against the binding rope like a soul possessed. Yet the villagers were not looking at her. Every eye was upon the lord Baldwin de Lench, with a knife in his hand, the short blade catching glints of evening sunlight. Before him, also bound and already half insensible, Fulk the Steward was stretched back over an upturned handcart, the pale skin of his belly exposed, and his braies torn down to his knees. It did not need any question to know what Baldwin intended to do. Bradecote scrambled from the saddle and drew his sword, as Baldwin, deciding that he was not going to stop after all, reached to Fulk's soft flesh.

'Touch him, de Lench, and your blood will flow more freely than his.' There was no bluster, just a grim promise.

'I have the right. You know I have the right. This filth betrayed my sire with that whore,' the knife flashed as he pointed it at the now-sobbing woman, 'in his own hall. What he would have done, I will do.'

'No, you will not.' Bradecote was firm. 'Walkelin, get the poor bastard way from here.'

Walkelin came forward silently, his eye upon the knife, cautious but determined. He tried to lift the steward, but the man was both in no position to gain purchase with his feet and help himself, nor with wits enough to try. It was the little priest who stepped out to take the other arm and help lift him upright, though the man's legs buckled, and he had, perforce, to be dragged away.

'This is my manor, and I decide—!' shouted Baldwin de Lench.

'No,' Bradecote interrupted him immediately. 'You do not decide. Your decisions are made in haste and heat, and are the acts of anger.'

'She admitted it. So did he, eventually.' The lord of Lench was livid with anger.

'Faced with your wrath and a knife, I doubt not they would admit anything.' Whatever he knew as truth, agreeing with de Lench was not going to help, and Bradecote felt no desire to shame the woman further. He caught sight of the girl Hild's oldmother, grim-faced, at the doorway of Gytha's cott. 'Oldmother, see to the lady. Take her within.'

The woman nodded and went to untie the bound lady and lead her, stumbling, into the hall.

'I will not have her in there!' Baldwin still had no other voice than a yell.

'It is not your decision. Put down the knife, de Lench, and for the sake of Heaven, muster what wit you possess.' He did not actually think that Baldwin would obey, but that was not important, since Catchpoll, at his most invisible, had quietly moved so that he was behind the ranting lord. Baldwin just stood there, and the undersheriff gave the very smallest of nods. In a moment the serjeant, with a nimbleness that defied his complaints about his creaking knees, had borne down the arm with the knife and twisted it so hard and far up Baldwin de Lench's back that he was forced onto tiptoe.

'There now,' said Catchpoll, soothingly, 'that's better, isn't it?'

Baldwin stared, panting, at Bradecote.

'As I said, not your decision.' The undersheriff was unsmiling. 'Now we could have done this the easy way, but you chose the hard. So be it. Serjeant, bring him to the church.'

Bradecote ignored the villagers and strode towards the church, with no doubt whatsoever that Catchpoll would bring de Lench with him. The undersheriff was thinking. For all his bluster and violence there was some truth in what the lord of the manor had said. He had the right to take action, but not this. He might thrash the steward and send him, lordless, from the village, an exile that would mean no other local lord would employ him, and he had no craft for town work. He might also cast out the lady. As he saw it, Bradecote could not prevent either for more than a few days, though the thrashing seemed to have already taken place. Until the killer of Osbern de Lench was taken, he would hold sway, but that might, and he hoped it was so, be only until the morrow.

He turned and stood before the chancel arch, his arms folded. Catchpoll, perhaps thinking that a penitential attitude was suitable for the church after such wrath, pushed Baldwin de Lench to his knees.

'Is this how Osbern de Lench ran his manors? Are you truly following his precepts, or just unable to control your temper, de Lench?' Bradecote was in no mood to be gentle with the man. 'You are their lord; you are meant to think more than they do. Act with decisiveness, yes, but with intelligence, not just rampage about like a goaded bull. If it is your decision that the lady de Lench leaves the manor, you have the right, and if you also choose to dismiss your steward, you have that right also, but what makes you so sure, other than confessions obtained at knife point, that what you claim is true?'

'I found them together.'

'You mean they were . . . ?' Bradecote could not imagine they would have been that foolish.

'He was holding her hand.'

'And that was it?'

'No, she was crying, but smiling at him, as if she was happy.'

'Which is proof of infidelity?' Bradecote privately agreed it gave a strong hint, but no more. 'Had it not occurred to you that the lady, already facing leaving her home, seeing her son go to the Benedictines and having just lost her husband, has been distressed? Your steward, whose manhood you are so keen to remove, is man enough to feel as many men do when a woman looks defenceless and alone. I have no doubt he sought to encourage her not to be dismal and offered some comfort.'

'It was not his place.'

'No, but she would get it neither from you nor the son of her own body.' It was then that Bradecote wondered about Hamo. 'Where is he, Hamo?'

'In the hall. He was praying as I brought her out.'

'Just praying? He was not injured?'

Undersheriff and serjeant exchanged glances. If ever final proof were needed that Hamo de Lench was not like ordinary folk it was the idea that he would stand by and see his mother mistreated before his very eyes.

'No. He came from the solar and asked what was happening, calm as you like, and I told him what his precious mother had been doing with that bastard steward, and he looked at her and said that adultery broke a commandment and he would pray for her soul. So he did, then and there.'

'Even when you shamed her?'

'She had shamed herself long since. I just wanted everyone to see her for the whore she is. My father would not keep a wife like that, and I will not suffer her to remain.'

'She can leave when all is settled, not before, and if you set foot in that hall—'

'It is mine.'

'It is the lord Sheriff's, from whom you hold, and I stand in his place. You do not enter it until I say so.' Bradecote looked Baldwin de Lench in the eye. 'And you do not place as much as a finger on the steward. When this is concluded, and only then, you may dismiss him, just as you may send your sire's widow from Lench, but you harm neither. Understood?'

'Where would you have me sleep? In the stable?'

'In the priest's house.' Bradecote could not much care by this point. He kept his gaze on de Lench but his words were for Catchpoll. 'Serjeant, Walkelin will sleep where the steward sleeps, and you and I will guard the hall.'

'Yes, my lord.'

'And take the lord Baldwin to the priest.'

'Yes, my lord.' It was not often Catchpoll was so obedient.

Chapter Fifteen

Bradecote waited until the serjeant had removed Baldwin de Lench, and then turned towards the altar and went upon his knees, silent in his prayers. After a few minutes he crossed himself and rose, and then went to seek out the lady of the manor.

The hall was both peaceful and yet showed signs of disruption. A stool was thrown over, a cup broken, and there, as Baldwin had said, was Hamo de Lench, down on his knees, hands together in the formality of prayer, intoning Latin as though he were already a monk professed. From the solar beyond came a sharp cry, an exclamation of pain that escaped through the gap where the oaken door was ajar, but the cadence of the prayer was not disrupted by as much as one breath. It felt unreal to Bradecote, who was suddenly very tired. It was as Catchpoll had said; everything tumbled upon them, one thing after another, and it seemed days since

Osbern de Lench had been interred. The praying youth was a distraction he did not want.

'Messire, go to the church if you wish to pray.' Hamo looked up but frowned as if questioning this.

'I could, but God hears prayers wherever they are said.'

'Assuredly, but yours will be interrupted when my men enter. Go to the church, and when you have finished your prayers, you may return.' Bradecote paused one moment and then asked the question to which, although he had had enough of the day, he could not rest without knowing the answer. 'Why did you not defend your lady mother when Baldwin . . . mishandled her?'

'She had sinned. It was a harsh penance, but chastisement is for the wicked, and adultery is a great wickedness, a breaking of God's commandment. If she suffers now, then perhaps it will not go so hard upon her with Him in the time to come.'

'It is also a commandment to honour your father and your mother.'

'Indeed, and I do. That is why I pray for her now. I think she will be forgiven, for it is not all her blame.'

'No.' Bradecote wondered at this flash of insight, but then Hamo continued.

'No, for she cannot help being a Daughter of Eve, and thus easily tempted, as Eve was by the Serpent.' He shook his head. 'Only a fool would be tempted by a snake, but women are fools.' With which statement he got up, dusted his knees and walked to the door without another word.

The lady de Lench had been right; Hamo would make a very bad priest, but a good monk.

* * *

Bradecote heard his stomach rumble, reminding him of his lack of sustenance, and then turned at the sound of footsteps. Walkelin entered, reporting that the steward was now fully conscious and very afraid.

'He got off more lightly than the Widow Brook, I will say that, my lord, when it comes to the beating.'

'I doubt not he could at least try and fight back, Walkelin, which is more than she could do.'

'Aye, my lord, but I think part was done when he was half strangled. He has cloudy memory of it all.'

'He is fortunate then.' He paused. 'Have you seen Serjeant Catchpoll?'

'No, my lord.'

Bradecote therefore explained how the lord of Lench would be kept from his potential victims.

'Bar the door to any but the girl Hild. Sweet Lady Mary, she is needed by too many this day.'

Catchpoll came in, a half-smile on his face.

'The priest was concerned that we wanted him to actually stand over his lord and prevent him leaving, but I reassured him that the guarding is with us.'

'Good.' Bradecote sighed, and ran a hand through his hair. 'What did we do to deserve all this, I ask myself,' he grumbled.

'Well, we takes the task seriously, and does it as well as we can. That means sometimes it gets all knotted, my lord.' The serjeant did not take the question as rhetorical.

'All I want is to eat, think, and sleep, and if I fall asleep thinking it will not be a surprise. Baldwin de Lench is like a bolt of lightning – you never know where he will come to earth and what damage he will do. I pity this manor.' He sighed. 'I have no idea if a meal is in preparation or not. Walkelin, go and find the cook and make sure it is yet to come. I would have words with the lady de Lench alone, but when you return, await me, both of you, and we will try, and I mean try, to make sense of what Parler has given us.'

Walkelin just nodded and went out, already thinking for himself so he could contribute upon his return. Catchpoll set the stool upon its legs, and sat on it, leaning forwards and with his hands loosely between his knees. He looked as though his mind was blank, but the mind of Serjeant Catchpoll was always working if he was awake, and sometimes even when he was asleep.

Bradecote went to the solar door and knocked upon it, though he entered straight after, and was prepared to avert his eyes if it was seemly. The lady was, however, laid upon the bed on her stomach, her face turned towards the door and her hand, clenched into a fist, pressed to her mouth. The old woman was not alone, for the youthful healer was now present, and placing strips of linen, soaked in some concoction, upon the red stripes of damaged flesh. He assumed she had been brought from Gytha in her travail. For a minute or so Bradecote said nothing, his mind filled with the thought that once, when Christina would have been no older than the girl Hild, she had been the victim left in the same position as the lady de Lench now. Had anyone even been allowed to tend her, solace her? Then he frowned, because a lash was not what a man commonly carried. De Malfleur would have sought out his child-wife and been prepared for what he had planned to do to her, but if Baldwin de Lench had simply discovered the lady and the steward together, how come that he had a whip to hand? He must also surely have rendered the steward incapable before he set about the lady, for a man, other than her strange son, would not stand by and see a woman he cared for being hurt and demeaned. Asking questions at this minute would be ridiculous, and so Bradecote simply turned away and waited, a silent presence in the chamber.

A short while later Hild came and begged his pardon, so he turned about. She had a bowl of torn strips and the remnants of her poultice, or whatever it was balanced on one hip, which made her obeisance clumsy.

'My lord, all is done as can be. I would be going back to the birthing now.'

'Yes, of course. I hope it goes well. Look in upon the steward when you have time, if you have time before . . .'

'It will be a time yet, so I can do that, my lord. Babes is oft born at night, and I think this one will be so. Mother Winflaed says . . . said . . . as it is good to keep the place dark, then the babe is not surprised by the light, nor fearful to come out into it. Too long a travail is bad for the mother and the child both.'

'Yes. To your duty then, Healer, and God aid you.'

'Thank you, my lord. I . . .' her voice became for a moment a confidential whisper, 'I wish I had had more time.'

'Your time is now, and you will learn from what you do, just as you learnt from watching. A score years hence all Lench will be saying "that is what Hild the Healer says" as if it was a law from the king.'

'Hild the Healer,' repeated the girl, with a dawning smile. 'It sounds right, don't it?'

'It does.' He smiled at her, and she bobbed again and departed, leaving the old woman and the lady upon the bed.

'You wants me to stay, my lord?' the oldmother questioned, unsure.

'There is no need. The lady is safe, and I would speak gently with her, but privately.'

The old woman looked at him, and what she saw confirmed the truth of his words. She could go with an eased heart.

'There's not been enough gentleness in this manor for far, far too long,' she commented, sagely and departed, shaking her head.

Bradecote approached the bed. The lady de Lench lay now upon her side, a coverlet drawn up to her neck, with the pale face, and a hand clutching a kerchief, the only parts of her visible.

'I warned your steward, and I see that I ought to have warned you, lady. Your husband's son leaps to thoughts that others come to slowly. What possessed you to be alone with the man Fulk? It could do no good and immense harm.'

'It was not intended.' Her voice was a whisper. 'I had thought to stay quiet and on my own, for I have much to think upon. But those thoughts brought me to weeping. I acknowledge my sin, will confess it and do whatever penance the Church sets me, but always the blame lies with the woman, the shame at least. Even Hamo thinks it. What happened between Fulk and me, it was the intent of neither to seduce, to betray. It just happened. The Church would not blame Osbern for being an uncaring and cruel husband, but would condemn me, the wife; one not simply neglected, which is bearable, but the wife he would hurt when he needed to take out his ire upon someone. It was never his sons, shout as he might, never them, only me. And though Baldwin wanted to act as Osbern would have acted with Fulk, to everyone else . . . he may even seem daring. It was not daring. He just cared a little.'

Hugh Bradecote did not want to listen to more, more with which he wanted to disagree, and yet felt sympathy. The killing of Osbern de Lench was that of a man, and assuredly by a man, but suffering women had been what they had faced since; this sad and almost unwilling adulteress; the worn out but loyal and betrayed wife of Raoul Parler; the Widow Brook reduced to selling herself to unpleasant but powerful men to survive. Winflaed the Healer had been strong, but right at the last, she had become a victim too. In comparison, the harm to Edgar of Flavel, and to Fulk the Steward, seemed so much less important. He gave himself a mental shake. He was becoming soft-hearted and Catchpoll would tell him how much that was to be avoided.

'Lady, I am not the Church, I am the Law, and what I ask is not judging, just truth-seeking. Baldwin found you and the steward together. You were, he said, holding hands, and you were smiling at the steward. Why does not matter, but what happened after may have importance. Tell me exactly what happened, from the moment Baldwin came in.'

'It seemed to happen so fast. Fulk told me that all this would pass, and that once I was not in this place, life could be better, would be so. He had no cause to say it, of course, but it was a nice thing to say. Then Baldwin was there, shouting, so loud and angry, and then my flesh stung as the end of the lash caught me.'

'So he had it in his hand when he entered.'

'Yes, I suppose he did, though why . . . Fulk pulled back, charged at him, Baldwin sidestepped and hit him with the butt of it and as he fell . . .' the woman closed her eyes at the remembered horror, 'he looped it about his neck and strangled him with it. I tried to stop him, but he pushed me away and I fell, and then he came and stood nigh on over me, and it began. All I could feel was the sting and the wet blood and hear screams, my own screams, and Baldwin shouting about "this time it is right". I think after a little while I was not aware, for I remember Hamo being there, and I do not know how or when he came, but he was blaming me, and then there was nothing, a blackness, nothing until I was outside and bound and Baldwin was going to . . .' She sobbed.

Bradecote set all she had said in order. He had mentally assumed that Fulk had been rendered unconscious trying to protect her, though it seemed she had risked as much to protect him. What was patently clear was that Baldwin had not been taken by surprise as much as he had implied. Had he suspected, and followed the steward into the hall? If so, how come this suspicion blossomed today of all days?

'He will touch neither the steward nor you, lady, but I think the steward was right. Your life will be better elsewhere. Rest your body and spirit, and face tomorrow when it comes.' He sounded solemn.

'I wish it might not come at all,' she murmured, and pressed the kerchief to her lips, stifling a sob that rose within her.

There was nothing that Bradecote could say in answer, and so he turned and left, closing the solar door behind him.

Both his subordinates awaited him in the hall, Catchpoll still upon the stool, and gazing into space. Walkelin looked a little uncomfortable, since disturbing his serjeant's cogitations would bring harsh words, and yet standing, pretending to be thinking as deeply, felt silly.

'How does the lady?' he asked, glad to speak.

'She'll mend, though I think it is her spirit that is more broken than her skin. What news of eating?'

'My lord, the cook says as there is some good, thick pottage and a spitted woodcock. It will be brought shortly. She says as the pottage did catch, on account of everyone going to see what was happening, but only at the very bottom, and she will see as you do not get that bit. It can be served as soon as you say.'

'Thank you, that will be soon, and I want you to eat with the steward. We speak now, but best you get to your guarding as soon as may be.'

'He can have the burnt bits,' suggested Walkelin, hopefully, and the undersheriff nodded, not fully attending.

'What the lady said that is interesting was that when she and the steward were discovered by the lord Baldwin, he had the whip already in his hand.'

'I had been a-wondering about that, my lord,' mumbled Catchpoll.

'But if he had an idea of what had been between them before, would he not have acted as we saw he did? Why wait?' Walkelin looked confused.

'Because, young Walkelin, today is when he found out, and if your mind was clear, not half asleep and full of woodcock, then you would not ask foolish questions,' chided Catchpoll. 'So either steward and lady have been more open than ever they were when the lord Osbern was living, and since we warned Fulk, mark you, or else the lord Baldwin has been told by someone. That might possibly have been by intent, but more probably by a slip of the tongue that gave him the thought.'

'Or,' added Bradecote, grimly, 'he obtained the knowledge by force.'

'You are thinking he might have learnt it from Mother Winflaed, my lord?' Catchpoll looked dubious.

'Is it not possible?'

'Aye, but he would need to have been thinking of it before that, or else why ask "What do you know of the lady and Fulk the Steward?", and we have seen as he does not take a thought beyond its first awakening, and just acts. He would have acted upon that first thought, not seeking proofs from anyone else.'

'That is true, Catchpoll. I think my head must be like Walkelin's. Yet it is firm in one thought, but that does not give enough to bring the man before the lord Sheriff, and then the justices.'

'You're right about the lord Parler, my lord, if you is thinking as I am sure you are. I've been sitting here looking at it every which way, and there is only one end it all comes to. If he got to the hilltop a mite early and thought to come across the lord Osbern on his way up, it was easy enough for him to have met him, killed him, cast the clothing aside, but kept the hat and the cloak, and lead the grey to the top, so that he might appear as the man everyone would expect to see. At that distance, and if he sat none so tall in the saddle, he would be the lord Osbern. If he then loosed the horse to amble home, and it knew the way after all these years, all he had to do was ride back down the other slope to join the Evesham road a little north of the village, cast hat and cloak away, and then, very pleased with himself, take his usual path to miss the village and head into Evesham and all its delights. That way the lord Baldwin, coming from Evesham, passed the track from the hill when his father lay dead upon it, and the false Osbern was near the top to be seen. Which is all wonderful, except for—'

'And, my lord, I was thinking too, and if the lord Parler killed the lord Osbern, when did he bury the dagger?' interrupted Walkelin, eager to show he too had pondered the matter, but earned a frown from Catchpoll.

'That is not all, either.' Bradecote grimaced. 'Come on, Catchpoll. I want you to make my day end well and give me the answer that makes it all work, but you were going to tell me it all falls to ruin if we have Parler as the killer, which is a shame, because the world would be the better without him.'

'As you say, my lord. While the lord Parler could have done the killing, and as we was coming away from the bastard it did seem a very good answer, we have the problem, one the size of the barn out yonder.'

'Which is, why would he bother with the deception at all?' Bradecote sighed. 'Why go to all the trouble to pretend to be Osbern when all he need do was kill him and carry on to Evesham? By that measure Parler must have been telling true, because of the hat and cloak north of Lench. Pox on it all. So Parler did not do it, I would swear oath Hamo did not do it, Fulk looks as if he did not do it because the lady sounded honest when she said he did not leave, which means that Baldwin de Lench must have killed his own sire. That is what happened, I am now fairly sure, but there is simply no reason.'

'Then let us see if it fits, my lord, and await a reason. If he came from Evesham and met his father coming down the hill after the lord Osbern's happy gazing upon his lands, then there is a mite of a problem in the grey getting back to the hall, and him arriving back to the harvest. It was close, but the horse had not far to come. If tethered it meant a risk. So we looks the other way round and as when we thought Parler might have done it. It would mean the lord Baldwin was not coming from Evesham, but from Tredington, and had cut up off the Alcester road on the same path Parler took, but earlier. He met his father as the man was on his way up the hill, not coming down, killed him, and to deceive all, kept the hat and cloak. Thing is, if he took but those things, it would lead us to think of that deceiving, so he also removed tunic and boots, as for a robbing, and trotted a short way so they would be not seen with the body, and threw them away. I am guessing he was urgent in this, for he did not stay to see where it all landed, with one boot a little in view, which it why Alnoth the Handless saw it. Then he cantered the grey up to the top of the hill, leading his own mount, to pose as the old lord.' He then left the grey and came down the northern way to discard the hat and cloak, hoping the horse would not come home swift like.'

'Do you not recall the groom spoke of the grey mare having bruised a foot the week before?' Bradecote was trying to make things fit smoothly. 'It might have been after Baldwin was sent to Tredington, but equally might have been something he knew of, and hoped it was still a little sore. Besides, the animal knew the track up and down the hill, took it every day, so would as likely just amble back at its usual pace.'

'That would make him more confident, yes, my lord.'

'The dagger and badge he could have kept, to supposedly find later, for he could have hidden them in his trappings from his stay in Tredington. It would also give him something to make Hamo look even more guilty, if he could not get him hanged for the crime straight away. So he enters from the north, which would mean even if the grey was there before him, he could just pretend to be surprised. Since the horse was not yet there, he went to the field so that he was seen by all and could be as stunned as they were when the riderless animal came home. He must have expected there to be a groom waiting, though not Fulk the Steward.'

'It does all fit, my lord,' exclaimed the eager Walkelin.

'Oh, it does. My sole problem is still why he did it. We could take him to Worcester on what we have, but the justices would come and ask why it was that this man was before them. What cause had he to kill the father from whom he would inherit anyway, especially if he thought him growing tired and morbid, rebuilding the church and such? Everything he has done since has been proving he is in his sire's mould, being the son of Osbern, and his defence of the man's honour today is one with that. He has admitted they were often angered with each other, as men of the same temper might well be, but if it was because of the refusal to accept the mercer's daughter as the future lady of Lench, then why did Baldwin not act earlier?'

'What if the woman is with child, my lord? If he is determined, as he says, that she is the only woman for him, and has reason to say she is carrying, he would want that child to inherit.' Walkelin proffered the thought, but Catchpoll sucked his teeth.

'Hmmm, might work, 'cepting I would think he would announce the news to his father and suggest that it would be better to have a wife who could definitely bear a child than one who was unknown, and hope he agreed.'

'Wait.' Bradecote held up a hand. 'Take that further. If she is with child, and he is not happy with her as his leman, he could wed her in Evesham. His sire would not be able to prevent it, and as Baldwin said, the alternative, even if Osbern wanted to disinherit him, was Hamo. We have seen Hamo de Lench. No man who cared for his land as passionately as Osbern would seek to have him hold Lench. So Baldwin would be taking a reasonable chance.'

'But then why did the lord Osbern die, my lord?' Walkelin sounded uncertain.

'Because we have seen what Baldwin is like when the anger takes him, and Hamo also. So however much sense says he would accept, grudgingly, this woman in his hall, he lets temper rule him, and in the argument, son kills father.' Bradecote sounded relieved as much as pleased.

'Far be it from me to say you are wrong, my lord,' declared Catchpoll, lying through his uneven teeth, 'but what the corpse told us from looking at it don't agree with that. There were no marks that said there had been blows other than the knife wounds.'

'I grant you that had they met in the hall, that would be a problem, Catchpoll, but they met on horseback, and so it grew from shouting to a stab wound in one, not flinging blows at one another.'

'And all that shouting, my lord, it did not upset the horses one little bit? The horses that stood one by the other, facing up the hill and down, did just that; they stood. If there had been an argument they would have sidled and disturbed the dust and earth more, but their feet was planted firm. Like so much in this, what sounds as though it must be so, ends up as dust.'

Bradecote swore. Reluctantly, he thought the serjeant was right.

'Yet still it surely has to be Baldwin, and there must be a cause.' He groaned, rubbing the back of his neck. Then he brightened. 'Tredington. The answer has to lie there. What it could be I cannot say, nor even guess, but he came back from there and straight away killed. Walkelin, at first light you . . . no, this time you go, Catchpoll. I would ride with you, but I get the feeling that keeping Baldwin under control will take a lot of shrieval authority, and besides, you have the greatest experience of drawing forth information. I am trusting to that. Return as soon as you can, and then, at last, we will be able to confront Baldwin de Lench with his guilt, and enough to put before sheriff and justices both.' He smiled. 'You go and have the cook bring the meal, Walkelin, and we will eat and rest, ready for the morrow, when this all ends.'

'Pray God you are right, my lord,' murmured Catchpoll, thinking of riding to Tredington and back in a day.

'I am. I have to be.'

Chapter Sixteen

Serjeant Catchpoll woke in the dark of the hall, and opened one eye. Thin slivers of pale light showed between the closed shutters on the narrow windows. It was the dawning hour, though he doubted the sun was over the horizon as yet. He ran his tongue round his teeth, stretched, groaned and sat up. He had actually stood up before Hugh Bradecote surfaced, though he was not trying to be quiet.

'Catchpoll?' The voice was sleep-laden.

'Nearly dawn, my lord. If I am away as soon as it is light, I can be there afore the sun is too high.'

'Yes, and if fortunate you can be back in time for us to end everything today. If I never enter Lench again I will be a happy man.' Bradecote threw back his blanket and got up. 'I will come with you to the stable.' He rubbed his stubbled jaw and yawned. 'I would rather be with you, but I think keeping Baldwin de

Lench on a short leash would be beyond Walkelin, unless he knocked him cold. He simply would not obey the instructions of one he considers inferior. I am a little surprised he obeys me, not being his overlord in person.'

'I would say as you have made a good act of being a man who does not expect to be ignored, my lord,' conceded Catchpoll.

'Aided by you and Walkelin all the while. You think I have not noticed how obedient you are when he is present?'

'Does no harm, my lord.' Catchpoll smiled, slowly.

'No, and I am well aware of the truth beneath, you insubordinate old bastard.'

Catchpoll chuckled, and the smile lengthened to a grin.

'I tries, my lord, I tries.'

With which the pair of them left the hall into the cool dawn, which had the faintest of chills to remind them that September was fast approaching.

The stable was warmer, and Bradecote's big grey greeted his master with a soft, low whicker of recognition and pricked ears.

'No, not you, my friend,' whispered Bradecote, rubbing his soft muzzle, and passing on to bridle Catchpoll's mount as the serjeant saddled it.

'I've not been out of the shire far eastward very often,' remarked Catchpoll. 'I can find my way across from Stratford though, I'll be bound.'

'I know Shipston lies on the road that runs south-west from Warwick, so keep heading south-east until you hit that road and then follow it southwards.'

'I'm too old to go galloping about like young Walkelin,' the serjeant sighed.

'But young Walkelin has not the skills to be sure of finding out what we need, not this time.'

'No, but he is learning well, my lord, I will say that for him.'

'He is, and a good choice he was, red hair notwithstanding.'

'Aye, 'tis a pity about that, but at least he has the brains beneath it.'

Catchpoll led his horse out into the yard and heaved himself up into the saddle. It was then they noticed Edmund, husband of Gytha, sat slumped against the wall of their cott. He was always easy to recognise, being, like Walkelin, red-haired, though his was more chestnut than flame. He scrambled to his feet as he saw the undersheriff, but his obeisance was perfunctory.

'How goes it within?' enquired Bradecote, cautiously, lest there be bad news.

'Slow. They's sent me out for bein' no use to 'em, and I think I would've slept better had I stayed out all night and risked the dew wetness.' The man looked haggard and Bradecote wondered how much worse his wife must look. 'But it must be close now, surely, and horrible to hear.' As if to prove this, a groaning, anguished cry came from within. 'Like a soul in torment it is.'

'Ah well, women are stronger than you think,' offered Catchpoll, and then looked down at Bradecote. 'I'll be back as soon as I can, my lord. Just hope I doesn't get lost and ends up in Warwick.'

'You'll find your way. Off with you.' Bradecote slapped the horse on the rump, and it trotted a few paces and was then urged into an easy loping canter. Another deep, howling groan came from inside the cott and Edmund covered his ears. He therefore missed the sound of a higher pitched voice, urging, commanding. Bradecote did not catch the words but knew it was the voice of the girl Hild, and it was not nervous or supplicating. In this, her own form of trial, it sounded as though she was winning. Bradecote gave up a silent prayer for her victory.

The road that led from Worcester to Stratford was good king's highway, not some half-overgrown track. From Alcester onwards there were still signs of the road the Romans had laid, the straightness and even some good cobbles, though now there were many parts where cart, horseman and even the fluctuations of British weather had worn it down, and earth had covered it, with weed and grasses giving it disguise. At such an early hour there was little sign of humanity upon it and Catchpoll saw more deer and fox and weasel than man until the last mile or so into Stratford. Once he had forded the Avon he asked a maid with a chicken under her arm if he was heading still upon the right road to Shipston, and followed her pointing finger with a word of thanks. He found it as straight as before and made good time, halting only to confirm he was upon the road from Warwick when he came to a junction. The carter he spoke with even gave him the good news that Tredington lay direct upon the road and before Shipston itself. Nevertheless, he reckoned he had been riding for three or four hours, when he finally dismounted, and his stiff legs made a good case for it feeling more.

The manor of Tredington was clearly not the caput of any honour. The hall was simple as had been at Bishampton, a longish building in stone to the height of a man's thigh but no more, and above that a timber structure with infill of daub and wattle and a thatched roof. Catchpoll announced himself as the serjeant to the lord Sheriff of Worcestershire, seeking the steward. He was come not to trespass upon the jurisdiction of the lord Sheriff of Warwickshire, but to seek information that would help the discovery of the killer of their lord, Osbern of Lench. If his first words had meant little, this stopped all who heard it. They stared at him.

'He's dead?' a young man asked, and it sounded as if he wanted to hear an affirmative.

'And buried yesterday. The steward now, I—'

'I am the steward.'

Catchpoll turned, and beheld a thin, care-worn-looking man, with stooping shoulders and rheumy eyes.

'Then I would ask my questions first of you, steward, and privily.'

'Will, take the serjeant's horse.' The steward addressed the young man who had spoken.

'But should I not—?'

'You can join us when you have seen to its care.' The youth scowled, but nodded, and came to take the horse from Catchpoll, and the steward resumed with the serjeant. 'We can speak within the lord's hall.'

He led the way into the hall, where the rushes had been swept away and left the hard earth bare. It looked a lifeless place, though wall and roof were both in good condition. It was simply wood and daub and stone. At one end was a table and a lord's seat, and to one side two long benches against the length of wall. The steward invited Catchpoll to sit.

'I am Guthlac, steward of Tredington. How can I help in anything to do with the death of the lord Osbern?' The man was not challenging, but curious. 'He has not been here since, let me see, a week after Easter that would be.'

'Did he bring his lady?'

'No. Haven't seen her in nigh on three years. He came as usual with the messire Baldwin, though I must gets used to calling him lord now.' He sighed and shook his head. 'The lord Osbern was not an easy man to please, and the son—'

'Aye, we have met the son.' Catchpoll did not need to say more. 'It was the son who has been here though, in this last week.'

'He came to see the harvest was brought in but I had it in hand before he arrived. Cuthwin, who is the weather-feeler, he swore the weather would break within a week, as it did, and so I had everyone out early. Our neighbours might scoff and say every extra day improves the grain, but I would rather it was a little less plump but not ruined by the wet. We was all gathered in two days before the storm broke, and there's no smile on the faces of those who mocked but have wheat all flattened and wet to rotting.' Guthlac gave a small, grim smile. 'Messire Baldwin berated me for starting too early, but better safe than sorry. I only wish my son Will was as cautious as I am, but it will come with years, no doubt.'

'So he is not as like unto his father as the messire to the lord Baldwin then,' observed Catchpoll, with a wry smile, indicative of age looking upon youth and finding it rash.

'No, not like me.' There was something, one note in that voice, that made Catchpoll wonder.

'Takes after his mother then.' The tone was cheerful, but the serjeant's eyes missed nothing.

'Aye, that would be it.' Guthlac did not seem the least cheered, nor believing, but resigned. It was the same look Catchpoll had seen on other faces before, faces like Edmund's in Lench.

'And think on that, friend, for a mother who sees a son in her image is proud as a cock at dawn, and a happier woman for it. We all likes happy wives; they chide the less.' Catchpoll thus set himself beside Guthlac in the unity of husbands.

'Mine will neither chide nor comfort for long.' Guthlac closed his eyes for a moment, then raised them. 'Not a mite of fat on 'er, and can scarce take a breath. She says as she feels she is drowning to death, poor soul.'

'Sorry I am then to make light,' Catchpoll looked serious once more, 'and I come at a bad time, but I has questions as needs answers, Master Steward, and only here can I find them.'

'Then ask, Serjeant.'

'The messire Baldwin came to the manor a bit over a week ago, he says. Was he here all the time?' It was a thought that had been growing in Catchpoll's mind as he rode.

'No, that he was not. He came, and in a foul mood, but that was common. If he came alone, and that was most of the time, he came scowling and finding fault. The lord Osbern, God rest him,' and Guthlac crossed himself, but it was perfunctory and a show only, 'would rant and rave at him, and he do the same back, and then father would send son here to calm down. We was the ones who suffered his lashing tongue, and not just tongue neither.'

'That also we have seen in Lench.' Catchpoll nodded.

'He has the Devil in him, that one. The Devil was in his mother, if ever she got stormy, which was often, but then she had a sort of life-fire about her when happy that was so bright, like sun at noon, that her temper was forgiven. I always thought as she died young because she lived all her life in few years.' Guthlac gave a sigh.

Catchpoll noted the adoration, the same that they had heard from Walter Pipard. The lady had cast a spell, on men at least.

'So the messire came, grumbled and did what?'

'He sat upon his horse and watched the harvesting for a day, and then grumbled that sitting in the saddle so long made his arse ache.' The steward gave a little snort. 'Ask us all if we would exchange that for our aching backs and blistered palms, eh?'

'You should not speak like that about the lord Baldwin.' The young man, the son Will, stood in the doorway, giving his new lord his title straight away.

'It is true, nonetheless, and to the sheriff's man one speaks true, son.'

'He will be a good lord,' declared Will, firmly.

'We hopes and prays so, but he does before he thinks and you need to be the voice that urges waiting.'

'Old men wait, and all they find is cold earth.' Will was clearly in the same mould as his new master.

'But the messire did not wait about here in Tredington after seeing the harvest was being brought in.'

240

'Not once he had complained and complained at me cutting early, no.' Guthlac sounded not just downtrodden but actually a little resentful, since he clearly thought his actions had been right.

'Did he go out riding in the day, or mayhap brought a hawk?' Catchpoll was pretty sure that the answer would be negative but would bring forth the one he expected.

'No, no. He left, and returned three days after, grim of face, which was unusual when he went off.'

'So he did this when he came to the manor; went off for a few days.'

'Since Candlemas I would say. Been here four times on his own, and never stayed more 'n two days. In truth I had not expected him back this time but he said he wanted to know the number of sheaves to report to his sire.'

'Do you know where he went?'

'No, serjeant, not know, but from the slightly better mood when he did return, my guess would be a woman.'

'And what do you say, Will? Young men like to boast to any who will attend.' Catchpoll looked at the young man, who still had some growing yet to do, and must be about seventeen or eighteen. It was an age when women figured a lot in the mind. Will blushed a little, so he was not as experienced as he might wish to be thought.

'He . . . he has a love in Evesham.'

'A love, boy?' Guthlac snorted. 'You mean he keeps a whore for his pleasure.'

'No, Father. He said it. He said she was his love and one day I would make my obeisance to her as his lady.'

Catchpoll kept his face expressionless. No wonder Baldwin liked the idea of the son rather than the father as steward. Here was a young man who would not just obey but be the faithful hound to the master. Baldwin would confuse that with respect.

'But you say this time he returned unhappy?' Catchpoll pressed on.

'A mixture of angry and thoughtful. Ha, never did I think to use that word for him. He got very drunk the night he came back, slept long and was sick as a dog all next morn. When that passed he was . . . unpleasant.' Guthlac pulled a face.

'In what way, specially?'

'Said as I was too old and when he was lord he would hand all to Will, here. Didn't seem that urgent, o' course, but . . . I took up stewardship when my father died, as he had his. I never did aught but right by this manor and . . .' Guthlac shook his head, 'I was fair upset, I grant you.'

'But no need to get Mother off her sickbed.' Will scowled at his father.

'Nor did I. It was her as was determined, and short o' tying her down I was not goin' to stop the woman.'

'She went to speak with the messire? What did she say?'

'That I know not, for she said as it was her and her alone would say what was to be said, for she would not be about long enough for him to make life hard, and how much harder could it be? All I know is he went off next day early, and silent.' The steward covered his face with his hands and spoke between his fingers in a whisper. 'My poor wife. She has been a good one, and a loyal one.'

'Master Steward, you will not like it, but I have to speak with your wife, however ailing, if she is still in senses.'

'She is too weak, and—'

'I am sorry, but it must be. Who killed the lord Osbern must be known, and whoever it was killed again: the village healing woman. There's deaths, and there is the Law.' Catchpoll rose, and the steward did also, as if to stop him, and then sat back down again.

'The priest is with her. He is there much of the day, in case . . .'

Catchpoll nodded and walked out.

Catchpoll had seen plenty of deaths, and plenty of dead. In the steward's home there was no doubt that the woman was dying and not far from the end. The priest was knelt at her side, holding her hand, speaking softly of the joys of Heaven to come for those that passed into its glories. The breathing was laboured but still regular, though her eyes were closed. The priest looked up, his eyes questioning.

'Father, I am Serjeant Catchpoll, the lord Sheriff of Worcestershire's man, and it is very important that I speak with Mistress Steward, if she can understand me. I would not do this without great cause.'

'Speak, but if she has strength to answer I do not know.'

'I understand, Father. I would have it just her and me, for all that your lips will not breathe of what is said.'

Catchpoll knelt at the other side of the pallid figure and squeezed her hand with his rough one. The priest got up from his knees and went out into the light, and life, and breathed it deeply for a few minutes.

'Mistress, I am Catchpoll, the lord Sheriff of Worcestershire's serjeant. I come because the lord Osbern de Lench is dead, by violence, these few days past. Squeeze my hand if you understand me.' There came a faint gripping of his hand. 'Good. Now, the killing took place right about the time messire Baldwin returned to Lench. He came from here, and you had hot words with him. Next morning he left, not a happy man. I have to ask what passed between you, mistress.'

It should not have been possible for one so pale to become more so, and yet he thought the cheeks lost even the vestige of colour remaining. The dying woman took a breath, which would normally have been a deep one, but was but a sipping of the air. Her words came in gasps.

'What he did . . . my Guthlac is a good steward. He was so . . . proud . . . so I told him . . . how would he like his brother . . . as steward?'

'Your Will?' She squeezed his hand in affirmation.

'Guthlac knew . . . from the first. The lord Osbern . . . no choice . . . some stayed . . . I could not face shame . . . he sent me here, told Guthlac . . . who had lost a wife, to wed me . . . and blessed I've been.' The woman paused, trying to get her breath enough to continue.

'Take it steadily, mistress. No need for haste now.'

'Yes, for there is . . . little time. I told him . . . about Will . . . and he laughed. Said a bastard was nothing. So I told him . . . told him what Osbern said in his troubled . . . sleep . . . that he killed Baldwin's . . . mother because she . . . had betrayed him.'

'But Baldwin was born some years before her death.' Catchpoll was surprised.

'Let him think . . . he found out late.' A slight smile touched lips that had a blue tinge. 'Osbern said once . . . I could do nothing.' She coughed. 'He was wrong . . . in the end.' She took several rapid, shallow breaths. 'I did not know . . . he would . . . after all . . . 'twas the mother as strayed then. I did not set him . . . to kill. 'Tis *wyrd*.'

'Aye, mistress, it is just *wyrd* and none of us can avoid that.'

'Should I confess . . . ? I . . .'

'I cannot say. If it gives your mind and soul ease, the priest will be a good listener. Thank you.' Catchpoll squeezed the hand, and let it go, getting up with a grimace at his creaking knees. He went to the doorway, and spoke quickly and low to the priest, who nodded and went back to his watch.

Will was standing in the yard. He had seemed confident when Catchpoll arrived, but now looked younger and less sure of himself. His face was clouded.

'My mother?'

'She gave good honest truth and breathes still. Why not go to her?'

'I . . . I am not brave enough.' Suddenly the mask of maturity slipped. Catchpoll clapped him on the shoulder in the manner of an oldfather.

'Yes, you are, lad, because you are a man, and it is the act of a man to face what he fears, and because it is the last gift you can give her, your presence, your hand. You run from that now and you will regret it always. Your father,' Catchpoll did not pause for even a breath, 'has duties as well as this, and one of you should be there now. She is giving a confession, but stand you by and close, and when you hear the absolution, you go in to her.'

'Yes. I shall.' Will took a gulp of air that was part sob, and then blurted out, 'His love is carrying his child.'

Catchpoll did not need to ask who 'he' might be.

'Is she now? Well, that is betwixt him and her, I say, so you just keep it nice and quiet, and look to your father in the days to come, for he will need a good son in his days of grief, as you will need a good father.' Catchpoll patted the shoulder once more, and went to the hall where Guthlac sat as he had been left.

'All is well, Master Steward, and the priest is with her again. I have said to your lad to go to her, and forgive me, I would say as you ought to be there soon. It won't be long now, by my guess.'

The steward just nodded, and Catchpoll went to fetch his horse, not relishing the long ride back, but confident he had all that the lord undersheriff would need.

He rode at a decent pace but was sensible enough to realise that forcing his horse to speed early on would leave it exhausted for the last miles, and curbed any urge to ride headlong. The steady canter also gave him the chance to go over and over the import of what he had learnt, making sure every last part of it fitted together like the shards of a broken jug. The steward's wife would be long-buried before she could give her oath on what she said, but she had no cause to lie, and he would vouch she then confessed all to her priest, which was as good as oath if one was dying and needed full absolution. What was more, the boy-man that was her son had the final reason why such a revelation might just tip a man to killing a father he feared, hated and admired all in one.

Stratford seemed closer on the return ride, and certainly

more lively. There was a woman wringing out her washing at the water's edge on one side of the ford, and a group of noisy children, stripped bare, splashing water at each other on the other side. The blacksmith was shoeing a horse, while the owner leant against the wall under the shade of the thatched overhang, and a girl was trying to shoo a goose from pecking at her skirts. It was peaceably normal, the way a serjeant liked things to be, even if it was not in his own jurisdiction.

He ran a finger along the inside of the neck of his tunic, feeling it sweat-wet, and let his horse halt and drink in the river's flow before urging it onward.

The sun was a little past its zenith when he passed through Alcester but he knew he would soon be in his own shire and that eased his saddle-weariness. He headed south-west to pass through Abbot's Morton and then kicked his now-sweating horse to take the shorter route and go up the top of the lord Osbern's hill to drop down into Lench. There was no reason to assume anyone would be there among the trees as he neared the top, and when suddenly a horse came at him from the side and rear he had no time to more than turn at the hoofbeats before he was shoved sideways to land, dazed, in the dust. For a moment he was dizzy and disorientated, and then he looked up and saw the face of Baldwin de Lench, and the stout branch gripped in his hand.

Chapter Seventeen

Hugh Bradecote sat upon a bench in the hall, tying up his blanket roll and with his thoughts elsewhere. Until Catchpoll's return there was little he could do, except keep the lord of Lench from committing acts of violence. What concerned him was the thought that the serjeant might return with nothing that would turn possibilities, opportunities and instincts into something solid that would remove any doubt and make any claim of innocence patently false. What would they do then? Returning to William de Beauchamp with a tale of 'we are reasonably sure he did this, but . . .' would bring down justifiably harsh words from the lord sheriff, not least because he would not want vassal service from a man who had almost certainly killed his own father and could not be trusted. The undersheriff therefore sat for some time, desperately seeking solutions and finding none. He sighed.

Hamo de Lench emerged from the solar, looking perfectly at ease and rested.

'How does your lady mother?' asked Bradecote.

'I think she sleeps, for there was no sound from behind the curtain.' The answer was given as though the enquiry had been a mere morning pleasantry, rather than about a woman with a torn back and distressed mind. 'Am I confined to the hall, or may I ride this morning? Now Baldwin is lord properly, and our father laid in the earth, he will be wedding that woman in Evesham and bringing her here. He will be glad to see me gone and so I can go to Abbot Reginald and seek admittance. I will miss riding and I will miss my hawks, but God asks us to make sacrifices and I will do so.' He paused. 'Do you think it would be kinder if I wrung their necks? Baldwin is a brutal man and would not treat them as I do.' He frowned.

'But you do not see to their daily care.'

'Of course not. Kenelm the Groom does that.'

'And he will continue to do so. Unless you think your brother would harm them when out hunting, if they miss the prey, there is no cause at all.'

'No, you are right. That is a good answer. I shall let them live. I cannot pray for them for they do not possess souls but I will think about them with kindness. So, may I go out today?'

'Messire, it would be better that you do not, for many reasons which I will not say, but tomorrow you may do as you wish.'

'What shall I do?'

'You could go to the church and prepare yourself for your admission to the abbey.'

'Yes.' Hamo walked out.

Bradecote shook his head. He had never met anyone quite like Hamo de Lench, and was thankful for it. Everything he said made perfect sense, except it had nothing to do with how things really were, for it did not include feelings, the natural emotions that pervaded life. With him it was either midnight or noon, no gloaming, no dawn, no sunset.

The undersheriff went back outside, and to the cook upon whom he lavished praise for the woodcock and from whom he obtained a beaker of small beer. He then went to stand with his back to the barn and feel the warmth of the morning sun on his face. From within the barn came the sound of voices and the threshing, and he relaxed, his eyes half closed for a moment. He drained his beaker and wished he were at home. He opened his eyes fully once more at the sound of footsteps. Walkelin was approaching to make his report of a peaceful night, if, he said, you could discount the groans from Fulk the Steward which had prevented the serjeanting apprentice from drifting into the slumber he deserved.

'But I had the door braced shut, my lord, so we could not have been surprised in the night.' Walkelin wanted to assure his superior that he had not been lax.

'I did not expect you to remain wakeful throughout, Walkelin. Ah,' the undersheriff looked past his junior, 'and here comes the lord Baldwin, and still not at peace with the world by the look of things.'

Baldwin de Lench was a man whose temper was not made the better by sleep, not as far as Bradecote could see. He had just emerged from the priest's humble dwelling with a scowling countenance, and was followed by the worthy Father Matthias who looked harassed. The priest cut away swiftly to the church like one seeking sanctuary, where Bradecote had little doubt he would not only say the Office but offer up heartfelt prayers to be delivered from Baldwin de Lench. Well, if Catchpoll returned with information that gave a reason for what they thought, then those prayers might indeed be answered, though not in a way the priest would find comforting.

'Did you sleep well in my hall?' growled Baldwin, showing just how much it rankled.

'Very well, thank you.' It might be a lie but it was one that was worth it to see the expression darken even more.

'And what happens now? Am I to live in exile upon mine own manor until you tire of all this and leave us in peace?'

'Until the matter of two killings is resolved, yes, though if you think I prefer being here to my own manor and with my wife, you are very much mistaken. But the way is now clear for you to wed your lady from Evesham, so I am surprised you are not in excellent spirits.'

'I saw my sire buried but yesterday. To leap into the marriage bed straight after looks unseemly.'

'I would not have thought you cared that much how things look, de Lench.'

'I care that much. You will not see grieving from his widow,' he spat the word, 'or her mad whelp.'

'Odd, yes, mad, no. He is keen to be away to the Benedictines in Evesham.'

'They are welcome to him,' Baldwin sneered. 'So are you going to tell me where I may and may not go today, my lord Undersheriff?'

'Yes. You will not enter the hall, nor the dwelling of the steward, nor the church, whilst your brother Hamo is in it.'

'The steward ought to be overseeing the threshing.'

'That is true. But you will not enter the barn once he is there, unless a sheriff's man is with you.'

'But this is madness. How long do you expect to keep everyone apart? You have to leave at some point.'

'That point is when we have the killer of Osbern de Lench and Mother Winflaed.'

'Which could be sometime never.' Baldwin sounded disgusted. 'What do I do all day?'

'You sound like your brother.'

'For the first time in our lives then.'

'Well, as lord you have a duty to attend the funeral rites for your village healer. You can be in the church with the lady, and everyone else present, because I will be at your side and my man Walkelin will be upon the other.'

'Do not tell me my duty.'

'I certainly should not need to do so. I expect the priest will wait until young Hild and her oldmother are finished with the birth, since they are closest in kinship to the dead, but the grave was dug yesterday afternoon and is ready, as I heard.'

'You do not mind me going to the kitchen and finding something to break my fast, then?'

'Not at all. By all means go.' Bradecote gave the permission airily, knowing it would irritate the more, and smiled as the man stalked away.

'You enjoyed that, my lord, don't say as you didn't,' remarked Walkelin, entirely forgetting his place, and grinning. Bradecote turned to look at him, coolly, and Walkelin gulped. 'Not that I, er, I mean . . .'

The undersheriff's lips twitched, and then he gave in.

'You are quite right, Walkelin, and I want you to be outside the kitchen and follow him about for a while. I do not see him attacking Fulk the Steward in the barn in front of the whole village, and I will see if the lady has risen, or indeed is in a condition to leave her bed this day. I think if she is able, she would like to attend church. He needs to know he is watched, however.'

'Yes, my lord.'

Walkelin dutifully went to stand before the kitchen, and Bradecote went back into the hall and knocked upon the solar door. A maidservant came and opened it, rather to his relief.

'My lord?' she bobbed in obeisance.

'Will you tell your lady that the Mother Winflaed is likely to be buried this morning, if she feels she could rise and attend.'

'Yes, my lord. The lady is awake but . . .' the maid's voice dropped to a whisper, 'I think she is afeard of what everyone will say.'

'What they will say is that the lord Baldwin gets ideas in his head and will not let them go, whether right or wrong, and has the Devil's temper.'

'True, my lord. Would you have me say that too?'

'Yes.' He turned away, since he was not sure the maid would close the door in his face, and went out of both hall and bailey. As he did so he saw the girl Hild emerge from Gytha's cott, and her oldmother followed and put an arm about her sagging

253

shoulders. His heart sank. Had it gone badly? He went towards them and then saw Hild smile, wearily.

'Mornin', my lord. I was wrong. This babe came later than the sunrise after all. Mind you it came not only slow but *earsling*, and them as comes out wrong way round will spend their lives looking behind 'em, so said Mother Winflaed,' at which Hild crossed herself.

'And the mother, she is recovering?'

'Aye, my lord. Most women does from the moment the babe is laid to the breast. They forgets the half of what passed. Mind you, Gytha is eased of more than the birthing pangs, for her son has a fine scalp of red hair.'

Bradecote smiled. Edmund need not go through life wondering, or worse, knowing, his son was not his own.

'You look worn,' he noted. 'When Mother Winflaed has been laid in the earth, you get some sleep for Lench cannot have you ill.'

'For I am Hild the Healer,' beamed the girl with a little more confidence than a day before. There would be failures and setbacks but her reputation would be founded upon this first, and not easy, birthing.

'For you are indeed Hild the Healer.' Whilst there was no need for it, none at all, Bradecote reached into his scrip, took out a silver penny and presented it to her. Coin was not something used much unless folk went into Evesham, and he did not suppose she had held many pennies of her own, if any.

'My lord?'

'That is a mark of respect from me, the lord Undersheriff, for your aid when I called upon you here, and because this was your first challenge and you did well.'

The girl blushed pink and turned the penny over in her hand.

'My lord, I would not spend this. I would have it strung so as I can wear it about my neck. That ways I can touch it and remember what you said. Thank you, my lord.' She stifled a yawn, and her oldmother told her to go and change her shift, which was soiled, and the girl nodded, bobbed her obeisance to Bradecote and went to do as bidden. The old woman smiled after her.

'She did well, my lord, and I am right proud of her. O' course others have experience with women in their hours of trial, but my sister was the best, and if things did not run smoothly, ah, then she came into her own. My girl kept her head when the babe showed wrong way about, and it does her credit. What you said, and did also, will stay with her and help her, for there will be days when folk see the girl's years and not her skills.' She sighed. 'Winflaed would be proud too. She said as she would see Hild take her place and be even better. Pity it is she did not, and the day came so swift.'

'You too must need rest. It was a long night.'

'Once Winflaed has hers, I will do as Hild and lay down my head then, my lord. You know, *wyrd* is strange. When we were girls, little ones, it was me as thought to follow as the Healer, but first time I went with my mother's sister, who was Healer then, I saw a man die horrible from the arching spasms, his back all bowed so only his heels and head touched the ground. Nothing could be done o' course, but it gave me such dreams I knew the *laececraeft* was not for me, and Winflaed began the learning of it instead. Could have been her here, and me lying in the church, but for *wyrd*.' She shook her head. 'Now I will go and speak with Father Matthias, and if he says all is ready, I will gather all from the barn.'

Bradecote nodded. A belief in fate gave reassurance that nothing could have been done to alter what had happened. Yet he felt that to accept it too much would mean that whatever he, Catchpoll and Walkelin might do, those who met a violent end were doomed, and by the same token, however inept they might be, they would save those who were destined to live longer. If he believed in *wyrd* too much he might as well not bother being undersheriff at all. He pulled a face at his own twisting thoughts. It came of having nothing to do but wait.

He went to the church.

Bradecote wondered if Baldwin de Lench was thick-skinned enough not to notice the almost palpable difference between the obsequies for Winflaed the Healer and his sire. This time there were sniffing women and sighing men, and a genuine sense of deep regret and sorrow. As the manor lord, Baldwin stood to the front, with Walkelin to one side and Bradecote on the other, and with the villagers at his back, but if Bradecote could feel it, how could he not do so? At least it meant he was not looking at the steward, or the lady de Lench, who had chosen to stand next to Hild and Winflaed's sister. Hamo stood upon Bradecote's other side, and Bradecote thought he was thinking about Evesham, not the healing woman.

The lord of Lench looked morose, but then he often looked that way. He mumbled about hoping it would not take long as he wanted everyone back to work, and got no answer from the undersheriff. When all was at an end, the villagers filed out and gathered about the second new grave in Lench, though Winflaed's was outside and Osbern had been laid beneath the earth in front of the altar, having been the man who had just paid for the church's rebuilding, and no tiles having yet been laid upon the chancel floor. Hugh Bradecote thought that Winflaed would have thought herself the more fortunate, with the sound of birdsong above her remains and the seasons passing overhead.

He sent Walkelin, with a nod, to dog the steps of Baldwin de Lench, who was still looking ill-tempered. Hild's oldmother, who felt that her previous conversation with such an elevated person as the lord undersheriff would raise her standing in the eyes of her neighbours, could not resist passing by close enough to comment.

'We will just have to make the best of things, I s'pose. We always knew, o' course, what with him being the lord Osbern's son and his mother as she was, and the lord Osbern was not a lord to be liked, just avoided as much as possible.'

'How was the mother?' Bradecote thought about what Raoul Parler and Walter Pipard had said of her.

'Ah, there was a beautiful lady, but with a fire, and that foolish way of seeing but one thing, true or not. Made for some fine arguments in the hall in those days, and 'twas sad how she paid so dear for it too.'

'What do you mean, oldmother?' Bradecote's brows drew together in curiosity, and he stood still.

'It don't matter now, them all bein' dead and buried,' murmured the old woman, half to herself, and then looked Bradecote in the eye. 'Winflaed knew, but the lord Osbern

257

knew she would not tell, and nor did she, not for years, but . . . I am kin, and old, and what secrets she told me were not like to spread. I would keep 'em still if it mattered.'

'What secrets?'

'Tragic ones, my lord, and all such a twisting and turning. The lord Osbern and the lady Judith loved one another, howsoever many pots were thrown and hot words shouted. There was a heat to them. She was unafraid, leastways not afraid of any man, but then when fear came, it ate her like a wolf devouring a lamb.' The woman shook her head. 'She began to have a loss of feeling in her fingers, two of her right hand. Winflaed told her not to worry but she was convinced it was the signs of leprosy. She had once seen a man cast from her home village, dead to the world and all those he loved, yet in it still. Now Winflaed had not seen the cruel disease, not up close, since a *hreófla* must keep at a distance with their clapper, but she had seen a lad who had the same tingles in his two fingers after he broke an arm. Her reasonin' was that it was somethin' in the arm, not a foulness like leprosy, but would the lady listen? No, not to Winflaed nor to the priest neither, so she fretted, and kept herself from her lord with excuses till he could scarce bear it more, and then she died. Well, it was a fall as was said. Years later Winflaed told me it could have been by her own intent, but that she had seen the poor lady's body when the lord Osbern brought her home. He begged her to find life, but what hope when it has already gone? What Winflaed saw, and swore to me as true years later, was marks upon her neck as told it never snapped in no fall. It was him what killed her, but she could not think why.' The old woman permitted herself a small smile, mostly because she could see she had the lord undersheriff hanging upon her every word.

258

'Go on. I can see there is more.'

'Well, I already had reason to know he had done for her. After the lady died, the lord Osbern did not wed for a year or so, but he was not a man to lie alone. He took one of the girls, old enough to wed mind, and she had told me he raved in his dreams, raved about his faithless whore-wife, raved of his love for her still though he snapped her neck. Well, that was words that would have got her an' me both dead, and so I told her. When the poor girl found herself with child she did not want to stay, and he would not keep her, so he sent her to his manor at Tredington and she wed the widower steward. I heard as it has been a happy union, and she deserved it. When I told Winflaed, she said as he had never cause and his lady was pure, and so she went and told him, she did, about the poor woman's fears. I thought her mad to do it, for he might have killed her on the spot, but she would have the lady's name restored. Near broke him, I think, knowing he had killed her innocent, not guilty, and that is why I think the church is new, and why that poor lady in the hall now could never please him. I think he made confession when he knew, mind you, because our young priest, Father Theodosius, he left us shortly after and went back to the monks in Evesham. The sort who is burdened by great confessing, he was.'

'And the steward of Tredington's wife knew only what the lord Osbern had said, that his wife betrayed him and he killed her.'

'She could not have known what Winflaed knew, and I was only told after the girl went to Tredington. I have told none, none but you, my lord, and that is because you are who you are.' She sighed.

'Go and rest, oldmother.' Bradecote did not tell her she had given him the answer he needed, or so near that he must guess what Catchpoll would bring back with him as knowledge. He smiled at the thought of how annoyed Catchpoll would feel having ridden to Tredington and back in a day, only to bring a tidying of ends, and went to ask the lady de Lench how she fared.

Walkelin did not follow Baldwin de Lench too closely, for that would be merely lighting the tinder of his wrath and inviting a boot, and Walkelin had a strong feeling Serjeant Catchpoll would tell him that a sheriff's man ought never to put himself in the position of making much of his rank whilst sprawled upon the ground chewing dust. He simply kept the man in view and within about ten paces, ignoring the occasional glare, as Baldwin prowled about his bailey and finally went into the barn, where the noise of the threshing flails declared the labour of the villagers. Fulk stood to one side, arms folded, and not stood as straight and tall as he would normally. When he saw the lord Baldwin enter his cheek paled a little, but he stood his ground.

Edmund the new father, secure in the knowledge that he was indeed a father, handed his flail to a lad and approached his lord to tell him, proudly, of the birth of his son. Walkelin watched but could not hear the words over the sound of the flails. The lord Baldwin merely grunted, which was all the congratulation Edmund would receive. Baldwin had things upon his mind and uppermost was the realisation that he had not seen that miserable bastard the lord sheriff's serjeant all day. The question was posed to Edmund and the answer given freely.

'Why he left before the sun was up proper, my lord, being off to Tredington and wanting to get back today, doubtless.'

Baldwin de Lench stared at the man, who lowered his eyes, gazed at the earth and then requested permission to return to the threshing. The lord of Lench remained staring, now into space, even after he had done so. Then he turned and left the barn, walked, without any sense of purpose, to the stable, whence the dutiful Walkelin followed him, entering not the darkness of a stable but of unconsciousness, as he was hit upon the head with a piece of wood.

Bradecote felt a huge sense of relief. What they had missed was not something they had failed to ask about, or see, but a tangle so old and deep it might well have remained hidden. At least they were right in thinking that the immediate cause lay in Tredington, though why the steward's wife would reveal her knowledge, that just happened to be wrong, Bradecote could not comprehend. Nor could he work out why it had made Baldwin ride off and avenge his mother, since he would not have faulted his sire's actions against a faithless wife, as he had since proved with a lash.

He went to the hall and found the lady in the solar, looking pensive and watching her son laying out his possessions upon his bed in neat order. He was telling her what he would take to Evesham for the Almoner to give to the poor, and what he would give to Kenelm the Groom, who had cared for his hawks.

'. . . and the blanket will go to the girl Hild, so that she can use it when the sick need to be kept very warm. That is a good act of charity. I will take my box with me, and show Abbot Reginald my writing. I would like to work in the scriptorium.'

'You are making your preparations straight away, messire?' Bradecote was a little surprised.

'You said that I could leave tomorrow, my lord.'

'Yes, I did.'

'Then I want to be ready. I will ride, not walk, for although humility is good, I am still Hamo de Lench until I enter the noviciate, and my father would not want me to arrive upon foot. Also, my horse is part of my gift to the Church.' Hamo had it all worked out, as neat as the piles of possessions on the bed.

Bradecote looked at the lady, who shrugged and gave a sad sigh.

'Tomorrow or the next day, does it matter, except to me, his mother?' She sounded defeated, as beaten in spirit as in her body.

'I came to ask how you did, lady.'

'As you see, my lord. Pain is transitory, shame lingers. Even if I could have remained here before, I cannot now. After my son departs, I will also.'

'I do not think you will be judged, not as you think.'

'But God will judge,' added Hamo, unhelpfully, and as a matter of fact.

'God judges everything we do, messire, and our charity as well as our sins.' It sounded a little priestly in the undersheriff's own ears, but the youth was irritating him.

'I give generously, my lord.'

'Of things, but what of thought?'

'Of thought?' For a moment Hamo looked puzzled. 'Ah, you mean not thinking badly of people. Well, I do not think that I do. I see what is, that is all.'

It was a lost cause. Hamo de Lench did indeed see, but never understood how ordinary folk thought. Bradecote gave up. What did occur to him was that if everything came together as looked likely, Hamo de Lench would not be able to depart on the morrow for Evesham, since the manor would be passing to him if his brother was destined for a noose. It was not something that could be declared beforehand, however, so Bradecote just shook his head and rather lamely instructed the lady to get as much rest as she could. Then he left and went out into the sunshine once more. The sparrows were chirruping and taking up trampled and shaken grain from the days of harvesting, making their own store of strength for the cold months that today seemed so far distant, and above them the martins and swallows added their high pitched voices. Just for a few minutes Hugh Bradecote let himself be enveloped by an English summer; then Walkelin emerged, staggering, from the stable. His face was sickly pale, in marked contrast to the scarlet trickle of blood that coursed down from his forehead and ran down the side of his nose. He tried to stand upright but simply collapsed into the dust, as the sparrows flew up in alarm. Bradecote rushed forward.

'Walkelin!' Bradecote went down on one knee, hauling the inert form into a sitting position. Walkelin screwed up his eyes.

'Hit me. Gone.' No more explanation was needed at that

moment. Bradecote yelled for aid, and after several shouts Fulk emerged from the barn.

'Look after him,' commanded Bradecote, loosening his hold upon Walkelin, who slumped a little forward, hands braced now upon his knees. The undersheriff rushed into the stable, bridled his grey and did not even bother to saddle it, trusting to his horsemanship for the sake of speed. It was only as he left the bailey that he realised that he had no certain knowledge of where, or indeed why, Baldwin de Lench had suddenly fled. Had he planned to do so and simply bided his time for the best opportunity? Why might he have thought he stood in any greater danger of being taken now than yesterday? Bradecote tried to think calmly, even as his heart raced. Baldwin could not have overheard what the oldmother had said, for he had not stayed for the burial. That might have sent him to Evesham and his lady-love, and then on in some mad flight but to what end? Lench, and lordship, would be lost to him, a man who for whom that meant so much. And there had been none who saw Catchpoll depart except . . . Edmund. Bradecote focused his thoughts. Yes, a sort of logic would work if that was the case. He threw himself off the horse and ran back towards the barn, leading it and calling for Edmund. The man came out looking frightened.

'Did the lord Baldwin speak with you today?'

'Yes, my lord. I told him of my son.'

'And did he ask any question of you?'

'Only if I had seen the serjeant, and I said as he had gone to Tredi—'

'Thank you.' Bradecote interrupted him. 'Give me a leg

up.' The grey was on the fret and sidling at all the shouting. Edmund threw the undersheriff onto the horse's back, and this time Bradecote left the bailey already leaning forward over the animal's withers and urging it to speed up the trackway to where the hill path left the Evesham road. As he rode, gripping tightly with his knees, he prayed. All morning his prayers had been for Serjeant Catchpoll to be swift, but now he implored Heaven that he might have been delayed. It took but a few minutes to reach the hilltop, though there was no sign of a horse or rider there, and he slowed to a trot as he took the descending track to the north, very aware that an ambush for Catchpoll could as easily be launched upon himself. At the first bend, however, he heard a cry and a thud, and kicked his horse to charge forward. Ahead of him Baldwin de Lench stood over a prostrate form and he had a large stick raised in one hand.

'Halt there!' screamed Bradecote, hoping the words alone might buy him a few precious moments. De Lench did halt and swing round, in time to be thrown back as Bradecote launched himself from his horse on top of him. The pair were equally winded, and Catchpoll was in no condition to move, so for a brief time there was a tableau of three men lying sprawled in various attitudes upon the twig-strewn earth. De Lench seemed first to recover, and rolled the undersheriff, who was half on top of him, to the side and scrambled to his feet, spitting dust. He leant to grab his staff but Bradecote, his senses as regained as his breath, took hold of the nearer end, and there followed a tussle as between two dogs with a bone. Neither had an advantage and so Bradecote suddenly let go, sending Baldwin de Lench stumbling backwards. Bradecote got up on one knee, just far enough to drag his sword from its scabbard.

'Put the staff down. It is over, de Lench, all over.'

'And have you put a rope about my neck? No thank you. It is not over, not yet.' Baldwin's eyes were wild with a furious desire to survive at any cost, and he was breathing through his mouth to get air into his lungs. He had the advantage of height, and swung the staff to drive the sword from the undersheriff's grasp, but although sword and arm were flung to the side, the hold was not lost. Bradecote felt the reverberation all the way up to his shoulder but yet managed to get fully to his feet, and as he did so Baldwin drew his knife from its hanger in a sweeping, outward stroke, and caught Bradecote's left arm even as the undersheriff pulled back, his arms bowed like a bull's horns. Bradecote took a hissing intake of breath, but his eyes remained locked to those of Baldwin.

'I think the fight fair enough,' growled Baldwin, his eyes narrowing to slits as he tried to second guess his opponent. 'You may have a sword, but the staff has longer reach and I am good with a knife.'

'As your father discovered.'

'But this I will enjoy. That . . .' for one moment Baldwin looked heartbroken, 'was dire need.'

'Why?'

'Because my woman carries my child and I would have a son born to inherit, and though my sire might have ignored the bitter truth about me because I was ever more a lord than the stripling Hamo, he would declare me bastard if I disobeyed him and wed her.'

266

'Yet he could have told you are indeed fully his own son. Did you not give him time to speak?' Bradecote's voice chided almost softly, and Baldwin's eyes widened in a sudden horror. 'The tale you had in Tredington was but the half-known there. Too late he discovered it and lived thereafter with the guilt of killing an innocent wife.'

'No.' It was a cry of denial, but to himself. Baldwin shook his head. 'You say it to unman me.' He lunged, using the staff as he would a sword, and Bradecote's blade parried and bit into the wood, where it stuck. Baldwin laughed, stepped suddenly close and thrust the knife towards Bradecote's throat.

Bradecote grabbed at the wrist with his free hand, though the strength in his arm was already sapped by the bleeding wound. It could not hold off the stronger arm for long, and Baldwin laughed again, but the laugh turned into a grunt of pain as Bradecote brought his knee up sharply into the man's groin. It was not a perfect contact but Baldwin's grip upon his weapons tightened convulsively, and the impulsion was lost. The inexorable advance of the blade to Bradecote's throat was halted, and the two men swayed for a moment, joined in a dance to the death. The pain in Bradecote's arm was an insistent thump now, but he overcame it just enough to push the knife away. Baldwin dropped the staff entirely, and grabbed the hilt of the knife so that he had a two hand advantage as the weight of the staff pulled Bradecote's sword arm instantly downward. Bradecote dropped his weapon and half stepped and half fell backwards, pushing up with his injured arm so that the knife, instead of entering his flesh, passed over his head. There was a flailing of limbs, the two men rolled over several times, and then there was a deep grunting noise and Bradecote lay very still. All he was aware of was the pounding of the blood in his ears and the pain in his arm, until Catchpoll, mumbling, pulled the corpse of Baldwin de Lench from across his body.

Chapter Eighteen

Bradecote stared up at the serjeant's grim face that slowly eased into his death's head smile.

'Mighty glad I am you arrived, my lord,' Catchpoll muttered, and took his superior by the good arm and dragged him to his feet. He swayed, still a little unsteady, and Bradecote swayed also, clamping his right hand to his left arm, and looked down at the crumpled heap that had been Baldwin de Lench.

'Bastard,' he growled, with feeling. Whether he was addressing the body or swearing at the pain in his arm was not clear.

'What you needs to remember, my lord,' sighed Catchpoll, sounding tired and rubbing the side of his head, 'is that lord or not, no man fights fair when his life depends upon it. A bit of you tries to do that. Thankful I am that it is not much, but it takes the edge.'

'But I did not want to have to kill him.'

'Ah, that is where the trouble lies. He,' and Catchpoll kicked the corpse, 'wanted to kill you or be killed by you, not go bound to Worcester and dangle at a rope's end. You needs to treat it like a true battle-fight, for sure as the sun sets the man you face will want your death. If you aims to take him just wounded you risk being the next one dead. Good job you got to fighting dirty and he landed on his own blade. Now, show me that arm.'

The undersheriff, feeling a little light-headed, obediently presented the arm to his serjeant. The slash ran down the arm from near the elbow to the wrist, and at the bottom end a tendon showed white amidst the scarlet.

'Ah, lucky you are that the knife did not cut through that,' remarked Catchpoll, and bent down, slowly, lifted the limp arm of the fallen man, and cut the sleeve from the tunic. 'Here, that will bind it till we gets back to Lench. The girl Hild ought to know enough to deal with a simple wound to the arm.' He wound the cloth about the forearm, and pushed a hand into the small of Bradecote's back to guide him to his horse. He stood by as the undersheriff leant across the animal's withers and with an ungainly hop and some colourful language, managed to get astride its back. He then went and lugged the body of Baldwin de Lench, with much swearing of his own, and contrived, with difficulty, to heave it over the withers of the man's horse before clambering onto his own.

They descended into Lench at walking pace. Of the two men living it was debatable who was the more focused upon what to do next. Catchpoll still felt dizzy and a bit sick, and the undersheriff was more than a little distracted by the pain in his left arm. His right hand was sticky with blood from staunching the wound that had soaked through parts of the binding, and he wiped it in his grey's mane. As they entered Lench, a woman came out of her home, rubbing her hands upon her skirts, and raised one to her mouth, then called out to her neighbours. It seemed to Bradecote that everyone appeared as from nowhere and very quickly, parting as Catchpoll's horse walked towards the bailey gate, crossing themselves, and then whispering in hushed, mumbling voices.

'Where's the girl Hild?' called Catchpoll.

'Here, but the lord be clear dead.' Hild pushed forward, a slightly more confident Hild in the wake of the last twenty-four hours.

'We knows that, but you get your salves and mosses or whatever, and come into the hall to tend the lord Undersheriff. Quick now.'

She paled a little, but since the undersheriff was patently conscious and able to sit upon his horse, she consoled herself with the fact that his wound could not be such as to tax her knowledge. She nodded, sighed with relief as she noted how he held his arm and darted away.

Catchpoll dismounted and went to assist Bradecote from the big grey, though the undersheriff muttered he needed no aid, and walked perfectly upright towards the hall. Walkelin, still a little concussed, stood at the doorway, relief upon his face as he stood to one side to let his superiors in.

'Bring the body into the hall also,' commanded Catchpoll, in charge of the situation, and looked to Edmund the new father, and Kenelm the Groom. He did not need to maintain the look to know they would obey. He entered the hall's dimness and found the lady de Lench fluttering about the lord Bradecote, not quite sure whether to offer wine, sympathy or a fresh binding for the wound. When the body of her unlamented stepson was brought in this distracted her enough to leave the undersheriff in peace. She was now uncertain as to whether she should rejoice openly or assume an appearance of distress. Father Matthias came in, crossed himself and knelt beside the body. The lady joined him, as out of habit.

Hild entered, followed by Fulk, bobbed a general obeisance and came before the undersheriff, requesting him to lay the arm and hand, palm up, upon a trestle table. He did as he was bid, and watched in a remarkably disengaged manner as she unwound the wrapped sleeve from about it and looked pensively at the long wound, now oozing sluggishly.

'Mother Winflaed, God rest her soul,' Hild crossed herself devoutly, 'did not like to shut up a wound with a needle and thread of any sort. She said as wounds went bad more, so unless really big she liked to bind 'em tight with a mash of garlic and leek upon the wound and moss over that for the first days, then honey once there was sign of it joining. And always used strips of yellow cloth cos it is dyed with onion skins and has the charm of 'em. The wound is not deep at the top, my lord, and that will heal fast, but near the hand will take longer. It is there I am not sure about stitching. Mother Winflaed,' she crossed herself again, and Bradecote wondered if it would become some form of totem to the girl to make her think the treatment would be more effective, 'loved to use the leek and garlic over all else with wounds, even cleavers. There is some as uses it but for the stye in the eye, but all in Lench would say the leek and garlic has worked well over the years, and,' she added, 'there is plenty of both hereabouts. Stings a lot o' course.' This was said in a casual way as she pounded both in a bowl which gave off a strong vapour that made her eyes water. 'Tis good, that is. When it brings tears to the mashing it is stronger in healing.' She sniffed, pounded some more, and then took a scoop of it with her fingers and laid it upon the wound. He winced but did not exclaim. She repeated the action until there was a pale greenish mulch all down the inside of the forearm, and then laid moss upon it and bound the arm as tightly as she dare, pushing the wound edges together with one hand as she bound it round and round with the efficacious yellow cloth.

Catchpoll, meantime, was sat upon a bench, and given a draught of ale and a cold compress for his sore head.

As the girl finished her ministrations Hamo de Lench burst in. He looked at the corpse.

'He is dead.' It was simply an observation.

'Yes, my son.' The priest was perhaps the only person who would sound regretful, and that because the man had died unshriven of the acts which had brought him to this end.

'Then I am lord of Lench.' Hamo sounded neither pleased nor sorrowful, but then frowned. 'I would still rather go to the monks. I do not want to be the lord. I do not want to have to marry and beget sons. Small children are strange. They make lots of noise and do odd things, and women are worse.' He looked at the undersheriff. 'Would the lord Sheriff let me pass the manor to my uncle? He has a son, a healthy son, nearly my age already. His name is Randulf. I need but enough to gift the abbey for my admittance.'

'My lord Hamo, it is your decision, but I doubt the lord Sheriff would object.' Bradecote intentionally gave him his title and saw him wince at it. No, William de Beauchamp would not mind at all. What use to him was this strange young man who did not understand people, who looked at everything through unemotional eyes?

'Then that is what I will do. I will go and write to the lord Sheriff. It seems fitting, and I will delay my journey to Evesham until my uncle takes seisin.' With which he walked out, not glancing again at the body nor his mother.

'And what of you, lady?' Bradecote addressed the lady of Lench. He realised he had never heard her name.

'I have already said that I will leave. I might return to my family, but then . . . I will not bear another child and lords want sons, as Hamo says. I have a cousin who was at Wherwell and escaped the burning. She is at Romsey now. It might be a better life.' She did not seem to have very great expectations, but then it was one where she was not going to be bruised and beaten upon the anger of a violent man. Yes, it would be a better life, though what was uppermost in Hugh Bradecote's mind was the image of the Sacrist of Romsey, and for the very first time since Ela died, he felt no twinge of guilt. What remained was a gratitude that he had met her and a prayerful thought that she prospered. His penance was complete.

'Lay Baldwin in the solar. He can have it as his now, and the lord's bed.' The lady smiled gently, but her eyes held a victory in this, if in nothing else.

Fulk went silently to the priest and between them they carried the body to the solar. The lady nodded at the undersheriff.

'I shall go to the church and pray . . . perhaps even for him. Come with me, Hild.'

The girl looked to her lady, and dipped in obedience and in obeisance to Bradecote, who thanked her and commended her for her skills. She blushed.

Thus within a few minutes the sheriff's men were alone. Walkelin permitted himself a small groan.

'Good. Now you have let that from you, no more complaining.' Catchpoll did not look sympathetic. 'At least it is all ended, and tidily so, all in all, my lord.'

'Yes, but . . . the healing woman did not deserve her fate.'

'Many a soul taken by a killer is not deserving of such an end, but God sees all, my lord, and I doubt not He looks kindly upon those who go to Him thus. And before you says it, no, we could not have foreseen it, not unless we had taken the lord Baldwin straight off, and without cause. I have been a-thinking it through whilst the maid tended you and though my head kept spinnin'.'

'Are you sure, Catchpoll?' Bradecote looked doubtful.

'Aye, my lord, as sure as I can be. When we came here we

got it wrong, and thought the lord Osbern was killed on his way down the hill, not on his way up, but even had we guessed so, and I cannot see how, it would not have helped us with his killer. We knew a bit after that his son, Baldwin, came to the harvesting not long afore the grey horse trotted home and was reported. Every action he took thereafter looked sound, and when we found out where he had been away, well, he would most like have come down from Alcester way and not ridden up over the top of that there hill to be in time to kill his sire. Nor did we have any reason for it, 'cepting they were tempersome bastards the both of 'em, and it was a cold-blooded killing, remember. No, we may not have liked him, but he was not our killer, not then. I grant that after finding the amber-bossed badge he looked likely, but Fulk was the more so, and it was then the healing woman met a sudden end. Fulk, well, he betrayed his lord, and betraying even a hard lord is a grievous thing. He had good cause to kill to save his skin. Meanwhile the lord Baldwin's lies were not wild, nor easy to see as falsehood.'

'And then there was the lord Parler, and not knowing all about him. That did not help. It all made the thing hard to untangle.' Walkelin had no regrets about how they had dealt with the killing of Osbern de Lench.

'We are finding excuses,' bemoaned Bradecote, ever one for self-blame.

'No, my lord, we are not. We are finding reasons, and I will put it down, charitable-like, that your paining wound makes you think wrong on it.' Catchpoll gave his superior a not unkind look, which from the sergeant was nigh on a benediction. 'It seems simple now, after it is over, to see it all, like a map laid out clear. Baldwin de Lench feared he would be declared a bastard by his father unless he married the woman chosen for him, and just when his Evesham lover was with child. He was angry and he was afraid, and when he met Osbern heading up the hill to his favourite spot, that anger led to a killing. Baldwin is the rash sort, so to imagine he had the clear head to take his father's place on the hilltop, and then arrive in Lench from the north, would not leap into our heads, but we got there in the end. When we are in the midst of it, we are in a forest and all looks the same. That we finds our way through it is down to hard work, thought, cunning, and a little luck also. Any fool could say "Yes this was easy, how it was done," when all is finished, but any fool would not have reached that end.'

'Just us fools, Serjeant.' Walkelin was rash enough to make the jest.

'Don't you be including me and the lord Undersheriff, young Walkelin,' Catchpoll chided, but then he smiled, and it lengthened across his face.

'Well, I have no wish to take Baldwin's corpse with us to Worcester when all was to do with this place. Let him have his six feet of Lench earth. We need not see the dead buried, and so there is no reason to remain. If we leave now, I can relieve my lady of worry, reach Worcester so we can report to the lord Sheriff and be home to eat in my own hall.' Bradecote stood, moved the fingers of his left hand and pulled a face. 'I do not want to ride at the gallop all the way either.'

'If we did, Walkelin here would most like fall off, or just get lost behind when his beast would not keep up. Yes, my lord, we will ride back at a gentle pace, and be glad of our own beds this night.'

It was late in the afternoon hour when Hugh Bradecote and his companions entered the bailey of his own manor. A child ran swiftly into the hall, and the undersheriff had no doubt his wife had given instruction that she was to be alerted the moment he returned. She emerged even as he dismounted, with a grimace and catch of breath. The smile froze upon her lips as she took in the binding about his forearm.

'My lord! You are hurt!'

'It is nothing serious, just a cut.'

'Yet the binding runs from elbow to near wrist.' She was a little pale.

'A slight wound, no more. The healing girl saw to it before we departed Lench.'

'A mere girl? But—'

'Their healing woman died.' Bradecote did not elaborate. 'The girl knew her craft well enough to salve and bind.'

Catchpoll and Walkelin dismounted, and stood a little to one side of their superior.

'It is none so deep as to weaken the sword grip, my lady, not when it is healed,' offered Catchpoll.

'Oh good.' The lady now had colour returning to her cheeks, but it was an anger pink, and her tone was sarcastic. 'My mind is now eased.'

'I swear it is nothing that need upset you, my lady.' Bradecote

278

smiled at his wife. 'You need not fret upon it. It was just what happens in matters like this.'

'But look at Serjeant Catchpoll. He has been involved in such matters for what, a score years or more, and he is still standing and looks to be hale and whole.' She ignored Walkelin's muttered comment on the serjeant's knees and continued with barely a pause for breath. 'You have been appointed barely more than a year, have a scar across your chest, nearly drowned in the Severn and now have this. Stop being some foolishly brave warrior . . . some *haeled* who throws himself thoughtlessly into danger.'

Catchpoll could not quite hide his grin, but Christina rounded upon him, pointing her finger accusingly.

'And what were you about, Serjeant, allowing him to get into that danger?'

'Well, on this occasion, my lady, I was in a fair way to being dead had not my lord arrived most timely and taken up the fight. I was stunned, and besides, I cannot be for ever holding him back for fear of a little scratch and . . .' Catchpoll realised his mistake as the words left his lips.

'You call that a little scratch?'

'Could be a lot worse, my lady.' This was also not the right response, for the lady took a sharp breath but then spoke very deliberately.

'Yes. It could. So know that I hold you responsible for my lord's safety, since he will not have a care to it himself.'

'I do not need a nursemaid,' objected Hugh Bradecote, half amused and half irritated.

'Be quiet. This has nothing to do with you.' She was

trembling a little, filled with anger, and an even greater fear of what might have been.

For a moment all three men looked stunned, then their eyes met, questioned, and finally answered.

'I will do as you command, my lady,' replied Catchpoll at last, in the colourless voice Bradecote was used to hearing when Catchpoll had no intention of obeying.

'It would be nice to be met by a solicitous wife,' opined Bradecote, softly, and then she turned back to him, her eyes filling with tears. 'Might I enter my hall and take a little wine?'

His regretful tone and plea did what remonstration could not.

'Oh, my poor lord. Yes, yes. Lean upon me and . . .' Suddenly the termagant was the epitome of the caring spouse, though in the event it was more that she leant upon him. Catchpoll and Walkelin did not follow. Catchpoll had a fair idea he and Walkelin would be offered good ale by Alcuin the Steward, and besides, this was a time for lord and lady to be alone.

'Not a soft lady, is she?' murmured Walkelin, more than a little in awe.

'A fine one, and caring. Better that heat than cold in a marriage bed.' Catchpoll, many years married to a woman who had reacted in a not dissimilar fashion in days long past when he had returned with less than a whole skin, was appreciative.

'But I doubt she is truly obedient.'

'If you wanted just obedience you would have a dog, not a wife, and you need a care. The Welsh are soft of lilting voice, if you can bear it, but swift of temper. When you take that Eluned of yours to wife, as opposed to just taking her, you will find that out. Biddable now, aye, she will be, but . . . you recall the Prince of Powys's lady.'

'But she was daughter to a king. They have pride and everything. My Eluned is—'

'Worth getting back to. Well, then, we take a draught of ale, wait a while, and then we goes back home to Worcester.'

Within the cool of the hall, Hugh Bradecote watched Christina take his son, delighted to see his sire, from the nurse and set him within his arm. The child smiled and patted the stubbled cheek.

'He has not pined in my absence. I swear oath he is heavier even after but a few days.'

'He eats well, and thrives.' Christina spoke with pride.

'And you?'

'I thrive also, my lord, and indeed am also no doubt the heavier.'

'Good.' He bent forward and kissed her cheek.

'Now, let me give Gilbert to his nurse and see to it that you have your wine, and arrange that there is a good meal for this evening. You must rest. Would you care to lie upon the bed?'

'With you? Yes. But I cannot, for I have not completed my task as yet.

'The killer is caught, surely. Are they dead? You bring none to Worcester.'

'He is dead, yes.'

'Then you can remain. You have a wound and—'

'No. I go into Worcester and report to William de Beauchamp.'

'Serjeant Catchpoll is quite able to do that.'

'He is, but I was sent in charge, and the killer was a lord and met his death at my hand. It is my report to make.' He saw the challenge in her look. 'Besides, the best healer I know is Brother Hubert at the Priory, and I swear I shall go and seek whatever he can produce for the pain, and see that the healing apprentice's work was good.' He smiled at her, though the smile was a little awry and there was still pain in his eyes. 'I know I disobeyed you, love, but not by intent. This is nothing. In a week or so it will be forgotten bar the mark.'

'I do try, my lord, not to be too worried, but now especially . . .'

'I know.' He pulled her close with his good arm.

'I am a solicitous wife, I promise. I have such a care to you, so much care . . .'

'I know that also, and expect nothing less than the most tender care,' his voice dropped to a husky whisper, 'and a great deal of personal attention once I return from Worcester. Then I will forget any pain.'

They emerged from the hall a not unseemly time later, lady touching-close to lord, and with Gilbert Bradecote on her hip. The undersheriff called for his horse, and Catchpoll, who had been sat upon a bench resting his eyes, opened them and stood slowly. Walkelin, who had been sat beside him whittling a piece of wood into a fair semblance of a hog, also rose, but without a grumble.

'Glad I am 'tis not far home,' murmured the serjeant, and went to unhitch his own horse.

A few minutes later and the three men were mounted. Christina stood beside the big grey and looked up at her husband.

Her hand touched his knee. 'Ride carefully, make your report and return to me before dark, my lord.' The look in her eyes held concern, but also a promise, which could be guaranteed to ensure he would make every effort to comply with her command. He smiled down at her and gave a small nod.

'Let us go and tell all to the lord Sheriff and hope he does not think we made a simple task difficult.' Bradecote gave a wry smile, which disguised a wince.

'I doubt he will, my lord, and if Roger de Lench is less of a prickly *hattefagol* than his father and brother, then he will be pleased enough.' Catchpoll knew William de Beauchamp too well.

'Ha, I would not say Baldwin de Lench curled up in a ball much.'

'No, but being close to him was not at all comfortable. I doubt the lord Sheriff liked it any more than anyone else. He will say we should have had it all trussed up neatly earlier, but then he always does that, eh? He thinks it makes us work harder if the praise is small or non-existent, and also gives the idea that if he had attended to it himself it would have been ended the sooner. Thing is, my lord, he can think what he likes, but we knows what we knows.'

'But this time, Catchpoll—'

'This time we got the answer and justice was done. 'Tis over, and we await the next duty.' Catchpoll was never one to lose sleep over what they did or had done. 'Come, my lord, or you will not be home as your lady here commands.'

'Ah, you noted that too, did you?' Bradecote grinned, and set his heel to his horse's flank, wheeling it about towards the gateway. Catchpoll just grinned.

The three horsemen urged their mounts to nothing more than a trot, aware of the lady Bradecote's eye upon them, and did not spur them to a canter until they were assuredly beyond her view.

SARAH HAWKSWOOD describes herself as a 'wordsmith' who is only really happy when writing. She read Modern History at Oxford and her Bradecote and Catchpoll medieval mysteries are her first foray into fiction. She is a member of the Crime Writers' Association, the Historical Writers' Association and the Historical Novel Society, and lives in Worcestershire.

bradecoteandcatchpoll.com   *@bradecote*

To discover more great books and to
place an order visit our website at
allisonandbusby.com

Don't forget to sign up to our free newsletter at
allisonandbusby.com/newsletter
for latest releases, events and exclusive offers

 Allison & Busby Books
 @AllisonandBusby

You can also call us on
020 3950 7834
for orders, queries
and reading recommendations